FORGOTTEN CITY

ALSO AVAILABLE BY CARRIE SMITH

Silent City

FORGOTTEN CITY

A Claire Codella Mystery

Carrie Smith

CROOKED
LANE

NEW YORK

Published in the United States by Crooked Lane Books, an imprint of The Quick Brown Fox & Company LLC.

Crooked Lane Books and its logo are trademarks of The Quick Brown Fox & Company LLC.

Library of Congress Catalog-in-Publication data available upon request.

ISBN (hardcover): 978-1-62953-767-2
ISBN (paperback): 978-1-62953-785-6
ISBN (ePub): 978-1-62953-786-3
ISBN (Kindle): 978-1-62953-787-0
ISBN (ePDF): 978-1-62953-788-7

Cover design by Lori Palmer.
Book design by Jennifer Canzone.

Printed in the United States.

www.crookedlanebooks.com

Crooked Lane Books
34 West 27th St., 10th Floor
New York, NY 10001

First Edition: December 2016

10 9 8 7 6 5 4 3 2 1

For Cyn

MONDAY

CHAPTER 1

The piercing ring startled Constance Hodges out of deep sleep. She groped for the phone, her blind fingers grazing the alarm clock, tissue box, and stack of nighttime reading. She lifted the receiver. "Yes?" Her voice was a gravelly whisper.

"Ms. Hodges?"

She cleared her throat. "Speaking."

"It's Cheryl O'Brien."

Hodges pushed herself up in the bed and glanced at the dial on the clock. Clarity quickly dispersed the fog in her brain. The Park Manor night nurse would not call her at four fifteen AM unless something was wrong. Had a resident with dementia rolled out of bed and hit their head? Had an independent living resident suffered a sudden heart attack or stroke and been rushed to the hospital in the private ambulance on call for just such occasions? Or had death—life's inevitable equalizer—once again visited their privileged confines? Based on Cheryl O'Brien's grave tone, Hodges sensed that the latter occurrence had precipitated this call. "Who is it?" she asked.

She held her breath and wondered which name the nurse would utter. Virtually every Park Manor resident was a once prominent New Yorker or relative of a now prominent New Yorker, and whenever one of them *passed the veil*, they prompted a lengthy *New York Times* obituary, a high-profile funeral at the Frank E. Campbell Funeral Chapel on Madison Avenue, where all of Manhattan's elite went out in style, and at least one new exposé about the obscenely privileged care given to Park Manor's "senior one percenters." Each of their deaths required Constance to play many parts—grief counselor, funeral planner, family therapist, and personal advisor—in addition to her official role as Park Manor's executive director.

"It's Lucy Merchant," Cheryl O'Brien answered.

The name ricocheted through Hodges's brain, and she was so surprised that she failed to edit her first reaction. "How can that *be*?"

"Maybelle Holder found her during the four AM check."

"Found her where? What happened?"

"We don't know. She was just lying in bed." The nurse's tone suggested that she was equally stunned by the turn of events and that she had enough insight into the dynamics of Park Manor's business to appreciate at least some of the consequences. Lucy Merchant was no frail octogenarian whose peaceful passing in the night would signal the sad but acceptable culmination of a long life lived to the fullest. Lucy Merchant was only fifty-six years old. Her obituary would tell the tale of a musical theater legend turned choreographer stricken with early onset Alzheimer's and dead within two years. It would spotlight her grieving daughter, Julia, and her high-profile husband, Thomas, chairman of the Bank of New Amsterdam.

Hodges turned on her bedside lamp and tried to focus on all the tasks Lucy Merchant's death would entail today, but the familiar death steps wouldn't crystallize into a coherent mental checklist. *Focus*, she thought, as if this silent admonition would magically shift her mind into gear.

As she scanned the room, her eyes registered the Courvoisier XO bottle and minisnifter sitting next to her clock. There was still an inch of cognac from last night in the bottom of the glass, and she imagined gulping it down right this minute. It would spread a soothing numbness through her extremities, she thought, like one of those heat-producing analgesic creams that athletes and arthritis sufferers used. She felt her left arm begin to reach for the snifter. But if she sipped the cognac now, before she was even out of bed, wouldn't it signal that she had crossed an invisible line, that she had a serious alcohol problem? Wouldn't it mean that she was out of control?

"Ms. Hodges?" Cheryl's voice brought her back to the moment.

Hodges picked up the snifter and swallowed. She closed her eyes and relished the hot burn down her esophagus. Her thoughts coalesced into a mental flowchart of what she must do: Get to Park Manor. Call Thomas Merchant. Speak to the physician on call. Debrief the night staff. "Is Baiba there?" she asked Cheryl.

"I've phoned her. She's on her way."

"Good. I'll be there shortly," she told the nurse in a now commanding voice. "Leave Mrs. Merchant where she is. Lock her door. Tell Baiba to let no one in. Keep the Nostalgia night staff on site until I have time to speak with them. And call Dr. Fisher immediately. Have him meet me there. We need him to certify the death as soon as possible."

CHAPTER 2

Detective Claire Codella was used to waking up at all hours of the night. After all, murders in this city—in any city—did not conveniently occur only between nine AM and five PM. But no call had come from Manhattan North this morning. No murder explained why she had been lying awake since four AM.

She slid her palm across the mattress to the other side of the bed where the sheet was cool to the touch, no body heat to warm it, and for an instant she regretted that she had sent Brian Haggerty home, that she had chosen to face this morning alone. In the very next instant, however, she reminded herself it was better this way. Wasn't it just naïve to think that anyone—even the person you were closest to—could ever really accompany you into your own dark places? And anyway, how close was she really to Brian? Until three months ago, they hadn't spoken in a year, since the night at the St. James Pub when he'd worked up his courage from way too much Knob Creek and told her— albeit inelegantly—how he felt about her. He'd expected her to admit her feelings, too. But she hadn't. Instead, she'd accepted a promotion and run all the way to Manhattan North. Then she got the lymphoma diagnosis and went through ten months of cancer treatment without even calling him—how could she? And he hadn't called her, either. Only later did she learn that he had come to the hospital to visit her, stood outside her room, and seen her at one of her lowest moments—when she was rattling the side rails on her bed and screaming for the nurse to bring morphine. He'd known she would be furious, that her dignity would be crushed, if she knew he'd seen her like that. And so he'd walked away, as hard as that had been to do.

Cancer had made her a little more vulnerable, she supposed, a little more receptive to him. She cared about him, of course, but she wasn't one of those women who needed someone around all the time, someone to tell her everything was going to be all right. She'd been taking care of herself for as long as she could remember. She'd gotten herself to New York on her own, she'd earned her gold shield without any help from an uncle in the ranks, and during her chemotherapy, she'd earned the equivalent of a PhD in self-reliance. She didn't need Haggerty or anyone to give her reassurance. She would be fine. And if she wasn't—well, then so be it.

She whipped back the blankets and sat up. The room was as cold as her fear. The frigid February air from her open window helped her sleep at night, but it did not make rising very easy or comfortable. She dragged herself to the bathroom, closed the door against the bedroom's cold front, flipped on the bright, uncompromising light, and stared into the medicine chest mirror. Her black hair was disheveled from Haggerty's hands. The pale skin around her lips was red from his wiry stubble. And the crow's feet at the outer edges of her eyes seemed to have disappeared. She remembered kissing him in her living room. And then she closed her eyes and relived the rest of the night with equal measures of satisfaction and apprehension. Her relationship with Haggerty was never going to be the same again.

She splashed warm water over her face. Did her need to forget about this morning explain why she had let him come here last night? Or had she simply given in to desire that had been on hold for too long? It was probably a little of the first, she admitted, and far more of the second. She had been a stranger in her body for more than a year. Cancer had moved in and evicted her desire, and when the cancer had moved out, she had been too terrified to reclaim what was rightfully hers.

To his credit, Haggerty had sensed this, and he had let her call the shots. Even when she was on top of him, even when he was inside of her, he had waited for her to make the first move. "Go ahead," he had whispered as if he knew she needed coaxing, as if he understood she was afraid to try this ultimate act of vulnerability and pleasure that she had not experienced since cancer had changed everything. And while he had whispered his permissions, she moved—tentatively at first, then with growing desire, and finally with need that erased self-consciousness—until she exploded into a mushroom cloud of sensations that fragmented her whole being like atoms dispersing. When she had finally rolled off of him, she felt her first moment of deep peace in almost two years.

But now that peace was decaying like a radioactive isotope, and in its place, cold dread was forming once again.

CHAPTER 3

Brandon Johnson found Baiba Lielkaja in the corridor that connected the east and west suites. "Can I go in Lucy's room, Baiba, just for a second? I want to say good-bye."

Baiba frowned. "Didn't you already see her?"

Brandon shook his head. "I drew the short straw—again. I've been sitting and walking with Mr. Lane for three hours. Please. This could be my only chance."

He touched the sleeve of Baiba's burgundy Park Manor blazer and stared into her blue eyes. She was wearing no makeup this morning, he observed, and her long blond hair was pulled back into a tight ponytail. She had rushed to work without taking her usual time in front of a mirror. Still, she looked perfect, he thought. She had always looked perfect to him, ever since the afternoon two years ago when she had interviewed him for the Park Manor job. He remembered staring across the desk at her. He had imagined how soft her pale, high cheekbones must be. He had felt mesmerized by the sound of her ever so slight Latvian accent.

"Please, Baiba," he repeated, and he sensed that she would grant his request—for the same reason she had pressed an envelope into his hand last week. Baiba's caregiving instincts didn't shut off after hours, and when he had told her his story—more of it than he'd ever told anyone other than his therapist Judith Greenwald—she had wanted to become a part of his happy ending. "I admire your strength and courage so much," she had told him as she'd reached across the diner table, covered his hand with her warm palm, and insisted he take her envelope containing three thousand dollars.

Now she glanced over her shoulder down the quiet east corridor. Six resident suites were situated on this side of the "Nostalgia Neighborhood," as Park Manor called its memory care unit. Lucy occupied the suite in the far corner overlooking Madison Avenue. Brandon could see her rooms clearly in his mind. He had tucked Lucy Merchant into her bed six nights a week for the past eighteen months, and now he found it impossible to accept that she was really gone. He had to see for himself. He had to bring her death to life.

Baiba fished in her blazer pocket. She was his manager and she was eight years his senior—he had organized the Park Manor party last month for her thirty-first birthday—but age and titles didn't matter. They were friends, and she would do this for him. "Come with me—quickly," she said as she pulled out her keys. He followed her down the carpeted corridor lined with photographs of turn-of-the-century New York City. As she unlocked Lucy's door, he stared at a photo of Fifth Avenue mansions on "Millionaire's Row." Some of those mansions still stood just blocks from Park Manor. "One minute, Brandon," she told him. "That's it. No more."

And then he was alone in Lucy's rooms. He took a deep breath. Despite the meticulous care provided by Park Manor's staff, some Nostalgia residents' suites had the faint odor of old age and incontinence, but Lucy's apartment always smelled like jasmine body lotion and the bouquets of fresh-cut flowers her family had delivered every four days. Her still-drawn curtains blocked the bright morning light. Lucy lay in the middle of the bed exactly where he had left her last night at ten thirty. She was on her back, and someone—Maybelle, he supposed—had arranged her hands neatly over her stomach. Maybelle would do something like that out of respect for the dead.

He kneeled next to Lucy's quiescent body. In death, as in life, she was an arrestingly attractive woman. Her brows arched symmetrically. Her skin was spotless. She had one of those rare, perfect noses that even the most sought-after Upper East Side cosmetic surgeons could never artificially sculpt. And unlike the other Nostalgia residents, she still looked youthful. Just last week, Park Manor's stylist had come to her room and given her a pixie cut. Only when Lucy smiled did you realize that something was wrong with her. Then you saw her straight but yellow stained teeth with hardened plaque and food particles at the gum lines. Even Brandon—who could coax Lucy to do almost anything—could rarely get her electric toothbrush into her mouth anymore.

He stroked her short hair. It was soft. It did not feel like the hair of a dead person. But then, wasn't the hair on your head already dead? Perhaps hair didn't change when you died. He touched Lucy's arm. Were the cells in her skin dead yet? He had once read that the body does not die all at once, that the cells give up their lives one by one. Were there any living cells in Lucy that still sensed his presence? "Good-bye, Lucy," he whispered to those invisible cells. "I'll miss you."

Baiba was tapping on the door. Brandon quickly kissed Lucy's cool forehead, rose from the carpet, and rejoined the Nostalgia Neighborhood care coordinator in the corridor. "Thank you, Baiba."

Baiba relocked the door. "I didn't just do that." She wagged her pale index finger at him and winked. "I'll have to deny it if you say I did."

"But I won't. You know I won't."

He returned to the kitchen where Maybelle and Josie were setting the dining room tables for the residents' breakfast. He slumped into a chair and Maybelle patted his shoulder. "At least she now with God," she consoled him in her booming Bajan patois. Maybelle was a tall, big-boned black woman who carried herself proudly through the Nostalgia Neighborhood of privileged white inhabitants. She was Brandon's favorite coworker because she was optimistic and kind to the residents. She always adjusted herself to the idiosyncrasies of their dementias instead of trying to force them to relinquish their delusions. When Mr. Morrow wandered the halls and repeatedly asked what time it was, she patiently answered, "Don't you worry yourself, Mr. Morrow, I not gonna let you miss that train to Scarsdale again!" And when Dr. Evelyn Bruce, a once prominent surgeon at Sloan Kettering, tried to follow Cheryl O'Brien into the dispensary while she prepared medications, Maybelle told her, "Let your nurse do her job, Doctor. Let her be. Now go read your new medical journal."

Maybelle told Brandon, "You just say a nice prayer for her. She gonna be fine where she gone to."

"What you crying about it?" Josie called out from the other side of the dining room where she was taking a sponge to a sticky spot someone must have missed during last night's dinner cleanup. Josie had only worked at Park Manor for two weeks, but she had taken an immediate dislike to Brandon and attacked him whenever she could. "Why you care?" she demanded. "They just a bunch of rich folk. It's not like they your family."

Brandon did not agree. How could you not become attached to someone you fed, changed, bathed, and rubbed with body lotion every night? In the past few months, Lucy had rarely uttered more than two or three words at a time, yet he had always known when she was hungry, thirsty, or upset. He had made her laugh. He could coax her to eat, play catch with an inflated beach ball, and swallow her medicine. And he had meant something to her, too. Why else had her face lit up whenever she saw him? She exuded no judgment, only gratitude for what he did for her.

Josie moved closer, shaking her head in disgust. "You call yourself a man, crying like that?"

Brandon let the comment go unanswered, but Maybelle snapped, "You stop that right now, Josie. When my mama pass, my brother cry like a baby in my arms—and he were a big six-foot-four-inch man. You let Brandon alone. Let him be. He got a right to *espress* his feeling."

"Well, he *espress* them like a *girl*." Josie returned to her work with a new hostile vigor.

Maybelle sat down and leaned in confidentially. "Don't you pay her no mind, Brandon. Josie from Jamaica, and the Jamaicans is different from the Bajans. We don't hate on nobody just because they different."

The irony of Maybelle's remark was not lost on Brandon. Everybody had his or her own brand of prejudice. At least Maybelle's wasn't directed at him. In fact, she had defended him in front of more than one caregiver who objected to working with "someone like him." Brandon knew he had done nothing overt to provoke Josie's outsized anger. Either he deeply offended her fixed and narrow definition of normal, he had concluded, or she felt personally insulted by his decision to abandon her gender for another.

"Thanks, Maybelle." He forced himself up and into the kitchen. He might as well stay busy, he thought, until Ms. Hodges debriefed them.

CHAPTER 4

Codella flashed her shield at the guards just inside the New York Presbyterian revolving doors. She opened her leather jacket to reveal the Glock in its holster, and the guards made way for her to step around the metal detector. It occurred to her that they probably thought she was here on a case. She wished she *were* here on a case.

She passed the waiting area, admissions office, and information desk. She glanced into a small glassed-in cafeteria where nurses, orderlies, and doctors stood like zombies in front of the caffeine options. She would have liked to stop and sip a green tea. Instead, she rode the elevator to the fifth floor and pushed open the door to the nuclear medicine department. She knew this drill all too well: check in at the desk, take a seat, and wait for the pitcher.

She chose the same couch she had occupied in October. Her scan then had been clean, and she was not immune to the superstitious belief that repeating her steps of that day might bring another good result. She looked out on the always-congested York Avenue and the East River just beyond. During her treatments, she had occupied rooms with views of the river and had watched for hours as cigarette boats, barges, tugs, and Circle Line tours plied the river's heavy currents. She had followed the movements of pedestrians on the footpath on Roosevelt Island. She had even found herself thinking, *I wish I could be taking a walk on that island right now*, although in precancer days and now, she dismissed that island as a depressing concrete outpost cut off from the lifeblood of Manhattan.

She checked her e-mails and opened a text from Haggerty. *Thanks for last night.* She still couldn't quite believe last night had actually happened, and she didn't want to think about what it meant to her or what Haggerty would think it meant. Not now. She looked out the window and searched her mind for something else to focus on.

She would have liked to distract herself in the tangled threads of a complex investigation, but she hadn't had a challenging case for three very long months. Dennis McGowan, her lieutenant, was making sure of that. When she had accepted the promotion to Manhattan North Homicide—just months before her cancer diagnosis—she'd felt like the teenager who finally graduated to the grown-ups' table. But the grown-ups weren't all that grown up, she had discovered, and they weren't enthusiastic about sharing their table with the detective who had solved a case they'd let go cold.

Four years ago, Elaine DeFarge, a nurse at Columbia Presbyterian, never made it home to her apartment in Fort Greene after her shift. Waste disposal workers found her body two days later, covered by rotting mangoes and bananas in a dumpster behind the uptown Fairway Market. The initial call came into the 171st, and Detective Marty Blackstone caught it. But Captain Reilly knew his detective squad didn't have the manpower to handle the case alone, so it was shifted up to Manhattan North, and Dan Fisk led a task force that worked the murder for six months without finding DeFarge's killer.

The files gathered dust for another year, and then Codella asked Reilly if she could study the file. She spent her evenings reading the reports. Manhattan North detectives had investigated family, friends, and hospital staff meticulously. They had considered and ultimately ruled out any connection to the unsolved murders of three other New York City hospital workers killed in the prior five years. Codella didn't retrace their steps. Instead, she zeroed in on a detail the detectives hadn't been able to explain and that they had ultimately dismissed as insignificant to the investigation—a three-inch-long lock of Elaine DeFarge's hair that was missing at the back of her head. Had she cut it off herself, or had someone else snipped a souvenir and left a signature the detectives hadn't been able to read?

Codella called up cold case murders from every database she could access. She ran keyword searches and looked for any link to the hair. She knew she was searching for a needle in a haystack, but if the needle were there, she was determined to find it. And then one night she had a breakthrough. Six years earlier, the Indianapolis Metropolitan Police Department had found the body of a woman whose hair appeared to have been snipped in the back—the forensic team had found strands of her cut hair next to the body. The victim was a rental manager at an apartment complex two blocks away from St. Vincent Hospital. The only link to DeFarge Codella could think of was the hospital, so she requested St. Vincent's employee records from that time period and cross-checked them with the staff working at Columbia Presbyterian when DeFarge had disappeared. A name came up—one name—Wainright Blake, a contract nurse in the postanesthesia care units of both hospitals.

When Codella discovered the connection, Blake had already moved on and was working at White Plains Hospital in Westchester County, twenty-five miles north of Manhattan. When she and county police showed up at his apartment with a warrant, she found a cigar box under his bed with six locks of hair—a souvenir from each of his victims. DNA from those locks helped police in five states put cold cases to rest. *New York* magazine dubbed her "a genius of deductive reasoning." The *Washington Post* featured her in a story on analytical detective work and the need for more integrated crime databases. The *LA Times* ran a three-part exposé focusing on all the uncorroborated conclusions that had led the original Manhattan North detectives to their dead end. And one night on MSNBC, Rachel Maddow asked her how it felt to bring closure to six families' grief. The NYPD brass really had no choice but to hand her the promotion Captain Reilly recommended.

So she had joined the "big leagues"—for a little while, at least, until cancer took her on a ten-month detour. And then she'd made her comeback solving the murder of Hector Sanchez. When McGowan had thrown her the body of that dead school principal, he hadn't counted on the case giving her the equivalent of a Broadway stage on which to make her comeback from cancer oblivion. He had assumed he was throwing her the smelly, days' old corpse of some unlucky New Yorker who had choked to death on his Seamless order or collapsed from cardiac arrest all alone in his West Side apartment. A detective had to go to the scene, and nobody wanted that job, so he had given it to her. But Sanchez had been anything but a natural death, and the case made not only the tabloids but also the front page of the *New York Times*. Three months later, op-ed writers were still debating whether Hector Sanchez was a flawed hero or a tyrant. And magazines like *People* and *Vanity Fair* had staked their claim on the story because it involved the box office star Dana Drew. McGowan's attempt to cast Codella as an insignificant extra in his homicide squad had been royally fucked, and now he was doing his utmost to make sure she never got on any stage again.

The pitcher of contrast arrived. The technician who delivered it was the same one who had prepped her for her October scan, and she decided this was another hopeful sign. "Your cocktail, Madam," he said as he lowered the plastic vessel to the coffee table with a flourish and handed her a paper cup.

"Did you spike it for me?"

"Don't think you're the first one to ask me that." He winked.

She poured some of the unpleasant liquid and held it up to him. "Here's to boring results."

Then he was gone, and she was left with her anxiety and the liter of liquid to drink. What if lymphoma cells lit up the scan this time? What if she had to go back to round one and begin the fight all over?

"Take off your jewelry," a nurse instructed her forty-five minutes later as they walked to the locker area. "Earrings, necklaces, rings. No metal."

Codella just nodded. Only the uninitiated came to scans naively adorned. She peeled out of her clothes, put on the blue hospital gown, and tucked her service revolver and backup gun below her other belongings in the tiny locker. Then she followed the nurse to a small room with three desks, the kind in high school classrooms. She slipped into a seat, propped her arm on the narrow desktop, and watched the focused, efficient nurse tie a tourniquet around her left bicep. While her veins expanded under the pressure, the nurse lifted the lid on a lead-lined box, removed the syringe within, and flicked it several times as she held it toward the light. Then she untied the elastic and pressed needle into flesh. Codella felt the electric prick. She watched the plunger push the radioactive tracer into her vein. She visualized the ionized particles heating her whole arm and spreading through her circulatory system, marking the scenes of any crime her B cells had committed in the last four months.

The nurse led her to a tiny room where she lay on her back while the tracer circulated. Thirty minutes later, she entered the chilly, windowless room that housed the state-of-the-art scanner. She knew this drill, too. Swing your legs up. Lie back. Hands over your head. Do not move. The technician pushed a button and the slab she was on retracted slowly. At this juncture in the familiar routine, she always had the impulse to pray. Instead, as usual, she closed her eyes and whispered, "Fuck, fuck, fuck!"

CHAPTER 5

Constance Hodges glanced up as Heather Granahan tiptoed into her office and set a clear glass mug on the desk. The first time Heather had made one of these unsolicited coffee deliveries, Hodges had assured her the task was not part of her job description, but the young administrative assistant had continued—apparently perceptive and ambitious enough to know that Hodges appreciated small acts of subservience—and this morning Hodges was more grateful than usual. She watched her assistant make a discreet exit, and then she took a sip. The taste was disappointing. She closed her eyes and wished for a little more of the steadying Courvoisier.

She stared at Thomas Merchant's cell number on her laptop screen. She did not look forward to calling him. Tolling the bell for Park Manor's fallen was not a vocation she had ever envisioned for herself, and she felt a sudden and unexpected longing for the Central Park West office where she had once counseled fifteen or more patients a week. Several large ad firms and financial companies sent her their executives who needed to do "penance" for sexual harassment, anger issues, or alcohol problems. They'd show up for eight or ten sessions to get "rehabilitated." And there were the self-involved artists and academics, the anxiety-ridden graduate students from Columbia University, and of course the clients questioning their sexual identities. These confused souls always stayed with her the longest. But it had been exhausting and mind-numbing to absorb everyone else's problems day in and day out. The *practice* of psychotherapy had never satisfied her as much as the *study* of human psychology. Her patients' predictable issues had never truly held her interest. Although she had been a skillful psychotherapist, she was not a woman who enjoyed the passive role of engaged and insightful listener. And even affluent clients had not paid her nearly as well as Park Manor did.

Hodges lifted the phone and dialed. Thomas Merchant picked up on the fourth ring. His "hello" sounded as groggy as hers had an hour ago, and she imagined him in his Fifth Avenue penthouse apartment lying in one of those luxurious handmade Savoir Beds. Was there a woman next to him listening to their call? She seriously doubted that Thomas had spent many solitary nights since his wife had moved into Park Manor—not that any of his overnight guests would last. She knew Thomas better than he knew himself, she thought. She knew exactly how to read people. Even in the superficial interviews she held with family members of prospective residents, she could distinguish between those who came to Park Manor because they wanted the best for a loved one and those who chose the venerable institution as a glorified Manhattan Mini Storage in which to stash an unwanted burden, freeing them from years of caregiving or freeing up a Park Avenue townhouse. A year and a half ago, when Thomas Merchant had entered her office wearing his bespoke suit and subtle, expensive cologne, she had known exactly what he wanted from her.

She cleared her throat and spoke in a calm, matter-of-fact voice. "Thomas, it's Constance. I'm sorry for the early call, but I'm afraid Lucy passed away early this morning." She had delivered end of life news to spouses and children of residents so many times that she knew getting directly to the point was the best way. Drawn-out condolences coming from her would only sound scripted and insincere, so she limited herself to "I'm sorry to have to give you this news over the phone."

"How? What happened, Constance?"

"She died in her sleep. Dr. Fisher is here now. I'll be able to tell you more when he's done examining her, but I wanted to call you right away."

In the silence, Merchant expelled a spontaneous sigh of what sounded to Hodges like unadulterated relief.

"Will you be coming over this morning?" she asked, carefully withholding expectation or judgment from her voice.

"I'm in DC. I have to meet with a Senate subcommittee in about an hour. I'll fly back after that. I should be able to get there by four PM."

"And Julia?"

"I'll call her right now."

"Okay," said Hodges. "We'll be ready for you." She ended the call, sat back, and took another sip of the unsatisfying coffee.

CHAPTER 6

The first floor of Park Manor was light-years from Nostalgia, Brandon thought as he, Maybelle Holder, and Josie Burns stepped off the elevator. On this floor, combination locks did not confine wandering sundowners. No one wore adult diapers, or at least they pretended that they didn't. These residents arranged daily outings through a concierge. They gathered for drinks at the Madison Bar off the main lobby and ordered spa cuisine at the Zagat-reviewed Manor Bistro. They were perpetually happy tourists at a five-star hotel.

Hodges was sitting behind her desk when the three caregivers entered. Maybelle and Josie claimed the two straight-backed chairs opposite Hodges, and Brandon stood just behind them. Hodges got right to the point. "The three of you were on duty when Mrs. Merchant passed away."

Brandon and Josie nodded.

"That's right." Maybelle's big voice resounded through the room. "She weren't breathing when I go in there. I always listen for the breathing."

"Can you tell me about Mrs. Merchant's evening?"

Maybelle turned to Josie. Then she twisted to make eye contact with Brandon. "It were like any evening," she said, assuming the role of spokesperson.

Josie nodded her agreement.

"How did she seem to you?"

"She seem just fine." Maybelle shrugged.

"Did she eat her dinner?"

Brandon spoke up. "Her daughter was there. She fed her for a while. Then I took over."

"At what time exactly?" Hodges's fingers tapped the keys on her laptop.

"Six thirty."

"She was there when Mrs. Lautner had her fall?"

"Yes."

Hodges frowned, and Brandon could guess what she was thinking: Why had Mrs. Lautner had to fall at mealtime while families were visiting? All Ms. Hodges cared about was appearances.

"What did she eat?" Hodges asked.

"Roast chicken. Mashed potatoes. Green beans. She had a good appetite."

"And her mood?"

"Happy. Alert."

"Especially when the daughter leave and you feed her the ice cream." Josie dropped this bomb with a heavy dose of sarcasm.

Maybelle shot Josie a look.

"Well, she did. You know she did."

"*He*," said Maybelle. "It's *he*, and *you* know that."

Brandon glanced down at Josie's purple-streaked hair. He found himself wanting to pluck every strand out of her scalp one by one so that she would be left with pinhole-sized blood spots where the follicles were. He felt a testosterone-fueled call to violence in every flexed muscle and tendon in his body. But he didn't so much as blink.

Hodges was staring at him. "Is that true, Brandon? You fed her ice cream?"

"Yes. I gave her half a scoop."

"On whose authority, may I ask?"

"On no one's," he admitted.

Hodges frowned again, and Brandon could read her disapproval of him in her strange yellow eyes. She had never liked or wanted him to work at *her* institution, and he supposed she didn't appreciate that he evidenced no fear of her now. "You are aware, aren't you," she said, "that Lucy Merchant is on a no-sugar, low-cholesterol diet?"

He didn't answer.

"And that giving her ice cream is a complete violation of her care plan?"

He stared at the meticulous image of middle-aged femininity she presented behind her antique Victorian desk. She must be very naïve, he thought, to think that her cold questioning could reach inside of him. Was she trying to blame him for Lucy's death? "I just fed her four bites of ice cream," he said. "Four bites. And she enjoyed them, by the way."

"That's not the point, though, is it?"

"I guess not." But it was *exactly* the point. As the vanilla ice cream had melted on Lucy's tongue, he'd watched a tiny miracle of cognition happen before his eyes. He played Lucy "Cell Block Tango," a number she had performed in the 1996 Broadway revival of *Chicago*—did Hodges even know Lucy had been in that production? Did she know anything about Lucy?—and Lucy's lips began to move. She remembered the words. She sang them. *He had it coming. He had it coming. He had it coming all along.* The ice cream and the music had combined to free a fossilized memory. Wasn't that more important than a glucose level?

He pictured Lucy's cool body still lying in the bed upstairs. He felt a sting of tears well up behind his eyes, and in that moment he understood for the first time why Lucy's life and death meant so much to him. He and Lucy were two of a kind, both imprisoned in bodies that didn't work as one with their minds.

Hodges narrowed her eyes. "You were not hired to make decisions for our residents. You had no right to do what you did."

It's not about who has the right, he wanted to say. *It's about what is right.* And he felt a blistering hot rage inside at this immaculate woman with her perfect hair and makeup. He wished he could telekinetically tear her limbs from her body. "Then fire me." He met her stare with a fierce resolve. "On second thought, don't bother. I quit. Right now." And he tore off his clip-on Park Manor ID badge and slapped it facedown on her desk.

CHAPTER 7

"Where the fuck were you at roll call?" McGowan growled when she came to his office. "You can't remember to tell me when you're going to be late? I should write you up. What is it? You still got chemo brain or something?"

"It's called chemo *fog*, and no, I don't." Codella did not keep the coldness out of her voice. Cancer, he knew very well, was her psychological Achilles' heel, and he liked to find snide little ways to bring it up, to remind her of her vulnerability. "I told you I had an appointment," she said.

"What appointment?"

He wanted to make her say it, she thought. Well, fine. She would say it. "I had a medical procedure."

"Jesus Christ, Codella. You have to stop all this doctor shit. It gets in the way."

She just looked at him. She had only missed three hours of work in more than three months. Dan Fisk, McGowan's lead homicide detective, had missed whole mornings due to his failed root canal, implant appointments, divorce and custody hearings—all of which he told her about ad nauseam as if she actually cared. McGowan never jumped on him. This wasn't about reality, she knew. This was McGowan's personal mission to cut her off at the knees. He leaned back in his chair. "But I guess you can't help it, can you?" He grinned. "That's the fucked

up thing about cancer, isn't it? Once it shows up on your doorstep, you can't ever really get rid of it, can you?"

Are you fucking serious? she wanted to say. People could *think*
those things—they did all the time, she could see it in their
eyes—but they weren't supposed to voice them. "When are you
going to let me catch a case of my own?"

"That's a whole different conversation, Codella. You want
to go there?"

"I want you to answer the question."

"Fine," he said. "When you learn to play by the rules." He
tapped his fingers on his desk. He had a new haircut with short
bangs that formed a reddish fringe across the top of his forehead.
With his freckled skin and full cheeks, he had to work extra hard
to look manly with that coiffure. Maybe that was why he was
such a son of a bitch lately.

"I have always played by the rules," she said.

He waved her away. "Go help out Fisk on the Hasbrouck
case, and next time you go see your doctor, you tell me personally. You got that?"

I hate your fucking guts, she thought as she stomped down the
hall to her office.

CHAPTER 8

The night caregiver with acne—Brandon, Julia Merchant remembered—pushed past her without a glance as she opened the door. Then three sets of eyes turned to stare at her. Two black women in burgundy Park Manor polo shirts strained the cane bottom chairs in front of Constance Hodges.

Hodges stood and addressed the two women. "Maybelle and Josie, I think we're done here, and I know you must be eager to get home."

Julia watched the caregivers lumber out. Then Hodges came around her desk and grasped Julia's arm. "I'm *so* sorry for your loss, Julia."

"Thank you," Julia responded mechanically.

"I wasn't expecting to see you till four. Your father said—"

"Yes, well, I can't live my life on my father's timetable. Maybe he doesn't want to see my mother before they take her away, but I do."

Hodges smiled tightly. "Of course. Shall I take you up right now?"

"I know the way, Constance." As soon as the words were out, Julia knew they had been too curt and that she would be offended. Constance did not exactly see herself as staff. She seemed to think that she and Julia were peers, that they had something approaching a *friendship*. She stared into Constance's piercing, yellow-brown eyes. Those eyes looked otherworldly.

Had her father ever fucked this woman? Did that explain why the director felt entitled to act like her stand-in mother? She certainly wasn't unattractive, but she was at least a decade too old to be in her father's sweet spot. No, he hadn't fucked her, she decided. Although he might have thought about it, and he might have channeled enough charm in her direction to make her think he wanted to or to make her *wish* he would. But no. She forced a conciliatory smile. "Thank you. I just want to be alone with her for a few moments. I'm sure you understand."

"Of course. Of *course*."

Julia turned toward the door. "I'll speak to you this afternoon when I come back with my father."

She rode the elevator up and made her way to her mother's suite. The lamps were off in her mother's bedroom, and Julia did not turn them on. In the grainy half-light that breached the curtains' barriers, she could just make out her mother's body lying on the bed under a blanket, her head on a pillow.

Julia sat on the edge of the bed and placed a palm tentatively over her mother's hand. She had never touched a dead body before. Her mother's skin had the cool, irregular texture of leather upholstery. Julia pressed harder, trying to find any warmth that remained below the uninviting surface, but there was none. She fought the overwhelming impulse to let go of the lifeless extremity. Instead, she gripped it with maniacal strength.

What should she do now? What was the *right* thing to do? Say a prayer? Whisper last words of love and gratitude? Enumerate all the details she would never forget about her mother? Try to connect with whatever metaphysical energy lingered here in this last space where her mother had breathed? Julia stretched out on the mattress next to her mother's body. With her face inches from her mother's, she listened to the silence. She sensed no energy in this room. She moved a little closer. She remembered the one time her mother had crawled into bed with her when she was a child and had trouble sleeping. And then she suddenly knew how to make this moment sacred and memorable.

The knowledge came in the form of lyrics her mother had sung to her on that occasion, and she whispered them now. *You are my sunshine, my only sunshine. You make me happy when skies are gray. You'll never know dear how much I love you. Please don't take my sunshine away.*

She shut her eyes. She wasn't sure how long she stayed there, but when she finally sat up, she thought she might have slept for a moment or two. When she stood, her body felt insubstantial, as if her cells had seeped through the confines of her flesh and mingled with the grainy light filtering in.

She brushed the wrinkles out of her skirt and blew her nose with a Kleenex from the box next to the bed. She opened the drawer of her mother's bedside table and looked inside. She closed it and turned to the photos in the windowsill—her mother as a twenty-three-year-old dancer in the Martha Graham Company, her mother as Velma Kelly in *Chicago*, her mother with Larry Hirschhorn, who had cast her in *Vegas Nights*. In the last two years, all these memories had evaporated from her mother's brain, and now her mother's entire narrative was just a fable encoded into *Julia's* brain. And how long would *her* memories last, she wondered.

She scooped up the photos and tucked them into her shoulder bag. And then she unplugged the sleek digital alarm clock next to the photos, stuffed that into her handbag as well, and left Park Manor.

CHAPTER 9

The shuttle was boarding by the time Thomas Merchant got through the TSA PreCheck line. As he walked down the Jetway, he texted Julia that he'd meet her in front of Park Manor. Then he rang Pamela, who had called three times while he was with the Senate banking subcommittee.

Pamela didn't bother with hello. "You could have told me yourself."

Merchant glanced into the cockpit as he stepped onto the plane. "Julia's better at breaking bad news." He supposed he should say something else, something consoling, but he was too tired from the subcommittee grilling, and Pamela would see right through whatever he said anyway and tell him he was full of shit. He certainly had to respect Lucy's sister professionally, but he'd never been a fan of hers. She was assertive and brassy—the polar opposite of his wife—and he had no interest in women who weren't interested in men.

"What happened?" she asked, as if Lucy's death were anything other than the simple calculus of inevitability.

"Her genes happened." He didn't even try to mask his sarcasm. "As I've said before, you really should get yourself tested, Pamela."

"Why? So I can spend my life worrying every time I forget a name? No thanks. Besides, I've read the studies too. Just because you have one of the mutations doesn't mean you'll get it."

"Tell yourself that if it makes you feel better, but it's like economic indicators. You ignore them at your financial peril. I'm on the board of Sloan Kettering. I can make a call for you. I can get you an appointment like that." He snapped his fingers even though she couldn't hear.

"I've defended three Sloan Kettering board members and one from Mount Sinai, too. I could ask them myself. You're an asshole, you know."

"I'm a realist." He smiled at an attractive blond in an aisle seat who was staring at him. He took the aisle seat right across from hers. "I say it's better to know what's coming." He tucked his briefcase under the row in front of his. "That's why I was so insistent with Julia."

"Yeah, and look how that turned out."

"She'll thank me some day."

"When are you planning to have the funeral?"

"We'll have a memorial service after the cremation. I don't know when. It'll be at Frank E. Campbell, of course."

"I want to be kept informed," Pamela asserted.

"Of course." He laughed inwardly at her puffed up tone, as if Pamela had any authority at all over the plans he made.

He ended that call and made the call he *wanted* to make.

"I really can't talk right now," she whispered, and again he detected that something in her voice. A cooling off. A pulling away.

"Come see me tonight."

"It's been a long day. And the snow is already starting here. I—"

"It's been a long day for me, too," he cut her off. "And I'm looking forward to an even longer night with you. I'll send Felipe for you at nine thirty." He pressed *End* before she could protest.

A flight attendant was demonstrating the safety features of the plane. The blond woman across the aisle was staring at him again. He met her gaze and she asked, "You're Thomas Merchant, aren't you?"

"Guilty as charged." He smiled and held out his hand.

CHAPTER 10

Despite their obvious age difference, father and daughter struck Constance Hodges as an unhappily married husband and wife reluctantly showing up for their weekly couple's session. Thomas claimed the long couch facing the fireplace. Julia staked out the smaller couch at a right angle to him. Hodges assumed a neutral position on the chair opposite Julia. "Shall I have some coffee or tea brought—"

"Not for me." Merchant cut her off. "I have to get downtown after this. Where do we stand, Constance?"

"Dr. Fisher certified the death this morning. I have some papers for you to sign. Frank E. Campbell came at one. They'll hold Mrs. Merchant until the death certificates are issued. We've alerted the media, per your request, and we're logging condolence messages as they stream in." Constance felt pleased by her succinct and thorough delivery.

"That's a big help, Constance. I'll have Roberta connect with you as soon as I get to my office. She'll take over arrangements from here."

Julia turned to him. "Don't you even want to know the cause of death?"

Ms. Hodges observed that Merchant seemed surprised by the question. "Coronary arrest." She supplied the answer quietly. "Her heart simply stopped while she was sleeping."

"Coronary arrest is not a *cause* of death," Julia snapped. "Coronary arrest is the *result* of something. Everyone knows that."

"True enough." Hodges strained not to sound patronizing or defensive as she pointed out that people with advanced dementia couldn't communicate their symptoms and often had undetected conditions.

"My mother was only fifty-six years old, Constance. And she looked fine at dinner last night." Julia turned to her father. "Not that *you* would know or care. When was the last time you came to see her?"

"I was here two days ago, Julia," he said evenly. "I brought your mother a few new things to wear."

"That Roberta picked out?"

If this had *truly* been a couple's session, Hodges thought now, she would interrupt Julia and ask her to reflect on the hostility in her last exchange, but she was *not* their therapist, she reminded herself. She was merely a facilitator, and all she could do right now was sit back and discreetly pretend not to hear their crossfire.

"That's out of line, Julia," Thomas Merchant told his daughter. He turned to Constance. "I'm sorry you have to sit through this."

"Whatever," Julia continued. "All I know is, my mother did *not* have a bad heart."

"We *don't* really know that," said Thomas.

"There's a *lot* we don't know." Julia turned back to Hodges. "Like why my mother's night caregiver—what's his name? Brandon Johnson?—ran out of here this morning and what he poured down my mother's throat in a medicine cup last night."

The words hit Hodges like a jolt of electric current, and she found herself too rattled to speak. She had felt this level of panic only one other time in her life, sitting in her Central Park West office, after an enraged patient had slammed her stained glass desk lamp on the floor and shattered the silence into thousands of tiny colored shards. He had brought his face so close to hers that she could feel his tensile fury. She had frozen then, and she froze now.

"I had a camera in her room, a motion-sensitive camera in her alarm clock."

"Jesus Christ, Julia." Merchant looked appalled.

Julia kept her eyes on Hodges. "When he moved my mother into Park Manor, I had the idea I'd protect her from caregiver abuse. The camera's been there all this time, and today I took it home and played it. I wanted to see my mother alive one last time. I didn't expect to see that caregiver forcing her to swallow something while the nurse stood by watching. I guess my instincts were right when I bought that camera. I'd really like to know what was in that medicine cup."

Hodges fought back her panic with deep, even breaths. At Park Manor, only the nurse on duty was authorized to administer medications. She wore an orange coat while she prepared and dispensed them. The coat signaled to the rest of the staff that she should not be approached, spoken to, or distracted. Hodges did not even want to think about the damage it would cause to Park Manor's reputation if news surfaced that a nurse and a caregiver had violated the sacrosanct protocol. Constance would *not* let that happen. She was Park Manor's lion at the gate. If the institution were tarnished, she would be the biggest loser. Park Manor, after all, was her passport into a world few regular New Yorkers like herself ever penetrated. She had attended cocktail parties in the private homes of the city's largest benefactors. She was invited to receptions and fundraisers in all the best venues of the city. She could pick up her phone and call heads of corporations, private school headmasters, Broadway producers, and city officials, and they would all take her calls. But her access would end without Park Manor.

"I can assure you, Julia," she said with as much conviction as she could summon, "that caregivers *never* administer medication to patients. Mrs. Merchant tended to get dehydrated. Dr. Fisher had instructed her caregivers to make every effort to get her to drink. This included giving her water at bedtime.

Brandon was Mrs. Merchant's primary night caregiver. This was his responsibility."

"Was it also his *responsibility* to kneel at her bedside and kiss her cold forehead this morning at five thirty-three AM?"

Hodges stared at her clear mug of cold, cloudy coffee. She had never felt so blindsided in her life. The effort to appear outwardly calm was straining every muscle in her body. She had always judged Julia Merchant as just one more unremarkable adult child of insanely accomplished parents, but now she wasn't so sure.

"And don't tell me you didn't think something was amiss," Julia continued. "Why else were those caregivers in your office this morning?"

At least Hodges could respond to this. "It's standard procedure to debrief the staff on duty when a death occurs."

"Do you check their pockets, too? Because I'd like to know where my mother's little gold charm is, the dancer charm she used to wear around her neck. It wasn't in her bedside drawer this morning when I went into her room. That charm had sentimental value to me and I want it back. I want to debrief that Brandon myself."

Hodges already knew what the unpleasant consequences of that would be. Julia Merchant would find out that Brandon had resigned. Hodges would have to acknowledge that he had violated Lucy's nutritional plan. Then Julia might leap to the conclusion that other, more serious violations had occurred. The grieving reacted to their losses in unpredictable ways, and Julia was evidently looking to cast blame. Hodges had no choice. "Brandon is off duty tonight and tomorrow," she lied. "But I'm sure he would never take anything from Mrs. Merchant's room."

"Oh? And how can you be so sure?"

Lies always begat more lies, Constance thought. But what choice did she have? "Because I have every confidence in Brandon. He is a wonderful caregiver. He was devoted to Mrs. Merchant."

CHAPTER 11

Fine icy snow crystals stabbed Julia's face as she pulled on the heavy glass door of Manhattan North. The nor'easter was intensifying and the wind wanted to keep the door shut. When she finally squeezed through, she felt swallowed up in this unfamiliar world within the Manhattan she knew. She supposed she had passed police precincts hundreds of times, but she had never, she realized now, actually entered one of them.

She stared through the wall of bulletproof glass ten feet in front of her. Behind the glass, uniformed officers soundlessly stared at computer screens, spoke into phones, and passed documents among themselves. They were like exotic fish in an aquarium, and she was an incidental visitor staring into their unfamiliar habitat. She hugged herself. Was it crazy to have come here? Would they believe her? Could she make them believe her? She took a step backward and slammed into a man coming through the door behind her. She lost her balance. He caught her. She turned. A shield was clipped to his belt. He asked, "Can I help you?"

"I'm looking for Detective Codella."

Then his squinting eyes traveled the length of her body, but not in a lurid way. She imagined he was wondering what event or circumstance required a woman dressed like her to seek out a homicide detective. He pointed to a counter at the far end of the bulletproof glass. "Talk to the desk sergeant."

Julia approached the counter. The desk sergeant stood with a phone wedged between his ear and shoulder. His bulging stomach pressed against the buttons of his blue shirt. Someone with so much belly fat was destined to suffer a massive heart attack and die in his early fifties, she thought. But maybe he wouldn't. Maybe he had protective genes that shielded him from his self-destructive appetites, unlike her mother, whose pernicious genes had prevailed over her ultrahealthy lifestyle. Julia found herself resenting this apparently undisciplined stranger, and by the time he hung up and acknowledged her, the resentment had fermented into disgust and rage. She struggled to hide these emotions. "I need to speak with Detective Codella."

"Is she expecting you?"

"Not exactly, but—" She couldn't admit that she had never once met Claire Codella or any other detective in Manhattan or any borough, city, or state. "I know her, and it's very important."

He jotted Julia's name on a pad. Then he turned and walked to a desk against the back wall of his aquarium. She could not hear what he said as he stood with the phone to his ear again. Finally he returned. "She doesn't recognize your name."

"She'll know me when she sees me. It's important I speak with her. Please, just tell her I need five minutes."

He frowned. "This is a police station. I'm not your messenger."

Julia pushed past her antipathy and summoned a respectful tone. "I realize that—" She read his name plate quickly. "—Sergeant Mills. And I wouldn't take your time like this if it weren't *extremely* important."

He returned to the phone grudgingly. She watched him punch numbers and speak again. She held her breath. If Detective Codella refused to see her, what then? Would she accept defeat, go home, and try to forget what had happened? Would she talk herself into believing that her mother had died a peaceful and natural death in her sleep? No. She would make a scene and demand the attention she deserved.

Finally Mills hung up and crossed the floor in her direction. He pointed to a bench against the wall behind her. "Sit over there. She'll get to you when she can."

The bench was hard. Maybe, she thought, it was meant to dissuade people like herself, people without an obvious, tangible emergency—blood dripping down their faces, angry purple bruises, knife cuts, gunshot wounds—from wasting the police department's time. But she wasn't going to be dissuaded, she told herself as the minutes passed. She would stay right here. She would stay as long as it took. She would make them so uncomfortable that they had to get the detective. If necessary, she would go back to the desk sergeant and say, "Do you have any idea who I am?"

Half an hour later, Claire Codella finally appeared. Julia guessed that she was about thirty-five years old. She was no more than five foot three, and her straight black hair was barely long enough to tuck behind her ears. She approached Julia with hands stuffed into the pockets of gray slacks. The sleeves of her black silk blouse had been rolled inelegantly to the elbows. Julia noticed the cold gray gun in her shoulder holster and the gleaming gold sunburst outlining the NYPD shield attached to her black leather belt. She couldn't decide if the detective looked stylish or terribly disheveled.

Codella stopped two feet in front of the bench and stared at her intently. "We've never met."

"No."

"You told the desk sergeant we had."

Julia heard the indictment implanted in the simple observation. *You lied. You tricked me down here.* "I know," she admitted, "but I've read about you."

"That's hardly the same thing."

Julia felt her confidence shrivel, but she pressed on. "My mother died this morning."

Codella's face registered no reaction to this. "And your mother is?"

"Lucy Merchant. Lucy Martinelli Merchant. Maybe you don't recognize the name, but—"

"I know who she is." The detective's tone seemed to say, *Do you think I don't read the papers? Do you suppose I never go to see a Broadway show?* "So what brings you to me, Ms. Merchant?"

"I think someone murdered her."

CHAPTER 12

Baiba Lielkaja punched the combination code and waited for the Nostalgia Neighborhood doors to open. She did not understand why Hodges had to speak to her right this minute. Hodges knew as well as she did that Nostalgia was chaotic between five and six o'clock and that she was needed to orchestrate the multitude of simultaneous activities. The dining room had to be arranged. Meals for a range of dietary restrictions were being delivered from the downstairs kitchen. Residents had to be changed, dressed, and coiffed in a way that would please family members who showed up unannounced to share the dinner hour with their "loved ones."

These family members knew the Nostalgia Neighborhood combination code and felt absolutely entitled—rightly so, Baiba supposed, given the exorbitant fees they paid—to treat the premises as they would their own home. Thus they went straight into the dining room and snapped their fingers for coffee while the caregivers were trying to seat residents and serve them the correct gluten-free, sugar-free, or sodium-free meal. Some of these visitors pushed tables together and moved chairs, changing the course of well-established walkways. Not only did this make transporting plates to tables more difficult for the servers, but it made navigation next to impossible for still-ambulatory residents whose neural pathways did not adjust well to sudden alterations in the physical landscape.

Just last night, Dottie Lautner, who was in a fairly advanced stage of Alzheimer's, had walked right into a rearranged chair, fallen onto her left elbow, and cried out in pain. Lorena Vivas, the young but highly competent day nurse, had rushed out of the dispensary in her orange coat and calmed Mrs. Lautner with her soothing voice. But the nurse had not liked the bruise under Mrs. Lautner's skin or the swelling around her elbow, and Mrs. Lautner could not string together enough coherent words to answer simple questions like "Where do you hurt?" or "Can you bend your arm?" Lorena had asked Baiba to summon the on-call ambulance crew, and then Baiba had faced the unenviable task of calling Mrs. Lautner's niece, who was only too ready to blame things on the staff.

What Nostalgia needed was a seating hostess for families, Baiba decided as she stepped off the elevator. In fact, she would mention this to Ms. Hodges right now, she thought. But when she reached Hodges's office, she saw Cheryl O'Brien seated in front of the director's desk. Why was she here two hours before her shift began? Baiba looked from Cheryl to the stony-faced Hodges and realized they would not be discussing seating hostesses today. Something was wrong. Something was *very* wrong.

"Close the door and have a seat," said the director in a calm, cool voice.

Baiba did as she had been instructed. "What is it?"

"A small complication. Nothing the three of us can't resolve together." Hodges turned to Cheryl. "It's come to my attention, Cheryl, that Julia Merchant had a hidden camera in her mother's bedroom."

"A *what*?"

"You heard me, Cheryl. A camera. Hidden in a clock radio. And that camera recorded you and Brandon last night. Apparently it shows you handing a medicine cup to Brandon and Brandon dispensing the contents to Mrs. Merchant."

Cheryl cringed. "I tried to do it my—"

"Stop!" Hodges raised her hand like a stern crossing guard. "Let me finish. Please."

Baiba felt a fireball combust in her chest. Heat spread to her shoulders and neck. Cheryl was going to get dismissed. And *she* would get fired, too. *She*, after all, was the one who had allowed Cheryl to violate the dispensation guidelines. What else was she supposed to have done? From her very first shift at Park Manor, Cheryl's unremarkable face had triggered inexplicable rage within Lucy Merchant. Every time Cheryl came near her, Lucy screamed the same words: *Get away from me, Daddy. You can't make me drink it. Get out. Get out!* And only Brandon's soothing voice could calm her. He alone could inveigle her to drink her meds. So he had accompanied Cheryl into Lucy's suite on virtually every night shift Cheryl had worked in her six months at Park Manor, and Baiba had allowed it to happen, because rules were one thing and reality was another.

Baiba glanced out the window where snow was falling onto the cedar-planked paths in the now flowerless courtyard. "Julia Merchant is upset by her mother's death," Ms. Hodges was saying. "She doesn't accept that her mother has passed away peacefully. And in her effort to explain the death, she may be reading into the images her camera recorded. I believe she's under the impression, Cheryl, that you handed Brandon *medicine* rather than a drink of *water* to give to her mother."

Cheryl opened her mouth to speak—to confess, Baiba supposed—but again Hodges raised a hand. "You don't need to explain, Cheryl. I *know* what happened. We all know what happened, and more importantly, we know what *didn't* happen. You filled the medicine cup with water, and Brandon helped Lucy drink it. All three of us know that you did not violate the dispensation protocol. We know you would *never* jeopardize your position or a patient's safety. Isn't that right?" She stared straight at Cheryl.

And now Baiba understood the purpose of this conclave. Hodges, who had the most to lose if Julia Merchant uploaded that video to the Internet or took it to the press, was proffering a conspiracy of self-preservation. She had crafted a life raft, but the raft would only float if they all climbed aboard.

Baiba held her breath. Cheryl's face was a pale canvas of panic, guilt, and indecision. Hodges repeated her invitation onto the raft. "You're a professional, Cheryl. You would *never* jeopardize a patient's well-being. Isn't that right?" And finally Cheryl's head began to nod, tentatively at first and then more decisively.

Hodges moved around the desk. She leaned on the front edge and continued to look directly into Cheryl's eyes. "Julia Merchant may ask you some questions." Her voice was gentle now. "And if she does, I don't want you to feel alarmed or defensive. I want you to tell her the *truth*. You gave Brandon *water*. You and Brandon did your job. You kept Mrs. Merchant hydrated according to Dr. Fisher's order. You followed the care plan, and I want you to know that Baiba and I have total confidence in you." She turned to Baiba. "Isn't that right?" Baiba heard the silent, serrated edge in Hodges's voice, the subtext intended just for her: *I'll get to you next.*

Then Cheryl was gone, and Hodges's granite eyes locked onto Baiba. Baiba's throat closed. She found that her muscles could not perform the simple involuntary reflex of swallowing. Hodges spoke in a voice that was simultaneously calm and chilling. "You have to make this right. You have to get him back here and get him on board with the narrative. Whatever it takes. Do you understand?"

CHAPTER 13

Julia Merchant tapped *Pause* and pointed to the image on her iPad screen. "Right there. You see? The nurse hands him the cup. Then she looks toward the door. You can tell she's afraid someone's going to come in."

Codella considered. Could you *really* tell that? Julia Merchant *believed* that her mother was the victim of a crime, and so she saw malice in a potentially innocuous turn of a nurse's head. "Maybe she just heard a noise. Maybe someone called her name."

"At Park Manor only a nurse gives out medicine. That's the rule, and I've seen how careful they are to keep the caregivers away from the nurse while she's dispensing. I'm telling you. This nurse knew she was doing something wrong."

"Did you share your concern with someone in charge?"

"The director. Constance Hodges. And she made up a lame story about how my mother gets dehydrated and the caregiver was only giving her water."

"How do you know it's a lame story?" Codella studied the young woman's spotless twenty-something skin, her highlighted hair, and the intricate links of the expensive gold chain around her neck. "Isn't dehydration a legitimate concern with people who can't take care of themselves?"

"I have other evidence." Julia Merchant reached for the Hermes bag hooked to the back of her chair. The bag's gold hardware gleamed as she set it on her lap and carefully extracted a bulky wad of paper toweling. She lay the toweling on the desk between them and slowly unraveled it to reveal beige balls of fuzz matted with a viscous substance. "*This* is what they poured down my mother's throat."

Codella waited for the explanation she knew was coming.

"After my father and I met with Constance Hodges, I went back to my mother's room, to the exact spot where the nurse and caregiver are standing in this video, and when I looked down, I saw a spill in the carpet—and not an old dried-up spill. What-ever they gave her last night is in these carpet fibers, and it isn't water, Detective."

Codella eyed the clotted beige fibers resting in the nest of toweling. Julia Merchant did not have enough evidence, she knew, on which to base her deduction. "Just because this was on her carpet doesn't mean it was in the caregiver's cup," she said.

"No, but isn't it likely?"

"And even if it's from the cup, that doesn't mean it had any-thing to do with her death."

"But it could, and given the circumstances, aren't you being a little dismissive?"

"I'm not being dismissive," said Codella. "I'm being objective."

As she said this, her iPhone lit up and her oncologist's name appeared. He was a single cell tower connection away from her Manhattan North office, she thought. He was ready to give her the results of her scan. All she had to do was swipe the surface of her screen. She rubbed her eyes. She weighed Julia Merchant's demand for attention against her own need for reas-surance. *Goddammit.* Then she turned the phone facedown and forced her focus back to the moment. "Let's review the *facts*," she said. "Just the *facts*. A caregiver found your mother in her bed around four this morning."

"Right."

"And no one performed CPR."

"Because my father signed a Do Not Resuscitate Order."

"And the Park Manor physician who certified her death attributed it to natural causes."

"He said her heart had *simply stopped*. But how could that be? Hearts don't just stop. She was perfectly healthy when I fed her dinner yesterday."

"To the best of your knowledge," Codella pointed out.

"What do you mean by that?" The young woman pressed her lips together.

"I mean you're not a doctor."

"Obviously. But I know my mother. I would know if something were wrong with her."

Would you? Codella wanted to ask. *Are you sure about that?* A year and a half ago, hadn't she been equally confident about her own diagnostic skills? Hadn't she dismissed the pain in her abdomen as a simple virus and delayed seeing a doctor for weeks and weeks because it never occurred to her that an aggressive lymphoma could be wrapping itself around *her* intestines? She glanced at her iPhone. She wanted those scan results. She wanted them *now*.

"And if you need more *facts*," Julia Merchant continued, "this morning the same caregiver went into my mother's room *after* she was dead. He kissed her forehead and talked to her for about two minutes. It's on the video. Doesn't that strike you as strange?"

Codella thought about that. "Maybe. Maybe not."

"I think he stole something, too—a little charm she had in her bedside table drawer, a little gold dancer. You can't see that part of the room on the video, but the charm was in the drawer yesterday, and this morning it wasn't."

"Have any other things gone missing while your mother's been at Park Manor?"

"I don't know. Honestly, I never thought to check."

"You've had the surveillance camera in your mother's room for how long?" Codella studied the sleek black piece of hardware sitting on her desk next to Julia Merchant's iPad.

"Eighteen months. Since she moved there."

"And in all that time, have you ever recorded anything else that disturbed you? Is this the first time you've seen a nurse and a caregiver together in your mother's room?"

"No, but—" Julia Merchant paused. "I only watched the recordings a couple of times."

"Just a couple?"

"Right after she moved in."

And now Codella waited again. She knew when to probe and when to let silence do the work. You posed your questions to lead a person to the brink of some unrehearsed revelation, and then you sat back in the demanding silence and observed the drama that unfolded.

"I was angry when my father put her in there," Julia Merchant confessed. "I wanted it to be a bad place, okay? So I bought this camera—top of the line, motion sensitive—and I *hoped* it would show them neglecting her. I *wanted* to prove he was wrong. I watched the video two or three times, but then I gave up."

"Because you saw no evidence of mistreatment."

"Because I knew he had won. He always wins. But that's history. What matters now is *this*." She pointed to the sticky carpet fibers. "What if that nurse and caregiver are a team of mercy killers who go into rest homes and euthanize people?"

"Have any other Park Manor residents died unexpectedly while this nurse and caregiver have been on staff?"

"Not that I know of, but . . ." Julia Merchant folded her arms. "Look, my mother was only fifty-six years old, and she didn't remember my name most of the time, but at least she was there. At least I could be with her, feed her, talk to her. Something bad has happened. I *know* it, even if I can't prove it. My mother can't speak for herself. I have to do it for her. She was always there for me; now I need to be there for her. You're a daughter too, Detective. Put yourself in my shoes. Wouldn't you want to know what they made her drink?"

Codella bristled at the presumed parallel between their lives and emotions. She leaned forward and spoke emphatically.

"Discuss this with your father. Ask him to arrange a post-mortem exam."

"I already did. He doesn't want one."

"Then request one yourself."

"He wants me to drop the issue. He made it clear." She paused, and then added, "But maybe *you* could talk to him."

Talk to him, Codella thought, *or investigate him?* She had enough complications to deal with right now, and she certainly didn't intend to become a pawn in whatever family drama was playing out between a grieving daughter and a powerful New York bank chairman. "No," she said. "You speak to him again. Share your concerns. Explain that an autopsy would help you accept your mother's death and move on."

"But—"

"I'm sorry." Codella pushed out her chair to signal that the conversation was over. "But the facts you've described just don't raise enough red flags to warrant a police inquiry. My advice to you is to ask for the autopsy."

The young woman stood, obviously displeased by Codella's response. "I expected more from you, Detective," she said with the brittle, arrogant tone of people used to getting what they wanted. And then she turned to leave.

When she was gone, Codella shut her door and immediately checked her voicemail. As usual, Dr. Abrams had not left her scan results on his message. He never did that. Good results or bad, you had to get them live. She phoned his office, but her call went straight to the after-hours message. She banged her fist against her desk. *Fuck.*

Then she stared at the nest of carpet fibers Julia Merchant had left behind. *You're a daughter, too, Detective. Put yourself in my shoes*, the young woman had said. *Wouldn't you want to know what they made her drink?* Why did people always assume you felt the same things they did? Why did they act as if filial connection was encoded into everyone's genome? Codella tried to summon an image of her own mother now, but the pixels of her memory were degraded by time. She had not seen her mother in eighteen years, and in that time, her mother had become a mere idea. *If I passed her on the street*, she wondered, *would I even recognize her?*

She shook her head, but she couldn't shake the thoughts. She had consoled the daughters and sons of true murder victims many times and never felt this pull toward her own past. For some reason, Julia Merchant's words had picked the lock on a maximum-security section of her brain where all the memories she didn't want to face were stored. Was it because she was nervous about the scan results? Was thinking about her mother easier than thinking about Haggerty and how she felt about him? She pounded her fist on the desk. She didn't give a damn about her mother.

She concentrated on the beige fibers glued together with yellowish coagulated syrup. Then she picked up the phone and dialed Detective Eduardo Muñoz. She didn't give him time for small talk. "You were a narc, Muñoz. You know how to do presumptive drug tests, right? Can you get your hands on some test kits right now?"

CHAPTER 14

Brandon felt the woman's eyes on him as soon as she stepped on the train. She was looking for clues. That's what people did when they saw him. First they stared into his eyes, as if his pupils were apertures that would reveal absolutes. Then they examined the shape of his eyebrows, the size of his nose, the outline of his lips. And when those features failed to deliver a verdict, their gaze dropped. Now he felt the woman's eyes pat down his chest, assess the veins on his hands, measure the size of his feet. He was, he supposed, an optical illusion to her—from this angle, man, from that angle, woman. And people, he had noticed, rarely tired of staring at optical illusions.

As the J Train groaned to a stop at Canal Street, the woman's eyes collided with his and he smiled at her. He always smiled at the people he caught midstare. Once in a while the overture disarmed them; their expression would soften, and he would feel as if he had affected a small change in their perceptions. But this woman quickly averted her gaze. When she got off at Delancey Street, Brandon closed his eyes and tried not to think as the train rattled over the Williamsburg Bridge.

The neighbor's baby was crying when he unlocked the door to his walk-up. He dropped his backpack just inside and crossed the small living room and kitchen alcove to his even smaller bedroom. He sat on the edge of the bed and plugged his phone into its charger. At this hour on a Monday, he would normally be at Park Manor. But he wasn't going to Park Manor ever again. He could have stayed in the library and done his homework there, but he hadn't felt like doing homework. He hadn't felt like doing anything. He still couldn't get Hodges's words out of his head. *You fed her ice cream? On whose authority?* And he couldn't stop thinking about Josie's betrayal or her contemptuous remark. *You call yourself a man?*

Fuck Josie, he told himself now. So what if he had cried about Lucy? Who was Josie or anyone to define the appropriate response to grief for a man or a woman? Who was she to categorize him?

He ran his palm against his jaw. He hadn't shaved for two days, and the scratchy stubble on his chin was a reassuring reality that counterbalanced the discomfort he felt when he lifted his shirt over his head, struggled out of his uncomfortable compression T-shirt, and confronted the reality of his breasts. After years of binding, they were like two deflated balloons.

He got in the shower. As the hot water beat against his hair, he told himself he would call Dr. Silverman's office first thing in the morning. He was *supposed* to make that call. Lucy's death was a sign that he needed to move forward in his journey. All the paperwork was done. Every penny he'd saved—along with Baiba's three thousand dollars—was sitting in a bank account waiting for him to make the call.

His phone was ringing as he turned off the shower. He yanked a towel off the rack and wrapped it around his hips as he went to answer. Baiba's voice in his ear said, "Brandon, where are you? I've been calling you all day."

"My phone died."

"I heard what happened in Ms. Hodges's office. I'm sorry."

"Don't be." He put the phone on speaker and set it on the bed so he could dry himself. "I'm glad it happened. Glad to be out of there. I only stayed for Lucy." As soon as he spoke the words, he realized his unintended slight. "And you, of course," he added, "but we'll still be friends, won't we?"

She didn't need to know that he wanted to be *more* than her friend. He could never tell her how he *really* felt about her. She might treat him differently if she knew that sometimes at night in his room, he imagined lying in bed with her. That he would sometimes touch himself while imagining *her* touching a part of him that didn't even exist. Baiba would never want him in that way, he supposed.

"Of course we'll still be friends," she said. "But you don't have to leave Park Manor like this."

"I turned in my badge, Baiba. And you know how Hodges feels about me anyway. She's not going to have me back, and besides, I don't want to come back."

"But I talked to her," Baiba said quickly. "I told her things don't run nearly as well when you're not there. I told her you're the best person we have in Nostalgia. That I need you—"

"You don't need me. You'll find someone else just as good. Park Manor is every caregiver's dream job—if you can stand wearing those burgundy polo shirts." He thought that would make her laugh, but it didn't.

"I don't *want* someone else. I want *you*. *Please* come back. *Please.*"

Brandon pulled boxers out of his drawer. He stared down at himself and replayed her words. *I don't want someone else. I want you.* If only she were saying those words about *him*, about her personal feelings for him. But she wasn't, of course. She wanted him back because of his competence and dependability, his willingness to do whatever she needed him to do. She knew her job would be much harder without him there. "How can you ask me that, Baiba?"

And then Baiba began to cry. She blurted out the whole story about Julia Merchant, her hidden camera, and what the camera had recorded. Brandon stopped dressing and sat on the edge of the bed.

"She thinks you gave medicine to her mother last night."

"Well, I did. You know that. So what?"

"So Julia Merchant is making a big deal out of it. Hodges is afraid she'll go to the press and say bad things about Park Manor. She told Julia there was only water in the cup. And she got Cheryl to promise that she'll go along with that story."

"And now she wants me to lie, too? Why would I do that for her?"

Baiba spoke very softly now. "Because I'm going to lose my job if you don't."

"She threatened you?"

"It was awful, Brandon. She knows I've been looking the other way while you helped Cheryl. And she knows I unlocked Lucy's room for you this morning. That was on Julia's video too. If Park Manor fires me after I've been there five years, where am I going to go? No other facility will touch me." She started to cry again.

She needed him right now, he thought, and he felt impelled by deeply ingrained protective instincts to respond to her need. He wished he could transport himself through the phone, hold her in his arms, and stroke her hair. She would let him do that, he thought. "Don't cry," he said. "Please. Just tell me what you need me to do."

She blew her nose. "I need you to come back," she said. "Only until this blows over. And tell anybody who asks that you gave Lucy water in that cup. I'm sorry, Brandon. I'm really sorry."

Brandon closed his eyes and sighed. "Okay," he finally said. "I'll do it. I'll come back tomorrow. But I'm doing it for *you*, Baiba. *Not* for her."

CHAPTER 15

Codella hadn't been in the detective's squad room of the 171st since the Sanchez case, but she still knew it as well as her own living room. To her left, immediately beyond the door, was the nondescript metal desk she had occupied for seven years before her promotion to Manhattan North Homicide. Now that desk belonged to Detective Sunil Ragavan. The small, handsome detective was hunched over the computer where he did his best forensic work. On the opposite side of the room, Vic Portino, the old man in the squad, was leaning back in his chair. He waved to her as he spoke into his phone, and she waved back. He was wearing one of his many Men's Wearhouse suits, and he hadn't lost an ounce of weight even though he'd supposedly gone on a diet since the last time she'd been there. He might have even gained a pound or two, she thought.

Detective Eduardo Muñoz stood up from his desk against the far wall. "It's good to see you, Detective." He gave her a big grin.

"Good to see you, too, Muñoz." She smiled up at him. His wavy black hair was short on top and faded at the temples. He had the broad shoulders and flat stomach of someone who worked out regularly. When she had first met him—at the Sanchez murder scene—she'd been a little unnerved by his height and build. That had been her first case after cancer treatment, and it was Muñoz's first case as a precinct detective after two years in undercover narcotics. She'd had to prove she was still in the game, and he'd had to prove he was more than just a buy and bust guy. To make matters worse, Marty Blackstone, the bully of the 171st, had christened him Rainbow Dick because he was gay. Luckily, Codella and Muñoz had recognized each other's vulnerabilities and helped each other.

"You have the tests?"

"Yes. For a range of narcotics. If it's something other than that, you'll have to send it to the lab." He pointed toward the door. "I've set things up in interview room A."

They walked across the hall. Muñoz had everything carefully arranged on the table. She watched him roll his shirtsleeves to the elbows, exposing thick honey-brown forearms. He slid his large hands into stretchy nitrile surgical gloves. Only then did he open the evidence bag with the fibers Julia Merchant had brought to Codella's office. He removed a clump with sterile tweezers and set it carefully on a clean paper surface. Then he opened the box of presumptive test kits and took out one of the clear plastic tubes containing a test ampule. He removed the ampule from its plastic tube, peeled off the protective paper over the tip, and carefully dabbed the sticky tip against the rug fiber. Then he replaced the ampule inside the clear tube, sealed the cap, and squeezed hard against the tube to break the ampule and release the test solution.

They watched the liquid change to violet. Muñoz moved the tube close to the test kit's color chart on which each small swatch signaled a different opiate. "I think we're looking at oxycodone here," he said. "What do you think?"

CHAPTER 16

Four inches of snow had fallen by the time Felipe pulled up in front of her building. He climbed out, came around the back of the Escalade, and opened the rear curbside door. She slid into the familiar passenger seat. The SUV had been warmed to a stifling degree, and she immediately wished that she were still standing on the street in the arctic winds. She closed her eyes. As Felipe drove, each surge of the accelerator, depression of the brake, and jerk of the steering wheel vibrated through her body as if she were melded with the vehicle's transmission. Why was she going back to Merchant when she'd promised herself that she wouldn't?

At his Fifth Avenue building, the night doorman helped her out and escorted her into the lobby. *I am like a FedEx shipment moving through a distribution chain,* she thought. The doorman announced her arrival and led her to an oak-lined elevator. A few seconds later, the elevator doors opened directly into Merchant's vast three-floor apartment and he received his "package" with a satisfied smile. "You see." He kissed her cheek. "A little snow isn't going to keep you from me." His palms traced the outline of her waist and hips, and she felt a twinge of revulsion. He must have sensed it, she thought, because he lowered his hands, and his look turned harder. His voice seemed cool when he said, "Go get comfortable. I have to make a call. I won't be long."

She felt his eyes follow her down the corridor to the room they shared each time she came here. She had never explored the other corridors of his residence. He had never invited her into those passageways or up the stairs to different levels. He had always steered her—*confined* her, she thought now—to this one particular room. The first time she'd entered it, she had judged it to be twice as large as her entire studio apartment. To the right was an elegant sitting area with two inviting love seats facing a working fireplace. A fire was lit tonight, she noticed, and on the coffee table between the love seats, two facedown glasses sat on a tray next to a champagne bottle in an ice bucket.

Her eyes moved left. In a room of these dimensions, even the king-size bed looked small. She turned away from it uneasily and stared at the windows on the wall opposite the door. She walked to the center window and pressed her forehead against the cold glass pane. The snowflakes falling through the darkness seemed to have soundproofed the city below. The lanterns lining Fifth Avenue illuminated spindly black branches of the trees in Central Park. *I shouldn't be here*, she thought.

But two months ago, Baiba had wanted to be here more than anything. She still vividly remembered the afternoon when Merchant had stopped her after his visit to Nostalgia and murmured, "Why don't you have dinner with me tonight." She could so easily have avoided that invitation by ignoring his smiles and subtle flirtations in the weeks leading up to it. But she had not ignored them. She had enjoyed his attention. She had encouraged it, she supposed. And by the time he extended the dinner invitation, she had already rationalized her acceptance. Yes, he was technically married, but he wasn't truly being unfaithful. Lucy Merchant didn't even know him anymore. And unlike some of the men with wives in Nostalgia, he had never attempted to make unseemly and inappropriate "conjugal" visits to a woman who couldn't legally consent. For all intents and purposes, he was a handsome, eligible, sexually attractive—and wealthy—widower.

They had dined at a discreet corner table in the Pool Room of the Four Seasons. On her empty stomach, the crisp white wine had gone quickly to her head. They'd shared oysters and tuna tartare before their main courses. He had commented on the hypnotic blueness of her eyes and asked about her childhood in Riga, her education, and her ambitions. And all during the meal his knee had lightly touched hers below the table.

When the meal was over, he had dropped his Black Card onto the check and leaned so close that Baiba felt his breath against her ear as he whispered, "I want to take you home with me. Tell me you want to come." She still felt that light touch of his breath after he sat up. For several seconds, she had stared at the glowing pool lights below the bubbling water in the center of the dining room. The wine and the warmth of those lights drowned out the warnings in her mind, and finally she met his eyes and said, "Yes. I want to come with you."

An hour later they entered this room for the first time. He'd sat on the edge of the bed, fully clothed, and said, "Take your dress off for me." And when her dress had fallen to the floor, he had gestured her over and pulled her face down across his lap in one practiced move, slipped his fingers under the edge of her panties, kneaded her buttocks, and murmured appreciatively. "You're a walking sin. You need a spanking for being so sexy. Tell me you want me to spank you."

For an instant Baiba had thought he must be joking. She tried to sit up, but he pressed her head back down. "Tell me," he demanded, and then she'd felt the first prick of fear, but something else, too, swimming just below it. Curiosity. Excitement. Desire. "I want to hear you say it," he repeated, and she heard herself say the words, and in saying them, she found that she did want him to do it. Her face had burned with deep self-consciousness and arousal as his fingers pulled back the fabric and his palm made contact with her flesh. Her arousal and her shame at it were so intricately entwined that she could not separate the two. Each sting of his palm against her skin had brought the two states closer and closer until the punishment was pleasure and the intensity of her desire was beyond anything she had ever felt. And in that state, it was suddenly so easy to rationalize what was happening. It was not strange at all, she told herself. Merchant was not actually *hurting* her. They were playing a sexual game. Everyone, she told herself as he ordered her onto her hands and knees and she heard the unzipping of his slacks, *everyone* explored their boundaries when it came to sex. How else did you ever really lose yourself to pleasure? How else did you reach a state of pure abandon in which you became nothing more than an ego-less organism hooked to a high voltage cable?

But two hours later, curled into the backseat as Felipe deposited her home, her arousal and shame had uncoiled into separate entities again and she felt something more like self-loathing. *I will never go back there*, she had told herself. *I will never let him do that to me again.* But even as she'd made the vow, she knew she would go back, that she wanted to go back. And here she was yet again.

Baiba lifted her forehead from the cold windowpane. When Merchant came in, he would expect to find her undressed, she thought, and her fingers instinctively reached for the top button of her blouse, but they were like the numb extremities of a frost-bite victim and would not cooperate. She should not be here, she thought again. Lucy Merchant had died less than twenty-four hours ago, and being here tonight was vulgar, tasteless, and unspeakable. *He* was unspeakable. He was not the same man she had dined with on that first night when he could not take his eyes off her. That night, she had believed she had a unique hold over him, that he wanted *her*—only her—and that Lucy Merchant's disease, her move to Park Manor, her quick deterioration over the past eighteen months, had all been preordained so that she and Thomas would be together.

But what if she had never been the real object of his longing? What if she had only seen what she wanted to see that night in the Four Seasons? If he truly cared about her, would he sequester her in this room? Would he keep her waiting while he made his phone calls? The truth, she finally allowed herself to recognize, was that she—Baiba—meant nothing to him. She had probably *never* meant anything to him. He might be content with *any* attractive blond willing to submit to his fantasy requirements—requirements that had grown steadily more demeaning.

She heard his footsteps. She watched the doorknob turn. She put her hand to her throat as the door swung open. She saw him look at her, take in the fact that she was still dressed, and frown.

"I have to go," she said quickly, reaching for her coat.

"Don't be silly. You just got here." He held out the glass in his hand and smiled. "Here. Drink this. Let's sit by the fire."

She stared at the clear, iced liquid in the tumbler. Her eyes darted to the two empty glasses on the coffee table.

"Go on," he coaxed.

She shook her head, or she thought that she was shaking her head. She couldn't be sure. Nothing seemed quite real. *She* did not feel quite real.

"Here." He stepped closer. "Have a little drink."

And then she felt fear in its undiluted form. *Get away from me,* she wanted to say. *You can't make me drink that. Get out.* And in a sudden synaptic explosion that finally destroyed whatever force had been pulling her here, she realized that she had mentally uttered Lucy Merchant's nightly refrain. The tips of her fingers tingled. Her legs felt weak. "I have to go. I really have to go."

He grabbed her arm. "That's fine," he said, "but you don't look well. Have this drink first. You'll feel better. Then Felipe can take you home."

He steered her to a love seat, placed the glass in her hand, and guided it to her lips.

CHAPTER 17

Their legs were still intertwined. Codella closed her eyes, and for an instant *all* of her was in the bed, between the sheets, with him. But in the very next instant, Julia Merchant's voice was in her mind pulling her away from this comfortable reality. *You're a daughter, too. A daughter. You're a daughter.* And then she was thinking about the oxycodone Muñoz had detected in the rug fibers. "I'm going over to that Park Manor place tomorrow," she told Haggerty. "I'm going to get my own carpet sample. I'll have Muñoz run a test on that one, too."

Haggerty's lips were against the back of her head. "Do you always mix business with pleasure?"

"Sorry."

He sighed. "Remember, those test kits can lie. It could be a false positive."

"I know, I know. And I vouchered the fibers and sent them to the lab, but it could take weeks to get confirmation, and Julia Merchant's evidence would never be admissible anyway. I have to get my own sample before there's no sample to get."

He rested his warm palm against her bare stomach. "Are you sure you're not just manufacturing a homicide case because McGowan won't give you one?"

His question was justified, she knew, because for three months he had been the sounding board for her frustration. He had listened patiently as she described every daily slight McGowan and

Fisk had dealt her. And he had talked her off the ledge the night the Manhattan North duty sergeant steered a homicide to Fisk when she was the detective on call. "That case was mine," she'd told Haggerty as they sat in a vegan restaurant on Amsterdam Avenue eating organic coconut açaí bowls. Well, *she* was eating hers and he was looking at his skeptically. "McGowan's got his people deliberately shutting me out. I should go over his head with a complaint on that."

"And then he'd really have it in for you," Haggerty had said as he tentatively sampled the muddy mixture in his bowl. "Listen, Claire. You've got to keep your cool. Don't let him see how you really feel. Remember, he's only there because he's got two uncles with captain shields. Wait him out. Sooner or later he'll do something really stupid and they'll ship him off to some other unlucky squad."

Now she placed her palm over Haggerty's hand. She looked out the window and tried to see the tip of the Empire State Building's spire—on very clear nights it was just visible over the rooftops—but tonight the falling snow concealed it. "Thanks," she said.

"For what?"

"I don't know. Just thanks for being here."

"Does that mean I get to spend the night?"

"Maybe. If you stop leaving the toilet seat up."

She could feel him grinning in the dark, and she thought about how she had liked that grin from the moment she had met him eight years ago, the day she had joined the 171st. Three detectives had been sitting in the squad room that day, she remembered, but only Haggerty had looked up at her.

"Which one of these desks is mine?" she'd asked.

He shrugged and patted the metal desk next to his. "This one's free—if you want to sit by your new partner."

The flirtation was harmless, but the last thing she wanted was a squad of male detectives infusing every word to her with sexual innuendo. "Thanks," she answered coolly.

He seemed to get the message. "Where you from, Codella?" he asked in a neutral voice, speaking low.

"Cranston, Rhode Island."

"Cranston, huh? Aren't you supposed to pronounce that Craaaaanston?" And then he had shown her that grin.

"Pretty good." She smiled. "But it needs to be a little more nasal."

"Don't you want to know where I'm from?"

Codella booted up the computer terminal at her new desk and wondered if it had been vacant because no one wanted to listen to his chatter.

"Staten Island," he volunteered.

"The borough nobody wants?"

"Hey, we don't get to choose where we're born, now do we?" He raised an eyebrow, and she had the uncanny sense that he was telling her, *I get you. I know who you are.*

Haggerty had been her partner her entire time at the 171st, and she had come to know all his habits as well as he knew hers. If he'd spent the night with some woman he'd picked up in a bar, he arrived the next morning in yesterday's clothes, shaved in the second floor precinct bathroom, and slapped on too much cologne, which she had to breathe all day. If he'd spent the night with a bottle of Knob Creek, his breakfast would be hard-boiled eggs and tea loaded with sugar. He smoked when he was thinking. And when he was depressed, he flirted with her to distract himself and she'd have to say, "Cut the bullshit." But Haggerty hadn't really opened up to her until three years ago when she and Vic Portino pulled him out of a pub after he picked a fight with a guy at the bar. She took him to her apartment, sat him on her couch with a cup of strong coffee, and just watched him.

"You got a boyfriend, Codella?" he asked her.

"You know I don't do *boyfriends*, Haggerty."

"You don't see yourself getting married, making a couple of babies, having the perfect life?"

"Who the fuck has the perfect life?"

"I don't know." His speech was thick from the alcohol. "I see these rich moms in their tight yoga outfits dropping kids off at private school every morning. Their lives seem pretty damn perfect."

"Drink the coffee, Haggerty."

But he didn't sip it once, and his eyes were so red and squinted she wondered if he could even bring her into focus.

He leaned forward and set down the untouched coffee. "I once thought I'd get married, have kids. Even bought an engagement ring. Cost me twelve big ones I didn't have, but I was in *love*." He laughed. His laughter turned almost uncontrollable.

"Drink some coffee," she said again.

He still didn't touch the coffee. "Her name was Cindy. Had a big apartment in Murray Hill—courtesy of Daddy." His head flopped back on her couch, and he stared at the ceiling. "God, I loved to go out with her, Codella. I loved to be seen with her. Stupid, huh? Shallow of me? But she was smart and beautiful. A law student. I couldn't believe my luck. Why would someone like her want to be with me, you know?" He lifted his head and looked over. "I fucking agonized over that ring. Would she like it? Was it impressive enough? And I must have rehearsed a hundred times how I was going to propose. I was so fucking nervous."

He was nervous now, she thought as she watched him bite his lower lip.

"So I showed up at her apartment one afternoon. Doorman always gave me the key. I had it in my head we'd make love and if it felt like the right time, I'd take the ring out and ask her the big question, but I never got the chance."

Codella watched his hand grip his jaw as he spoke. She didn't know why he had chosen this moment to tell her this story, but she sensed he was determined to get it out, even if he woke up tomorrow and regretted it.

"She was in bed with another guy. They were naked. Her hair's all tangled. They've obviously just finished fucking. I'm too stunned to think clearly. So I say, 'What's going on?' She just looked at me with her mouth gaping, but the guy, he smiles, pulls her close, and says, 'What do you think's going on? She's done slumming with an Irish cop. Now get the fuck out of here.' I can still hear how that fucker laughed as I turned to leave." Haggerty leaned forward and stared at Codella's rug as if he were looking at an enormous, shiny cockroach. "That motherfucking bastard. Bet he dumped her the same way she dumped me."

"Why are you telling me this, Haggerty?" she asked him gently.

He met her eyes, and he looked absolutely sober. "Because that asshole in the bar tonight—that was him."

After that Haggerty went to the bathroom, vomited, and fell asleep on her couch.

He was gone when she woke up the next morning, and he didn't say a word to her when she walked into the squad room, so she knew he remembered his confession. He still hadn't spoken to her when they signed out a car and drove to the BMW dealership on Eleventh Avenue to investigate a string of car thefts. He was embarrassed, she figured, and she gave him his space until they returned to the precinct two hours later and he still wasn't talking to her. She motioned him into an interrogation room, closed the door, and stood right in front of him so he had to meet her eyes. "Look, you've been holding that rejection inside of you for a long time. It had to come out. It's a good thing."

"If you ever tell anyone, Codella—"

And then she grabbed both his shoulders and pushed him up against the wall. "Stop. Don't even say it."

She wasn't sure if he was stunned by her grip on him or by the words, but he just stood there.

"Look, I'll tell you something," she said still holding onto him. "I don't have a bunch of girlfriends I shoot the shit with. I don't do friends or boyfriends very well. You want the truth? You're the closest thing I have to a best friend. And I would never humiliate you. Get that straight." Then she'd released him and walked out of the room, and they'd never spoken about Cindy again.

The drone of a garbage truck on the street below brought Codella back into the bed. She twisted around to face Haggerty. "My father's out of prison, by the way. He and my mother are back together."

"Huh?" Haggerty propped himself on his elbow. "Did I just miss a transition?"

Codella sat up. "When Julia Merchant showed up this after-noon, I took an instant dislike to her. She made me feel ashamed of myself."

"You? Ashamed of yourself?"

"It's strange, I know. But she's the devoted daughter I never was. When I left Cranston, I didn't look back. I haven't seen my mother in eighteen years. After Muñoz did the presumptive tests for me tonight, I went back uptown and ran a DMV on my mother. She's got a suspended license on a DUI—her taste for alcohol hasn't changed—and she's still living in the same yellow cracker box on Pleasant Street where I grew up."

"Love that name. Pleasant Street." Haggerty combed his fin-gers through her hair.

"Trust me. It didn't deserve the name. I checked my father's incarceration status, too. He was paroled four years ago and he's back on Pleasant Street. My mother waited for him for twenty-two fucking years, and now they're back together. Nothing has changed for her."

"But it has for you." Haggerty's hairy legs brushed against her smooth ones. He kissed her lips gently. "Go to sleep, Detective."

Five minutes later, *he* was sleeping soundly, and she slipped out of the bed, pulled on an NYPD sweatshirt and shorts, and tiptoed into the dark living room. She hadn't been on Pleasant Street in Cranston for twenty-six years—since she was ten—but she still remembered her last night there. And that wasn't so surprising, she reflected. Didn't people always remember the childhood events that caused them spectacular joy or profound sadness? She could only summon a fuzzy, featureless image of her mother standing at the kitchen sink that night, but she effortlessly reconstituted every detail of her father's face—his puffy jowls with a dark five o'clock shadow, his thick chest hair coiling over the V-neck of his T-shirt, the sheen of sweat on his forehead below his combed-back hair. Claire had been sitting next to him at the round faux-marble kitchen table that night as he ate his meal in silence. When he finished, he wiped his mouth on a white paper napkin, crumpled it, and tossed it on his plate. Then he pushed out his chair. "I gotta go."

"What else is new?" Her mother slammed her shot glass on the Formica counter. "You must think I'm running a restaurant here or something. You think you can just pay the check and go every night?"

Claire watched the napkin on her father's plate absorb the pool of red marinara.

"What's got into you?" he snapped.

"I'm up to here. That's what." Her mother raised her palm to chest level.

"What do you want from me? I got a *job*."

"Yeah, sure. And what's your *job's* name?"

"Shut up, Maureen."

"Because I'm not one of those ditsy little Italian housewives who looks the other way, remember? I'm *Irish*, even if I make a better gravy than your mother." She waved a disdainful hand at his dinner plate and poured herself another shot. Her father's expression was cold and implacable, but her mother refused to heed the warning signs. She continued, "What does she do for you, huh? What's *her* job?"

He pounded the table with both fists. His plate jumped. "I said shut up, Maureen." He turned to Claire. "Don't you have school work? Go do it."

Claire got up.

"Does she get on her knees?" Her mother's taunts were fueled by cheap vodka. "Does she get down there and say, 'Oh baby, it's so big'?"

From the next room, Claire heard her father shout, "Shut your fucking mouth, you stupid Irish cunt, or I'll shut it for you!" She heard the familiar crack of his hand across her mother's face. She moved reflexively back into the doorway as her mother staggered, lost balance, hit the Formica counter, and fell. When her mother got back on her feet, blood was rolling down her forehead. She was smiling. "I see I touched a nerve, huh? I guess I got it right," she said in a scornful voice that precipitated another blow to her jaw. Then Claire's father turned and saw Claire in the doorway. "Get the fuck out of here." He raised his fist. "Unless you want some too."

Claire could have run upstairs and crawled under her bed. She could have hidden in the basement or at the back of a closet. But in the panic of the moment, she ran out the front door to the silence of the street. To the end of screaming and slapping. She was breathing fast. She stood at the end of the driveway and looked both ways down the block. The neighbors' houses appeared warm and inviting, but then, so did hers. She walked to the end of the dark block and back, hugging herself. She had not thought to grab her jacket, and in the biting winter air, her teeth were chattering. The bottoms of her feet absorbed the coldness of the concrete sidewalk through her thin sneakers. Her fingers grew stiff. She tugged at the heavy garage door—it would be warmer in there—but she did not have enough strength to lift it. She could no longer feel her toes. Her ears burned. She looked into the next-door neighbor's house. Mrs. Nardallillo was sitting in front of her television. But Claire knew that knocking at a neighbor's door was not an option, that exposing her family's secret violence would have dire consequences she could not quite articulate.

Then she remembered the old blanket in the back of her father's Impala. She opened the rear passenger-side door. The blanket was balled up on the floor behind the driver's seat. She crawled into the car and closed the door behind her so the dome light wouldn't draw attention to her. She was draping the blanket over her shoulders when the front door slammed. She dropped to the floorboard and pulled the blanket over her head. The driver's door opened and shut and the driver's seat pressed into her shoulder as her father adjusted his position. She was too terrified to breathe. Her teeth began to chatter from fear, not cold. She bit into her hand hard to stop them. The car rolled down the driveway, and she stayed beneath the scratchy wool blanket, her cramped, rigid body in agony, as they twisted and turned through the dimly lit streets of Cranston.

Finally the car came to a stop. The driver's door opened and slammed shut again. Her father's heavy footsteps moved away from the car and faded into the night. She remained under the blanket for several minutes. Then she peeked out, sat up slowly, and peered over the driver's seat. Through the front windshield she was staring at an unfamiliar street. She looked over her shoulder, through the rear windshield, and saw that her father had backed the car into the driveway of a small, aluminum-sided house. He had popped the trunk of the car, obstructing part of her view.

She waited and waited. Each exhalation became a small cloud in front of her mouth. She stuffed her hands between her legs to warm them. Her shivering made her aware that she needed to go to the bathroom, and the more she tried to ignore this need, the more it intensified. She held her legs tightly together and rocked in time to a song she had learned in school. *O Mary, we crown thee with roses today. Queen of the Angels, Queen of the May.* She mumbled the words over and over until the song ceased to distract her from her physical discomfort, and she opened her door, walked up the driveway at the side of the house, and peered through a window into a small living room.

She saw it all like a silent movie. The woman's terrified face. Her mouth forming words. *No. No. Please.* Her arms moving up to shield her face. Her father's surprisingly placid expression as he swung the bat into her stomach so hard that she bent forward and vomited. The second swing that bent the woman's knees unnaturally and sent her to the floor. The third and fourth blows that must have broken vertebrae. Her father mouthing some words while the woman writhed in pain and pleaded for mercy at his feet. And then the home run hit that crushed the left side of her skull.

Claire did not realize she was screaming until her father looked up and their eyes met through the windowpane. He dropped the bat and came outside. He clamped one latex-gloved hand over her mouth and dragged her into the house as she kicked and screamed. "You stupid little shit." He launched her into a corner, and her head slammed against the wall. Only then, as she watched him unfurl an industrial-size black plastic bag, did she realize that she had urinated. Her father worked the trash bag around the body, stuffed the bloody bat inside, and carried out his handiwork. Then he came back for her, and when they emerged, two Cranston police cars were blocking the driveway.

At the Cranston Station, they called Claire's mother. When she showed up, she was so inebriated that they refused to let her take Claire home. She slapped Claire's face over and over in the station bullpen and screamed "Look what you've done! This is *your* fault!" until two officers pulled her off and arrested her on a DUI and child endangerment. Then a social worker was called and Claire had to talk to a detective, and then she began her odyssey through the Child Protective Services system while her mother "stood by her man"—unlike Joanie Carlucci, the woman Claire's father had punished for not standing by hers.

Now Codella stared through her living room window at the snow blanketing Broadway. She touched the side of her abdomen where the lymphoma had been. In the wake of cancer, this touch had become habitual, a way of reassuring herself that the cancer was gone. She saw a yellow cab—the only vehicle on the snow-covered street—fishtail when the light turned green. She thought of her mother and father, now in their sixties, whose only intimacy had ever been violence and a shared bottle of cheap vodka. Codella had been an afterthought in their lives. She had existed in their physical space but not in their emotional world. When she had left, her mother never reached out in an effort to reclaim her. She had discarded Claire as easily as New Yorkers let go of flyers people shoved at them in Times Square. Codella supposed it was natural to feel sadness about that, but she had compartmentalized her sadness well—or at least, she thought she had. But this afternoon, Julia Merchant had flaunted her mother-daughter bond and reminded Codella that *her* mother had chosen a bottle and a monster over her.

Codella exhaled a deep breath. She was lucky her mother had let her go. She had escaped and made herself into the opposite of her mother. She had never allowed herself to become someone else's victim, and now it was her job to avenge those who were victims.

She turned away from the window. If someone had killed Julia Merchant's mother, she told herself, she would find out who. And then she returned to the bed and fitted her body against Haggerty's warmth.

TUESDAY

CHAPTER 18

Haggerty flipped on the gas. "Hey, where's the coffee?"

Codella opened the cupboard and smiled. "Have some tea."

He frowned. "I'll pass."

She went to the front door while he examined the contents of her refrigerator. This morning, her *New York Times* lay on the floor tiles in front of her neighbor Jean's door. Speed, not accuracy, was the main concern of the delivery guy who hurled papers from the elevator each morning. Codella picked it up and was carrying it back to the kitchen when she noticed the headline on the front page just above the fold. "Hey, check this out," she called to Haggerty, who was slipping two slices of bread into the toaster. He came behind her to read.

Broadway Dance Legend Dead at Age 56

One of Broadway's shining stars, Lucy Martinelli Merchant, died yesterday of Alzheimer's related complications. Fans of musical theater remember her best as Noreen Shipley, the big-hearted showgirl in *Vegas Nights*, a performance that *New Yorker* critic Marty O'Kane described as a "dazzling, heart-stopping display of art in motion." In 1993, *Vegas Nights* won Merchant her third of five Tony Awards for Best Lead Actress in a Musical. During her 386 consecutive performances, Merchant famously signed autographs every night, often lingering at the stage door for more than an hour. In a *Vanity Fair* interview that year, she explained her devotion to fans: "The theatergoers are my real employers. Without their passion and dedication, the magic on stage could never happen. I owe my joy to them. Why wouldn't I give some back?"

Codella turned to the inside page where the article continued. She poured boiling water over the green tea bag in her mug while Haggerty pulled the toast out and buttered it. Then they continued to read.

During her career, Merchant electrified Broadway and West End stages in hit after hit. Choreographers loved to work with her. "She's not just an artist and a superb athlete; she's the ultimate risk taker," choreographer Gabriel Salzman commented during previews for *Vegas Nights*.

Haggerty took a bite of his toast. "You ever see her?"
"I wish I had."
"I once dated a dancer. She had an amazing body." He grinned.
"Dated or picked up?"
He kissed her cheek. "It was a long time ago."
Codella rolled her eyes at him and sipped her tea. She skimmed through the details of Lucy Merchant's first four Tony Awards until she got to something more interesting.

In 1994, Merchant gave birth to only daughter, Julia Merchant, and in 1996, she married the father, newly divorced financier Thomas Merchant. That same year, she won her fourth Tony Award in *Harbinger of Love*. She went on to win a fifth in 2001 for *Filibuster*, in which she played the role of Helen, the spiteful wife of a U.S. senator, opposite a delightfully abhorrent Malcolm Walsh, who also won a Tony for his performance.

In a freak accident six months into that show's run, Merchant fell from a structural platform during a performance and broke her leg in two places. She never returned to the stage as a dancer, but in the wake of the tragedy, she transformed herself into one of the most prolific and innovative choreographers of her time, staging back-to-back hits such as *Dance Until Dawn* and *Fever Dream*.

"You ever wonder what your obit will say?" Haggerty asked.

"I wrote mine in my head several times while I was in the hospital." She sipped her tea. "Lucy Merchant's was probably written by some *New York Times* staff writer the day she moved into Park Manor. I'm sure all those celebrity obits are sitting in a file years in advance."

Haggerty held a piece of toast up to her mouth. "Eat something, Detective. You're still too thin. Let's keep your obit in the file."

Codella pushed the toast away and kept reading instead. Haggerty lowered the toast to a plate, rested his chin on her shoulder, and read along.

In a 2014 interview with *New York Times* arts columnist John Avery, Merchant acknowledged that she was a carrier of a rare genetic presenilin mutation associated with inherited early onset Alzheimer's disease. "This is obviously devastating news. I'll face it with as much stage presence as possible and do whatever I can while I can to advocate for those who still have time to benefit from a cure."

Broadway marquee lights were dimmed at 8:00 PM last night in Merchant's honor. She is survived by her husband, Thomas Merchant, daughter, Julia Merchant, and younger sister, Pamela Martinelli.

Codella lowered the paper. "Shit, that's worse than cancer."

"We're all ticking time bombs." Haggerty raised the toast to her mouth again.

Were any diseases purely accidental, she wondered as she took a bite, or were they all blueprinted in the primordial language of DNA the moment your life began? She had experienced the awfulness of the body's betrayal. But how could that begin to compare with the mind's? Had all of Lucy Merchant's memories dissolved before she died? Had she lived her last days with no storyline at all, robbed of her darkest secrets, her deepest disappointments, and her failed romances as well as her moments of glory on the stage, at a curtain call, when thunderous applause must have made her feel omnipotent?

Codella recalled her own vivid memories of childhood. The sights, sounds, and smells of that last evening on Pleasant Street in Cranston were hardly pleasant, but they were part of *her* narrative, part of who she was today. They were like the light from a burned out sun still barreling through time and space to make an impact on the present. What would be left of her when those memories faded away?

Haggerty was rinsing his plate. Then he put it in the dishwasher. He was on his best behavior, she thought. Trying to make this work—whatever this was. She put her hand on his back. He turned, smiled, and wrapped his arms around her waist. His hands found the backup gun in the holster tucked into her waistband, and he frowned. "Since when do you carry your backup on duty?"

"Since the last time I could have used one," she said. "Since Sanchez."

He kissed her lightly on the lips. "Well, let's hope you don't need one today, Detective Codella. Now, I've got to go. Reilly's out until next Monday, and I'm playing captain all week."

CHAPTER 19

At first, the noise was a loose catgut string vibrating in slow motion in the back of her mind. Then, little by little, the vibrations sped up and the pitch grew higher so that the sound perforated her awareness. Eventually her dreaming self could not dampen the noise or sleep around it any longer, and her eyes opened.

She was aware of the light, brilliant and blinding. She felt the grip of invisible fingers compressing her skull. Then sights and sensations emerged from the black hole of her mind. They were like jump cuts in a movie, too quick to process. Black tires circling gleaming hubcaps. The needle pricks of falling snowflakes on skin. The snap of burning logs in a fireplace. Her limp legs and arms falling into soft sheets. The hard cracking sound of flesh slapping flesh. Hot, lacerating pain. Suffocation. Terrible pressure.

She shut her eyes to seal out the images, but they persisted on the insides of her lids. Over and over, the same flashes, surreal, indecipherable. She hugged the pillow. The fabric felt familiar. This was *her* pillow, she thought, which meant that this must be *her* bed. She squeezed her forearm to make sure that she was real. She ran her hand up and over her shoulder to her neck. She felt her naked stomach and legs. But who was she? What was her name? She squeezed her eyes together and tried to grasp the answer through a thick mental sludge. And then it came to her.

Baiba Lielkaja. My name is Baiba Lielkaja. And this most basic fact became a tenuous bridge to others. *I come from Latvia. My mother lives in Riga. My father is dead. I have a sister. I live in New York City.*

This reconstruction of her basic identity exhausted her. She curled on her side and brought her knees up to her breasts. The insistent noise continued to assault her eardrums. Was she only imagining it? She pulled the covers over her naked body. Her mouth was so dry. Her chin and cheeks felt chapped and raw against the pillowcase. Her neck was stiff, and it was hard to swallow. When her knees brushed against her breasts, the nipples felt sore. She lowered her knees, straightening her legs between the sheets, and realized that her thighs and abdomen ached.

The awareness of pain made her more alert. The offensive noise, she finally realized, was the ringing of an alarm clock, *her* alarm clock, and she reached out to turn it off. In the subsequent silence, her confusion turned to terror. She was afraid to move, to take further inventory of her body. She did not want to think. She did not want to know what had happened in the dark emptiness of her amnesia, and yet she knew without remembering. She knew it all in a sudden upsurge of awareness that made her curl into an even tighter ball, like a primitive pill bug reacting to danger. *Now what do I do?* she asked herself, and the answer tracing the circumference of her consciousness was, *Nothing. Block it out. Forget it before you remember.*

CHAPTER 20

"Thank you, Heather." Constance Hodges lifted her eyes as her assistant set the clear mug of coffee on her desk. She stared at the headline. *Park Manor: Lucy Merchant's Last Address.* She was not surprised to see it. In these waning days of print media, disclosing the excesses of the privileged was still a sure way to sell tabloids, and Lucy Merchant's death was the predictable excuse for another Park Manor exposé.

Hodges sipped her coffee and studied the byline. The reporter's name wasn't familiar to her, and that meant it was unlikely he had ever set foot in Park Manor. If he had, she would know it, because no one gained admittance without signing in and showing a valid ID card. His article, she concluded, must be a tapestry of tabloid fabrications and rehashed rumors. Still, there was the possibility he had sniffed around. He might have "befriended" a talkative resident leaving the building. And many of those residents had no filters. There was no telling what they would say.

She read the first paragraph.

Park Manor. The name evokes an idyllic estate in the English countryside, a Downton Abbey for New York City's aging gentry—retired hedge fund managers, successful entrepreneurs, investment bankers, box-office stars, and Botoxed heiresses.

The Downton Abbey reference was such a cheap allusion. *Leave it to the* Post, she thought, and continued reading.

> Situated on the first three floors of a lesser-known Emery Roth building between Fifth Avenue and Madison, Park Manor has served New York's privileged for almost three-quarters of a century. The institution is now the crown jewel of health care empire Foster Health Enterprises. Competing health care conglomerate Eldercare Elite recently made an offer to acquire Park Manor. According to an unnamed source at Eldercare Elite headquarters, "Park Manor has breathtaking facilities and amenities beyond belief, but its management is bloated and shortsighted. Folding the operation into Eldercare Elite's portfolio would save money, improve care, and benefit shareholders."

Hodges reached for her coffee and wanted to slosh it all over the tabloid. Sam Davidson, the Eldercare Elite CEO, was an egocentric maniac willing to trample over anyone in his path, and Hodges hoped Renee Foster would not let the bastard get his hands on Park Manor. He would cheapen the institution's name by creating a chain of Park Manors in upscale markets— and Hodges would certainly be out of a job.

> What is life like in this rarified world of the privileged senior set? Park Manor is highly protective of its clientele, but many celebrities, politicians, and business moguls are known to have spent their last days here. No one who's worked at Park Manor will speak on the record—employees sign a no-exceptions confidentiality agreement for life—but by all accounts, these high-achieving seniors like nothing better than to reenact their glory days.

Hodges skimmed the familiar anecdotes about high-profile Park Manor residents: Vera Pressley, the invalid actress who clutched a pen in her arthritic hand at all times to sign auto-graphs, and chain-smoking inside-trader Chuck Rose, who rolled his oxygen tank around the first floor giving investment advice until his dementia advanced and he had to move upstairs to the Nostalgia Neighborhood.

These anecdotes, Hodges was pleased to see, were the tried and true tales regurgitated periodically for the masses who loved to envy or hate the rich. *She* could tell far more interesting tales—like the night just six months ago when former Federal Appeals Court justice Mark Gallop ordered a prostitute off the Internet and she had to be turned away at the front desk, or the day last month when declining socialite Erika Speers refused to allow two other residents to dine at *her* table, saying, "You're just old, you're not *old money*," and a golden girl fight had ensued.

Hodges skimmed the over-the-top description of Park Manor's perks.

Need a quick Buddhist chant to make you forget that your legs don't work? At Park Manor, a Tibetan monk is a snap of the fingers away, and so are the nutritionist and Hollywood-trained makeup artist.

Hodges imagined straphangers eating up this exaggerated drivel as their subways slammed through tunnels taking them to their low five-figure jobs. Finally she got to the part about Lucy Merchant.

Sadly, the musical theater legend did not qualify for life on the vibrant first and second floors. She did, however, receive a standard of care few dementia sufferers enjoy. Sequestered above the socially stimulating world of Park Manor Village is the Nostalgia Neighborhood, a state-of-the-art dementia care unit where the well-heeled participate in brain research studies and pharmaceutical trials that make potentially effective drugs available to them long before they are approved by the FDA.

And at Park Manor, the specially trained caregivers outnumber their charges by a ratio of almost 2 to 1.

Hodges tossed the article onto her desk and sighed with relief. Michael Berger, the Foster Health Enterprises chief of operations, would not be calling her to complain about leaked information. And there was no mention of Julia Merchant's surveillance video, either. Hopefully, Thomas Merchant had calmed down his daughter since yesterday.

Hodges smiled when Heather Granahan appeared in her doorway. "Yes, Heather?"

"Baiba—Ms. Lielkaja, I mean—she just called. She said she's not feeling well. She won't be in today."

CHAPTER 21

Codella waved to the desk sergeant, took the stairs two at a time, and walked straight to Dennis McGowan's office. "You read the paper this morning, Lieutenant?"

He looked up from his cell phone. "What is this? A quiz?"

"Did you happen to read about Lucy Merchant?"

He gave her a blank look.

"Wife of Thomas Merchant. Bank of New Amsterdam?"

"I know who he is. What about him?"

"His wife was Lucy Martinelli Merchant. A five-time Tony Award winner." She waited for a sign of interest that did not come. When was the last time he had even seen a Broadway show, she wondered. "They dimmed the lights for her last night."

"So? Get to the point, Codella."

"She died yesterday at Park Manor, that exclusive Upper East Side senior home."

"Okay, and why should I give a shit about that?"

"Because her daughter came to see me yesterday."

"Thomas Merchant's daughter was here?"

"And told me she thought her mother had been murdered."

McGowan was suddenly alert. "And you didn't bring it to my attention?"

"There was really nothing to bring you, except her unsubstantiated theories. But I did a little checking, and there may be something there. Maybe not." She told him about the carpet fibers and Muñoz's unofficial field test results.

"Jesus, Codella." McGowan leaned back, crossed his thick arms, and squinted at her. "We send things to the lab. We don't go running color tests."

"If I waited for lab analysis, I'd be waiting weeks and her ashes would be in an urn," she told him. "This is a Broadway legend. If something happened to her and we didn't take action, imagine what the press would say."

"And imagine what they'd say if one of my detectives launched an investigation based on a field test kit."

"We make narcotics arrests that way all the time."

He rolled his eyes. "As I've said before, you just don't like to play by the rules."

"And as I've said before, I consider the rules to be very important, sir." She kept her voice even, remembering Haggerty's advice. "In this case, I figured it was my job to screen things before I raised an alarm."

"Oh, you did, huh?"

She observed his show of sarcasm as if she were a spectator at a sporting event. His intense dislike of her, she reminded herself, could not be explained by anything she had ever done to him. Reilly, her former captain at the 171st, would not have criticized her for showing initiative, and she wished she could be talking to him right now. Maybe McGowan just felt threatened by competent women reporting to him. Maybe he grew up with a sister who had always upstaged him. Whatever the explanation, she told herself for the hundredth time, it was *his* problem and it blinded him to the importance of the situation. "I'd like to open a case," she stated firmly. "I want to go to Park Manor and have a look around."

"No."

"No? Just like that?"

"It's above your pay grade, Codella."

"Above my pay grade?"

"You heard me." His arms were crossed over his worn blue suit jacket.

You're the one above your pay grade, she wanted to say. She took a deep breath and held it in for a moment while she dialed down her emotions. If she let her frustration show, he would seize on that. "I don't understand." She worked hard to sound innocent. "How exactly is it above my pay grade?"

"He's Mr. Page Six," McGowan said. "The guy's worth millions."

"Billions, actually, but so what? If something happened to his wife, don't you think he'd want to know? Don't you think he'd be pissed if we *didn't* look into it?" According to Julia Merchant, he'd be more upset if they did look into it, but she wasn't going to tell McGowan that. "The daughter came to see me. She brought a suspicious substance. Considering the field test results, I think we'd be remiss if we didn't take a closer look. I've sent the fibers to the crime lab, and I want to pay a visit to Park Manor. Do I have your permission?"

Then she held his eyes and waited. The silence stretched on. He would be considering a multitude of reasons—excuses—for denying her request. She waited as impassively as she could. Any outward sign of desire, she sensed, would only fuel his denials. Finally he spoke. "One visit. If there's nothing there, you drop it. Understood?"

CHAPTER 22

Brandon's phone vibrated as he entered Judith Greenwald's waiting room. "Hey, Baiba, I can't talk right now."

"But—"

Judith was signaling him into her office. "I've got therapy," he cut Baiba off. "I'll call you in an hour or so." He stuffed the phone in his back pocket and took his usual spot on the far right cushion of the olive green couch. Judith sat across from him in her leather swivel chair, and then she waited for him to break the silence, the way she had at the start of every session for the past three years. He stared at her shoulder-length hair, equal parts black and gray. She never wore makeup, but she always accessorized with bold jewelry—thick sterling silver bracelets and pendants with semi-precious stones that he imagined had been crafted in places like Taos or Santa Fe. He had concluded long ago that she must be a lesbian, although she never talked about herself.

"I set the date for my surgery this morning," he said. "Three weeks from tomorrow. They had a cancellation."

"You've been talking about doing that for more than a year, Brandon. Why this morning?"

He shrugged. "It just feels like the right time. I start my first respiratory therapy internship in May. If I do the surgery soon, I'll have three whole months to recuperate."

"How do you feel about your decision?"

"Good. A little impatient, too. Dr. Silverman is going to be my surgeon."

"I had another client who used him."

"He wants a letter from you, stating I'm psychologically stable and ready for this." Brandon watched her reaction.

She leaned forward. "I'll draft it today." She smiled. "I really can't think of anyone who's more sure of him- or herself than you are."

"I have *you* to thank for that."

Judith shook her head. "No, you have *yourself* to thank. You've done hard work in here. You haven't let the world define you."

As she said this, Brandon felt the vibration of his phone in his pocket. He pulled it out. Baiba was calling him again. He tapped *Ignore* and set it on the floor so he would not feel its intrusion. When he was in here, he didn't want to think about anything or anyone *out there*—not even Baiba. He pushed his thoughts of her to the back of his mind and let Judith's words sink in. *You've done hard work in here. You haven't let the world define you.*

He remembered meeting Judith two weeks after he'd come to New York. He had gone to a clinic in the Village seeking hormone therapy, and they had referred him to her for an evaluation. "I don't like therapists," he had announced at that first visit, standing before her defiantly with his dark blond hair cut short for the first time in his life.

"Okay. Well, I'm Judith. What shall I call you?"

Beth Ann was the name on the tip of his tongue because he had been forced to say and write that name his whole fucking life. "I don't like my name," he said instead.

"Well, if you don't like it, why don't you give yourself a new one? What do you want me to call you?"

"Brandon," he had whispered, and in saying the name to someone else for the first time, he had felt instantly different, like a quadriplegic experiencing a first hopeful muscle twitch.

"I didn't hear you. Can you say that louder?"

"Brandon," he had repeated.

"Well, I'm pleased to meet you, Brandon. And I'm sorry if you've encountered a therapist who put our profession in a negative light, but let's give each other a chance, shall we? I don't like to be judged on the basis of stereotypes, and I expect you don't, either."

She had offered him no pity or sympathy. Her words had been a challenge. He had responded with his own challenge. "I don't have a lot of money. I don't even have my own bed. I'm sleeping at a friend's place. Actually, it's not even a friend. It's a girl I met. She thinks I'm a lesbian. She's into me. I lied to her. My parents named me Beth Ann. But I'm not a girl. I've never been a girl."

They'd met every week since then at a reduced fee he could still barely afford, and he'd told her things he'd never discussed with anyone. How he felt whenever he looked at his body in the mirror. How his father had punished him if he didn't wear a skirt or dress and carry a purse like a proper teenaged girl. He let himself cry and admit how jealous he was of other gender nonconforming kids with parents who at least *tried* to understand. And finally he told her about the other "therapist" his parents had forced him to see, Pastor John Sutter, who had promised Brandon's father he would "put the girl back on God's glorious path."

At their first "therapy session," Sutter had pointed his finger at Brandon and said, "You have disrespected God's plan for you, Beth Ann Johnson. You've caused heartache to your family and embarrassed them in our faith community. But God is merciful. He's sent you to me. And I am going to be your spiritual guide. Now take my hand and let's get on our knees and pray together for God's blessing as we start our journey."

They had knelt side by side on the speckled linoleum in a windowless basement room of the Church of Salvation in Jackson, Michigan. Sutter's hand felt pudgy and moist, and it was trembling slightly. Brandon watched the pastor gaze heavenward at the low chipped ceiling. He heard Sutter call out, "Dear Lord, this lamb of God, Beth Ann Johnson, has strayed from the path you chose for her." As Sutter continued the endless prayer, Brandon imagined sitting in a window seat on a Greyhound bus to New York City. He wondered how much money he would need to save up before he took that ride. He calculated how many additional hours he could clock as an EMT.

"Lord, help me be a shepherd to Beth Ann Johnson." Sutter reached an emotional crescendo, pulling Brandon's hand to the front of his sweaty shirt. "Pour into me the power to help her embrace the beauty of her God-given sex." And Brandon thought about the lockers at the Jackson bus depot and how he could store a set of clothes there for when he was ready to make his escape. Finally, Sutter stood and stared down at him with crossed arms. "Now repeat after me, girl." His voice turned hard. "My name is Beth Ann Johnson—go on now, say it— and I need God's help."

When Brandon arrived for their sixth session, Sutter locked the door of the little room and gently said, "Get on your knees, Beth Ann." Brandon figured another long prayer was coming, but Sutter just leaned against the locked door and stared at him. "God came to me last night in a dream," he said. "And he told me my prayers haven't touched you one bit. He said I need to pray a different way with Beth Ann Johnson." He moved within inches of Brandon's face and pushed down on his shoulders.

Brandon wasn't stupid. He knew where this was going, and dry terror crackled in his throat. He jerked back and rose to his feet. Sutter said, "Get back on your knees, honey," in an ice-cold voice as he reached one hand below his big gut to tug down his fly.

Brandon's rage propelled him forward. He charged Sutter, slamming his head and fist into the pastor's stomach. Sutter doubled over in front of the door, and Brandon pushed him off balance. The pastor landed on the worn linoleum, and Brandon kicked his ribs. Sutter curled up protectively. Brandon kicked his knees and shins. Sutter shrieked in a high-pitched wail. "Stop it, Beth Ann!" And Brandon kicked all the harder. "Say that name one more time, and I'll kill you, you motherfucking pervert." He might have been screaming, but he wasn't sure. Finally, he pried the door open and left. He never went home again.

Judith Greenwald was pressing her palm against the back of his hand. He guessed she knew he was remembering again. "You're right here with me, Brandon," she said as tears rolled down his cheeks.

When he left Judith's office half an hour later, the sky looked intensely blue, and the winter sun glistening off the snow-covered brownstone roofs was blinding. He walked west toward the Borough of Manhattan Community College feeling understood and optimistic. As he crossed Seventh Avenue, he pulled his phone out of his back pocket and called Baiba. "I'm sorry I couldn't talk before."

The sound of her sobbing erupted in his ear.

"What is it?" he asked. "Tell me."

"Oh God, Brandon," she said. "I've been so stupid."

CHAPTER 23

Only a small brass plate mounted on the limestone exterior marked the entrance to Park Manor. The building looked like any Upper East Side white glove address, home to titans of industry or heirs to fortune. Beyond the doors, however, understatement immediately gave way to opulence in the form of intricately patterned prewar floor tiles and marble colonnades. A hanging water sculpture assured visitors they had entered a place of serenity, and a granite desk staffed by two men in burgundy Park Manor blazers promised attentive service to those who called this place their last home.

Codella showed her shield to the concierge whose nameplate read Oscar. "I'd like to speak to your director."

While Oscar lifted the house phone, Codella checked messages. Dr. Abrams had not called her yet. When was he going to get to her again with her results? She turned to watch water seep from the top of the hanging fountain and flow gently down the surface of the burnt red rock in an endless mechanical cycle that evoked the natural trickling of a glacial spring. Park Manor, she surmised, was a purveyor of artful and expensive illusions.

Oscar escorted her to the director's office, and Constance Hodges stood as Codella entered. She appeared to be in her late forties or early fifties. She was trim and immaculately dressed in a short beige jacket and navy pencil skirt. Her artificially blond hair was shoulder-length and straight. Her eyes were almost golden, like a feline's, Codella thought, and they transformed her otherwise generic middle-aged attractiveness into something more compelling.

Codella held out her hand, and Hodges gripped it across her desk in an impressively muscular handshake. "Please have a seat, Detective. What brings you to Park Manor?"

Codella sat in one of the two chairs facing Hodges. "There was a death here yesterday. Lucy Merchant."

"Yes. Very sad."

"And unexpected, I take it."

Hodges frowned. "Not really. Mrs. Merchant was in a late stage of Alzheimer's. She had a terminal condition."

"She was receiving hospice care?"

"Well, no."

"Then what were the circumstances surrounding her death?"

Hodges crossed her arms, tilted her head, and knitted her brows. "I'm curious, Detective. Did someone send you here?"

Codella wanted to say, *People don't* send *me, Ms. Hodges. And they don't ask me the questions, either.* Instead she just repeated, "What were the circumstances?"

Hodges picked up a yellow pencil and twirled it between thin manicured fingers that shook ever so slightly. "Mrs. Merchant died in her sleep," she answered. "Her heart gave out, according to our house physician. He certified her death early yesterday morning."

"He didn't feel the need to understand what *caused* her heart to give out?"

Hodges frowned. "I'm sorry, Detective, but should I assume from your questions that you are investigating Lucy Merchant's death?"

Codella leaned forward. "Let's just say I'm investigating whether or not I *should* investigate it." She met the director's golden eyes.

"And why is that?" Hodges's tone turned demanding.

Codella kept hers calm and casual. "Julia Merchant paid me a visit yesterday."

"Oh." Hodges nodded, and her tone softened again. "I see." She steepled her hands on the desk like a sympathetic funeral director. "I've watched many families lose a loved one, Detective. Even when they know the end is near, they're often unprepared. Julia is very young—just twenty-two or three—and she was extremely close to her mother. This is hard for her. She was here yesterday, as I assume you already know. She was upset. She told me about the video she had. She obviously misconstrued what she saw."

"What did she think she saw?"

Hodges's tight mouth betrayed the fact that she obviously didn't want to discuss this. "She was under the impression that a caregiver administered medication to her mother, but in fact he only gave her mother a drink of water."

"How do you know that?"

"Because I questioned my staff thoroughly."

"And you trust them to tell you the truth?"

"Intrinsically," said the director.

Codella considered the choice of words. Could trust ever be *intrinsic*? "Were you here on Sunday night when Lucy Merchant's last medication was administered?"

"No. I only pop in sporadically on the weekends, and her medication was given after ten PM."

Codella tapped this information into the notes app on her iPhone. "Who was the senior person on duty when Lucy Merchant died?"

Hodges answered quickly. "Baiba Lielkaja, the Nostalgia Neighborhood care coordinator, went home around eight PM that evening, so Cheryl O'Brien, our night nurse, was the senior staff member on duty."

"And what did she tell you about the death?"

"That Maybelle Holder—one of our overnight caregivers—discovered Mrs. Merchant at four AM. Mrs. Merchant wasn't breathing. Maybelle summoned Cheryl, and Cheryl phoned Baiba and me. Baiba got here within half an hour. I arrived within the hour."

Codella nodded. "Can you ask these two employees to join us—Cheryl O'Brien and Baiba Lielkaja? I'd like to ask them some questions as well."

"I'd be happy to, Detective," said Hodges, "but Cheryl won't be here until seven PM tonight—her hours are seven to seven—and Baiba called in sick today."

Codella made another note in her iPhone. "Does she call in sick often?"

Hodges narrowed her eyes. "What are you implying, Detective?"

Codella only smiled. "I'm just asking questions. It's my job. I'm sure you understand." She shifted to a different line of inquiry. "You mentioned that Julia was close to her mother. How do you know that?"

"I'm in a position to observe how family members interact. For the past month, Julia has visited her mother almost daily."

"At what time of day did she come?"

"Lunchtime usually. She'd sit and feed her. During the past week, she's been here at dinnertime, too."

"She was there on Sunday night?"

Hodges nodded. "You see, on some level I'm sure she knew the end was coming, but she didn't want to let go."

Codella watched the director pick up a clear glass mug of cloudy coffee.

"I've been at Park Manor for twelve years, Detective, and one thing I've learned is that we humans don't like to accept our losses." Hodges took a sip. "We do many unpredictable things when we're grieving."

Codella supposed the director's observations about loss were perfectly reasonable, but they didn't negate the possibility that a homicide had occurred. "Tell me about Lucy Merchant."

Hodges sat back in her chair and was silent for a few seconds. Finally she said, "By the time Mrs. Merchant came to

Park Manor, she was already exhibiting pronounced cognitive difficulties."

"Such as?"

"Short term memory loss. Sequencing problems. Confusion about her surroundings. Anomic aphasia."

"What is that?"

"The inability to recall names of people and things. Lucy would start a sentence but couldn't retrieve the words to get out her thought. The Alzheimer's had already affected the part of her brain that controls speech."

"Did you know Mrs. Merchant before she developed her illness?"

"I knew *of* her," said Hodges. "And I had been introduced to her once or twice. She and Thomas—Mr. Merchant—were active in a number of charities, and I represent Park Manor at many of those events."

Was it evasion or defensiveness Codella detected in the director's answer? Either way, she backed off again. Alienating the woman wasn't going to help her get what she needed right now. She said, "I wish I'd seen her in that 1996 revival of *Chicago*. Unfortunately that was a few years year before I came to the city." She smiled and leaned forward. "Look, Ms. Hodges, despite what you or I might think, Julia Merchant has for some reason convinced herself that her mother's death wasn't the result of natural causes. Whether or not that's true, she could stir up a lot of unpleasant publicity that I'm sure you don't want. But I can't put her concerns to rest unless I perform my due diligence. I'd like to take a quick look around Mrs. Merchant's room. Would that be okay with you?"

Codella willed her face into a facade of nonchalance. Lucy Merchant was dead, so technically she no longer had a right to privacy, but that was a gray area Codella preferred not to face if the case ever ended up in a courtroom. Without a warrant, she wanted the director's explicit permission to enter Lucy Merchant's quarters. If Hodges knew her caregiver had administered a lethal dose of oxycodone, then surely she would find a way to keep Codella out of that room. Then again, she might know that oxycodone was in the cup without knowing that it had spilled onto the carpet. She might presume it was safe to take her upstairs.

Codella took a deep breath and let it out slowly. In the prolonged pause, Ms. Hodges's stiff shoulders and straight spine announced her discomfort. Finally the director gave what appeared to be a forced smile. "Of course, Detective. I agree. By all means, let's put this to rest. I'll take you up myself."

The elevator was large enough to accommodate multiple wheelchairs or stretchers. It ascended in slow motion, as if it had been purposefully calibrated to the pace of Park Manor's residents. Codella followed the director out onto cushioned carpet, turned left, and stopped in front of solid double doors. Hodges punched a five-digit code into a keypad on the wall, and the doors opened slowly like the gates to a heavenly kingdom or a maximum-security prison. "This is our Nostalgia Neighborhood, Detective."

As the double doors closed behind them, Codella surveyed a spacious room to her left. She had seen impressively appointed rooms like this in cavernous prewar apartments. Decorative molding framed panels of elegant wallpaper. Against the far wall stood a cast-iron fireplace. Fresh-cut flowers in blown glass vases sat at either end of the mantel. Overhead, ornamental plaster made the ceiling a work of art.

"This is our parlor, Detective." Hodges smiled with satisfaction. "This is where our Nostalgia residents read, watch movies, or listen to guest speakers and performers."

Codella had the impression Ms. Hodges was reciting the script she used with wealthy families of potential Nostalgia residents. The four vacant, watery-eyed seniors sitting in the room with their caregivers hardly looked capable of tracking print, following a movie plot, or interacting with a speaker. Codella guessed that she was about to get the grand tour, so she nodded her appreciation and followed where Hodges led.

Beyond a restaurant-style dining area, they entered a sunroom where five seniors swayed awkwardly to Chubby Checker singing "Let's Twist Again," but the only ones actually twisting were the Park Manor caregivers in their burgundy polo shirts. Hodges apparently felt the need to comment on this scene, too. "For many sufferers of dementia, music is the one stimulus that still connects them to their vibrant pasts. Music etches deep memories in our brains, Detective."

Codella nodded like an attentive acolyte. She had seen her share of old shut-ins on the West Side. When they died and a foul odor finally announced their demise, a detective usually had to confirm that their death was not suspicious. She remembered the unrenovated rooms of one old woman five or six years ago. The smell of urine throughout the apartment was so pungent that Codella had not wanted to breathe. A thick layer of dust blanketed every surface. The old woman had hoarded hundreds of plastic containers, grocery bags, and condiment jars. And her cat, who had not been fed for days, lay dead on the cracked linoleum.

By comparison, these dancing dementia sufferers lived in luxury, but were they any happier than that old woman? Codella wasn't fooled by the illusion of this place, and she doubted anyone else could be fooled by it, either. As artfully arranged as it was, it was still depressing, the same way even the most state-of-the-art cancer ward was depressing. The "Nostalgia Neighborhood" was a place you would never willingly go to—and a place you would never walk out of.

Hodges led her to a quiet corridor that felt like a guest floor at a Ritz Carlton. Mounted on the wall next to each door they passed was an engraved brass nameplate, and Codella skimmed the names. Dr. Evelyn Bruce. Mr. Arthur Lane, Esq. Senator Phillip Prinz. Tomasina Knight. Mrs. Dottie Lautner. The placards suggested permanence, except that none of them were permanent, she realized when they arrived at the last door on the wing and she saw the Velcro wall strip where Lucy Merchant's nameplate must have been.

Hodges unlocked the door, and Codella stepped into Lucy Merchant's sitting room. Coaster-sized depressions in the plush beige carpet marked where furniture had been. Enlarged Playbill covers in gold frames leaned against the walls where they had hung. "We don't usually remove a resident's belongings so quickly," Hodges explained, "but there is a Park Manor Village resident who now needs Nostalgia's services. We're moving Mrs. Merchant's furniture downstairs until the Merchants can arrange to have it picked up."

As she entered the bedroom beyond, Codella gave an "I-understand-perfectly" nod to conceal her suspicion. Had Hodges's staff already combed this place for evidence? Three taped and labeled moving boxes in the far left corner were the only indication that Lucy Merchant had been here. The queen-size mattress had been stripped. Personal artifacts that might have rested on the built-in shelves or window ledge were gone. The open closet across from the bed was empty except for several smooth wooden hangers.

Codella closed her eyes and mentally replayed the surveillance video Julia Merchant had shown her yesterday. In that video, the nurse and caregiver had stood on the far side of the bed in front of the window. The caregiver had been closest to the bed, holding the cup to Lucy Merchant's lips. Codella moved to the window now and stared down at the carpet. At first, she saw nothing in the shiny nylon fibers. But as she continued to scan the length of the bed, a small matted and faintly discolored patch caught her attention. Hodges, it seemed, had *not* brought the carpet cleaners in yet.

With the director watching her from the doorway, Codella pulled her iPhone out of her pocket, bent down, and photographed the patch. Then she pulled nitrile gloves out of her jacket pocket and ran a gloved index finger over the patch.

The fibers felt rough. Whatever substance had spilled was now dry and crusty. She removed sterile tweezers from her jacket pocket, unwrapped them, and yanked up some of the carpet fibers.

Hodges stepped closer. "What are you doing?"

Codella dropped the fibers into a small evidence bag and tucked the bag and the tweezers back into her pocket. "There was a spill in the carpet. I lifted a few fibers."

Codella rose. Hodges's eyes remained glued to her as she crossed the bedroom and stepped into the bathroom doorway. She could sense the director's unspoken questions about to erupt, and she raised her hand up to hold them back. The bathroom, too, had been completely emptied, and she imagined that the now immaculate shelves built into the tiled back wall had once held large packages of adult diapers, toilet paper, and tissue. The towel rack was empty. And the small trash receptacle below the sink had been emptied. She turned to Hodges. "Do you have an incinerator on site?"

Hodges shook her head. "We have a waste disposal service that comes two times a week."

"Have they come since Sunday?"

"No. They'll be here tonight."

Codella visualized Lucy Merchant's Sunday night medicine cup sitting in an industrial sized garbage bag resting in the bowels of Park Manor. The rug fibers in her pocket might test positive for oxycodone, but she couldn't prove they had entered Lucy Merchant's body. If, on the other hand, the residue in her cup matched the substance spilled on the carpet, and if Lucy Merchant's DNA were on the rim of the cup, then she had a much tighter case for possible homicide.

If she did not leave Park Manor with the cup right now, she knew, it would be lost forever. On the other hand, if she found it and it tested positive, she would have enough evidence to demand an autopsy of Lucy Merchant's body. She glanced up at Constance Hodges. "Can you take me to where you keep your trash?"

"Why?"

"We need the cup she drank from on Sunday night."

Hodges looked skeptical. "It will be mixed up with all the others."

"But it will have her name on it, won't it?"

The director nodded.

"You need to help me," said Codella. "I won't be able to dismiss this inquiry until I can assure Julia Merchant I've looked into the matter. Let's just get it done."

Hodges led Codella out of Nostalgia, and they rode a service elevator into the underbelly of Park Manor. The thick smell of petroleum told her that the enormous boiler ran on fossil fuel. They passed a loud, steamy laundry room in which three tired-looking Hispanic women were folding towels and tablecloths. A labyrinth of narrow cinderblock passages led them to the back of the basement where large bags of garbage were sorted for pickup. At one end of the room were red hazardous waste bags. Black garbage bags sat on the other side.

"Which bags contain the trash from residents' garbage cans?"

Hodges pointed to the black bags. "They are considered general medical waste. The small trash bins get emptied into white bags that are labeled by floor. The white bags go into the large black bags, so they are separate from the garbage that comes from the kitchen. Still, there's no telling how many bags you would need to pick through to find the cup you're looking for."

Codella considered. The task could take fifteen minutes or it could take hours, and it wouldn't be a pleasant interlude. "Can I get some bodies to help?" she asked.

Hodges disappeared briefly. When she returned, two porters wearing work gloves were following her. Hodges asked the shorter Hispanic porter which bags might contain the Nostalgia Neighborhood's general waste from Sunday night.

The porter held up his index finger in a "wait here" gesture. Then he spoke Spanish to the other porter, a thin man with an olive complexion, high cheekbones, and bristly black hair, and they disappeared through the outer door. They returned three or four minutes later carrying two overstuffed black bags they had removed from a dumpster beyond. The younger porter opened one of the bags, and inside were four medium-size white bags. Under Codella's direction, the porter opened one white bag at a time and dumped its contents into a bin. Codella studied the used tissues, Q-tips, old toothbrushes, dental floss, and other debris from the Nostalgia residents' trash. The first bag held only two medicine cups, but neither was Lucy Merchant's. The porter stuffed the debris back into the bag and dumped out the contents of six more white bags before Codella saw what she was looking for—a clear polypropylene cup with a white label on the side that read "3F Merchant" and the date it had been administered. She carefully lifted the cup from the bin with her gloved hand. In the bottom of the cup were the crystalized remains of a liquid.

As the porters rebagged the garbage and returned it to the dumpster, Codella moved closer to Hodges. The woman's face was now a flat screen of panic. Codella showed her the inside of the cup. "That caregiver on the video didn't give Lucy Merchant water, did he?"

Hodges eyed the remains of medicine in the cup.

"You might as well tell me the truth right now," said Codella. "Because it's going to come out sooner or later."

Hodges sighed. "No. It was diazepam—Mrs. Merchant's nightly sedative."

"And you knew that when you told Julia Merchant otherwise?"

Hodges rubbed her left shoulder over and over. Her nod was almost imperceptible.

"You need to tell me what happened."

Hodges breathed deeply and sighed. "Cheryl O'Brien—the night nurse—had trouble administering meds to Mrs. Merchant," she explained in a pained, confessional tone. "Lucy didn't like her for some reason, so Lucy Merchant's caregiver—his name is Brandon Johnson—gave the meds to her."

"Which is against Park Manor policy, of course."

"Yes."

"And you didn't want Julia Merchant to find that out?"

"No," Hodges acknowledged. "I didn't."

Codella shrugged in what she hoped was a convincing display of indifference. "Fine. I can understand that. I mean, I'm sure these families let you have it for every little infraction, don't they?"

Hodges's squinting eyes conveyed her mistrust of Codella's empathy.

"You broke a house rule. You didn't break the law. And as you say, Julia's grieving. She'll do anything to keep her mother front and center in her mind—even if it means thinking the worst about others—about *you*." She paused, giving Hodges time to process. "Fortunately we now have a way out of this."

Hodges squinted. "What do you mean?"

Codella held up the cup. "This is our way out."

The director still looked confused.

"If I take this cup, the rug fibers I collected, and Lucy Merchant's prescription medications, I can run some quick tests on them. They're called presumptive tests. I can show that there was nothing in her cup or on her floor except her medicine. And that should be enough to put Julia's concerns to rest."

Hodges took another deep breath and sighed again. "But I told her there was only water in the cup. I—"

"You lied to her. True." Codella shrugged again. "But once I show her there's nothing lethal in the cup, it won't matter. She'll give up her crusade—and you and I both know there's nothing in this cup except the diazepam." She waited. She didn't believe any such thing.

The woman nodded.

Codella removed another evidence bag from her pocket and placed the cup inside it carefully. "Let's go get her meds," she said.

They threaded their way through the winding basement passages until they were standing in front of the service elevator again. They rode back to the third floor and returned to the Nostalgia Neighborhood. Hodges led her past a small windowless office with "Baiba Lielkaja, Care Coordinator" etched on a brass nameplate. The office was empty, and Codella heard Hodges's voice in her head. *She called in sick today.* Was the care coordinator's absence coincidental, or had she called in because she wasn't ready to answer questions that might be posed to her? Was she taking time to construct a story or communicate with others—conspirators—about deeds they had done? If Lielkaja had a role in whatever had happened to Lucy Merchant, she would have been smart to come to work and maintain her usual routines, Codella thought. But the guilty often panicked and violated that obvious rule of thumb. Codella made a mental note to look carefully into Baiba Lielkaja.

The closed door next to Lielkaja's office had a nameplate that read "Dispensary." Hodges stopped and said, "Wait here. I'll get the day nurse to open up."

A moment later, she returned with an attractive young Filipino woman wearing burgundy nurses' scrubs. Hodges introduced the nurse as Lorena Vivas. Codella shook her hand and explained that she needed to take medications belonging to Lucy Merchant.

Vivas unlocked the dispensary, opened a file drawer, and removed Lucy Merchant's medicine chart. The nurse's large brown eyes scanned the page. "She takes a multivitamin and Benefiber at breakfast, like most of the residents. There's only one prescription drug ordered for her."

"What is that medication?" Codella glanced at the chart over Vivas's shoulder and photographed it with her iPhone.

"Diazepam," said Vivas.

"That's her nightly sedative?"

Vivas nodded. "It used to be known as Valium."

"It's not a narcotic. Correct?"

"That's correct. It's a benzodiazepine."

"Tell me more about that."

"Benzos are psychoactive drugs," explained Vivas. "Tranquilizers. They work on a neurotransmitter in the brain. They have a calming effect. We don't use diazepam with most residents—we prefer to give them a different psychoactive drug, Atavan—but Lucy Merchant didn't respond well to that. It didn't help her sleep. She had a lot of trouble sleeping."

"I need to take that bottle," said Codella, and she reached in her pocket for an evidence bag and the same nitrile glove she had worn in Lucy Merchant's suite. "Just point to it. Please don't touch it. I'll pick it up and put it in the bag, and then you'll sign the bag to confirm that I have the right one."

Five minutes later, Codella followed Hodges out of the Nostalgia Neighborhood with three sealed evidence bags. They sat in armchairs near the elevator, and Codella unfolded a consent form she'd brought with her. "I need you to sign this form, Ms. Hodges. It gives me permission to remove these items from Park Manor. It's just a necessary formality." She willed indifference onto her face yet again. If Hodges refused to sign the document, then Codella would have to leave the fibers, the cup, and the diazepam bottle behind. She would be forced to call in a uniformed officer to safeguard the items while she tried to convince a judge to grant her a search warrant based on scant evidence— Julia Merchant's video and the results of a presumptive drug test on fibers that didn't meet chain of custody standards. And how many judges would go out on a limb based on that, especially when someone like Thomas Merchant of BNA was involved?

Hodges stared at the form, and Codella could see the director wavering. She needed to hear that everything would turn out all right for her, and only that certainty would result in her signature on the line. "If you sign," Codella said, "I can do the field tests and I can put Julia Merchant's concerns to rest within hours." She stared into the woman's golden eyes and smiled. *You did what you had to do to get to the truth—and sometimes that involved lying.*

Hodges continued to vacillate.

"It's up to you," Codella added, "but I suspect there are many other matters you'd prefer to concentrate on, and I certainly have more pressing investigations to attend to." *If only that were true,* she thought.

"And you'll know something today?"

"That is my intention." Codella pulled a pen out of her pocket and waited for Hodges's trembling fingers to take it.

CHAPTER 24

Julia saw her aunt enter the restaurant at precisely twelve thirty. Pamela scanned the tables, spotted Julia, and crossed the dining room as if it belonged to her. They kissed on both cheeks—only the Martinelli side of the family did that—and her aunt announced, "I have a deposition at two," as she sat and pulled in her chair. "We should order right away."

"They have good salads here," Julia said.

Pamela seemed unmoved by this information. She placed her cloth napkin on her lap and gestured to the waiter with an expression that signaled, *Hurry up and do your job*. Pamela never just let things happen, Julia thought. Maybe she knew she wouldn't get what she wanted if she did. She had none of Julia's mother's physical grace, flair, or feminine seductiveness. It wasn't that Pamela couldn't afford to look stylish—she was, after all, a highly paid trial attorney with an impressive record of keeping guilty white-collar felons out of federal prison. But she wore only minimal makeup—haphazardly applied mascara and a dark shade of lipstick that was completely wrong for her complexion—and she gravitated to tailored suits in dark colors. Today she wore navy pinstripes. Brooks Brothers, Julia guessed from the cut. Not Armani.

The waiter brought stiff, leather-bound menus and stood there while they decided. When he left, Julia said, "Thanks for meeting me."

"How are you holding up, sweetheart?"

That was all the invitation Julia needed. While they waited for their salads, she told her aunt everything that had happened since her father had called her yesterday morning. "What if I hadn't watched that video? We would never have known."

Pamela registered no opinion. "What did the detective say to you?"

"That there weren't enough *red flags*—her words—to warrant police involvement. She said I should ask for an autopsy—to put my mind at ease."

Pamela glanced at the iPhone in her lap.

"I thought she was very dismissive," Julia added. "The police never want to go out of their way, do they?"

Pamela looked up again. "They need solid evidence to open a case, honey. You're speculating. But she's right, you could request an autopsy if you want one. They would have to perform it."

"I do want one, but my father would never forgive me. He'd take away—" Julia regretted the words instantly. "Never mind."

But Pamela was already jumping on them like a seasoned cross-examiner. "He'd cut you off. Isn't that what you were about to say?" She leaned in and stared at Julia. "The same way he threatened to cut you off if you didn't get tested. Am I right?"

Julia twisted the napkin in her lap and shrugged.

"You're too dependent on him. You have to stop living off his monthly checks, Julia. It's bad for you. It's the worst possible thing. You have to get a job—and not at BNA."

"It's only because of Park City," Julia said. *Park City* was her way of referring to the accident. She preferred not to say accident, because every time she did, she visualized her body wiping out in the powder and doing three-sixties until her skis flew off and she slammed into a tree. "I'm going to start looking soon. I am." But just saying these words terrified her, and she knew she would do anything imaginable *not* to have to face stony sets of interviewer eyes looking for excuses to disqualify her. *You've been out of college for a year. What have you done since then? What skills do you have? What are you passionate about? Where do you see yourself in five years?* Did other people really know where they wanted to end up or were they just better liars than she was? She was afraid she would never get a job without using the one qualification she didn't want to use—the fact that she was the daughter of Thomas A. Merchant and Lucy Martinelli Merchant.

"I know you want the best for me," she told her aunt. "But right now, I can only focus on my mother. There should be an autopsy, and I can't demand one." She paused. "But *you* could."

Pamela sat back and laughed so loudly that the two women at the table behind her turned their heads. "Is that why you asked me to lunch?"

Julia hedged. "Don't you want to know the truth?"

Pamela's smile turned into a penetrating stare that made Julia squirm. Witnesses on the stand probably felt this way under her aunt's cross-examination. "You forget one thing, Julia. Your mother and I were not close. Why should I pretend to be her grieving sister? When she didn't attend my wedding three years ago, it was the last straw for me. You know that."

The waiter arrived with their salads. Neither of them spoke while he set down the plates, offered freshly ground pepper, and asked if he could get them anything else. When he departed, Julia told her aunt, "My father didn't want her to go. He said you were using her to get your wedding on *Page Six*."

"That's ridiculous." Pamela picked up her fork. "I don't give a fuck about *Page Six* and he knows it. He didn't want Lucy associated with her lesbian sister—he was afraid to offend his rich conservative clients. I may defend them, but I don't pander to them. Your father has no spine. And he still believes that rich white men are going to call the shots forever. I can't wait for him to find out how it feels not to have a seat at the table. I hope I live to see the look on his face when no one takes his calls." She stabbed a heart of palm. "And Lucy went along with him—my own sister, whose most ardent fans were gay men, for God's sake."

"I think the dementia was affecting her judgment even then," suggested Julia.

"Possibly." Pamela chewed as she spoke. "But that doesn't justify her behavior for twenty-five years. She treated her fans better than she ever treated me—or you, for that matter. Hardly anyone in her circle even knew she had a sister—and plenty of them didn't know she had a daughter, either."

"That's not true. Don't say that."

Pamela set down her fork, wiped her lip with her napkin, and leaned her elbows on the table. "You can live in your fantasy, Julia, but I don't. I went through a lot of therapy to deal with my resentments of your mother, and you know what my therapist called her?"

"What?"

"A malignant narcissist."

"What's that?"

"Look it up." She glanced at her watch. "I know this is a tough time for you, but my advice is move on with your life. Let her go. Stop trying to prove you deserved her love. It's too late. It was always too late."

Julia couldn't think of anything to say.

Pamela set her napkin next to her plate. "I've got to go." She picked up her purse, took out her wallet, and laid five crisp twenties on the table. "That should do it," she said as she pushed out her chair.

CHAPTER 25

Baiba opened her door. Brandon took one look at her and froze. Broken capillaries charted a road map across the whites of her eyes. Red marks ringed her neck. Her hands trembled. Her face was pale and damp.

Baiba turned without a word and went back to her pull-out couch. She crawled between the sheets and hugged a pillow against her baggy T-shirt as if it were a stuffed animal. He followed her to the foot of the mattress. "What happened? Are you okay?" He sat on the edge of the bed.

Her chin quivered. She covered her face and began to cry softly. Soon her sobs intensified. She gasped for air, coughed, and rocked back and forth with the pillow clasped tightly against her breasts. He didn't know what to do except wait. When her sobs finally turned into muffled moans, he went to the sink, poured her a glass of water, and brought it back to the bed. Then he found a box of tissues in her bathroom and set it down beside her.

Questions multiplied in his mind. He sat next to her again, placed his hand on her back, and felt her ragged inhalations. He watched her alarm clock for three unbearably long minutes. *Give her time*, he told himself. *Give her time*. And finally she said, "I went out last night and someone drugged me and—"

"Oh my God, Baiba. That's terrible." He put his arm around her shoulder and she moved a little closer to him. "What can I do?"

"I shouldn't have bothered you," she said, "but—I just woke up so foggy. I couldn't remember anything and—"

"Of course you should have called. You can always call me."

She put her hand on his knee. "You're a good friend, Brandon."

"You need to report this, you know. Where were you when it happened? In a bar?"

"Something like that."

Brandon sensed her evasion. "Who did it? Did you know him?"

Baiba covered her face. "Oh, God, Brandon."

"What? What is it, Baiba?"

"If I tell you something, do you promise you won't say anything?"

"Of course."

And then she blurted out, "It was Merchant. Thomas Merchant."

Brandon felt the name like a punch in the solar plexus. "*What?*"

"I've been seeing him, okay?"

"*Seeing* him? You mean having an—" He stopped and considered his words. "A relationship with him?"

"Yes. But no one knows, okay? I wanted to tell you, but I couldn't. You can understand why, can't you?"

Brandon was too stunned to answer. He managed to nod his head.

"He asked me to dinner last month. I shouldn't have agreed to go. I know that. But I wanted to."

Brandon's body was humming. He imagined his pores constricting so that his skin became a protective membrane shielding him from the words.

"He took me to the Four Seasons. God, that place is amazing. It was so romantic."

"I bet." Brandon's mouth felt dry.

"And then he took me home," she continued.

And fucked you, Brandon thought. He didn't breathe. He had to fight the urge to pull his hand away from her, as if she were suddenly infectious. In the space of an instant, his whole conception of who she was began to crumble. He shook his head as if this movement could reset his thoughts and emotions. *How could you do this to me?* he wanted to say, and then a hot lump of shame formed in his throat.

Two years ago, Baiba had introduced herself to him across a desk in the small first-floor office where prospective caregivers were interviewed at Park Manor. They had talked for half an hour, and at the end of the interview, he had felt certain that she would hire him. Later he learned that she had had to advocate on his behalf because Constance Hodges had not wanted him on her staff. And since then, she had never asked him to be anything other than what he was. No one—not even Maybelle—had tried to understand him the way Baiba had. Whether out of discomfort, repulsion, or politeness, the others had astutely avoided the issue of who and what he was. But not Baiba. One evening while they were in Arthur Lane's bedroom sorting through the clothes, jewelry, and photos he regularly pilfered from other residents' suites, she had asked him, "When did you first realize you were, you know, a man in a woman's body?"

Brandon was surprised by her directness, but he was also grateful for the invitation to reveal more of himself. "I always knew," he admitted.

"What was it like for you growing up?"

And as they painstakingly traced the provenance of each article Arthur Lane had stolen, Brandon told her about the Church of Salvation in Jackson, Michigan. Once a month, the congregants gathered in the church basement to stuff envelopes with brochures pleading for money to stop the Queer Agenda. The covers of these brochures featured tattooed men in leather and butch-looking women in men's clothing, and the headlines asked *Do you want perverts living on your street? Do you want males sharing the restroom with your teenage daughter?* Every June, he told Baiba,

Pastor Sutter rented two buses and the congregation rode from Jackson, Michigan, to New York City to hold up protest signs at the LGBT pride march. "I helped make those signs," he told her. "I painted banners that said *Burn in hell for your sins*. And the whole time I knew I was condemning people just like me."

When he told Baiba about his surgery plans, she didn't say, "Oh my God, how could you do that to yourself?" She said, "You're going to look very handsome on the beach." And a week later—just last Wednesday—she gave him three thousand dollars to help him pay for the procedure.

Now Brandon hugged her tightly and kissed the top of her head. "Go on, Baiba. Tell me what happened. You need to tell someone."

"It was really good that first time," she said. "Different, but good."

He nodded.

"And the next day he came over to my apartment with flowers and a little Tiffany bag. There was a jewelry box inside. He gave me a gold chain with a beautiful diamond pendant."

Brandon stared out the window as her head rested against his shoulder. His jaw ached. He didn't want to hear any of this. He wanted to be anywhere else.

"And a few days after that he called me again and, well, I couldn't really say no. I didn't want to say no, and this time it got a little—" She shook her head.

"A little more *different*?" he supplied.

"I promised myself that was the last time," she said, "but he brought more flowers. He gave me another little Tiffany bag. He told me he had to see me or he would go crazy. And I went back."

"And you went back again last night?"

She nodded. "He sent his car for me."

"What happened?"

And then she told him everything she remembered, from the moment Felipe had opened the Escalade door for her in the snow until the moment when she had sipped the drink Merchant gave her and all her memories dissolved.

"He drugged you. He took advantage of you."

Baiba stared down.

"And he choked you, too. I see the marks. Was that one of his *differences*? Did he like to tie you up?"

Her silence was the answer.

"I think I should take you to the hospital," he said. "I should take you to the police."

Baiba shook her head and gripped his arm so hard that it ached. "No! You promised. You can't tell anyone," she nearly shouted. "What happened was my own fault. *I'm* to blame for this."

"That's what women always say, Baiba. But you're not."

"Yes, I am!" She punched her legs with her fists. She gripped her skull as if it might crack open if she didn't hold it together. "Oh, God, Brandon. Don't you see? I went right along with it. I let him do those things to me—until last night I *liked* it. I *enjoyed* it."

He held his breath. How much more would he have to hear?

"I know what that must sound like to you, but—"

"It's okay," he said weakly. "It doesn't change how I feel about you." But it did. Her fucking Merchant like that changed everything. He would never, he realized, be able to give her what she wanted. Rough sex. Expensive jewelry from Tiffany's. Dinners at the Four Seasons. She would never want him.

Baiba grabbed his arm. "You won't tell anyone, will you? I just want it to all go away. Promise me."

"I promise. Of course." But you couldn't just pretend things hadn't happened, he wanted to say. The worst events in your life had a way of carving the deepest grooves in your memory. Even dementia victims seemed to hold onto their traumas. How many times had he sat up with them at night while they tried in vain to fit fragments of haunting memories into cohesive narratives? He thought of Lucy and the things she had said. *No, Daddy. No!*

I don't want it. Please, Daddy. Take it away. Even Lucy had bad childhood memories. She was always talking to her daddy.

Brandon glanced down at his worn Converses. He could already predict the memories that would plague him decades from now. His father landing a hook on his jaw when he refused to wear a dress. Reverend John Sutter unzipping the fly below his tumor-like gut. Shivering on the front steps of the LGBT Community Center his first night in Manhattan when he had nowhere to go. Despite three years on Judith Greenwald's couch, those memories were still vivid. They still got in his way sometimes. He stared into Baiba's tropical blue eyes and softly caressed the rash on her chin where Merchant's stubble had burned her. He understood perfectly why Merchant had wanted her. But he could never do what Merchant had done. He knew a little too well what it felt like to be the woman in that equation, to be the object of someone's self-serving desires. For as long as he could remember, he had experienced and interpreted every human interaction through two simultaneous points of view—male and female. That was the one dubious superpower, he supposed, that came with living in the fluid nexus of genders.

"Why don't you sleep," he said gently, to cover his ambivalence. He didn't want to talk to Baiba anymore. He needed to think, to sort out his feelings. "Go to sleep. I'll stay with you for a while."

"And then you'll go to Park Manor, right? You promised you would go. I told Hodges you would be there tonight. I told her you would tell anyone who asks that you only gave Lucy water to drink. I don't want to lose my job, Brandon. Please."

He nodded reluctantly. Merchant had used her, he thought, and now she was using him.

CHAPTER 26

Codella stood on the front steps of the 171st and called Dr. Abrams again. This time the receptionist put her on hold, and a moment later Abrams came on. His gentle voice in her ear said, "You're persistent, Detective Codella. I want you if I ever need a homicide detective—which I hope I don't."

"Well, I hoped I'd never need an oncologist," she answered. "So? What's my verdict?"

"You're boring. Quit calling my office, and don't come back for six months this time."

She took a deep breath and felt her mind reconnecting with the body she had feared might fail her again. "Thank you."

"My pleasure. Now go solve some murders." She could hear the smile in his voice.

She opened the precinct door and went inside. Just like yesterday, Muñoz had everything precisely arranged on the table in interview room A. He slid his hands into the green nitrile gloves and took the three evidence bags she held out. "I see you went in there like a one-woman CSU team," he said.

"Just don't tell Banks." She frowned. "He might try to recruit me, and sifting through garbage isn't really my thing."

Muñoz tested the rug fibers first. As he pinched the tube to release the test solution, they watched the liquid change to violet. "Same as last time," said Muñoz.

Codella felt a sense of exhilaration even more intense than what she had felt after hanging up from Abrams. It was an exhilaration she knew she shouldn't feel. She *wanted* Lucy Merchant's death to be a homicide. But all detectives were guilty of hoping their instincts were correct. And you mitigated your guilt by telling yourself you were only confirming a terrible deed that had already been perpetrated. Wishing for someone's murder *after* the fact was different from wishing for it before they were dead.

Muñoz unwrapped a second ampule and repeated the procedure with residue from the medicine cup. Haggerty slipped into the room in time to watch the third test on the liquid from Lucy Merchant's diazepam prescription bottle. When Muñoz was finished, three clear plastic test kit tubes lay on the table, all three containing the same violet liquid. Codella photographed the ampules. She looked at Muñoz. "How often do these test kits lie?"

He shrugged. "In my experience, they're right more often than wrong, but it's always possible something in the sample screws up the results. It happens."

"We'll voucher the evidence and send it to the lab for confirmation, but we won't get results for weeks. And I can't wait that long."

"So what's your plan?" asked Haggerty.

Codella pulled out a chair on one side of the interrogation table, and Muñoz and Haggerty sat across from her. "Let's assume for the moment that the tests *aren't* lying. If they're not, then we just traced oxycodone from Lucy Merchant's diazepam bottle into her medicine cup and onto her bedroom carpet. That's fairly compelling circumstantial evidence that someone tried to drug her—considering that her only prescribed medication is diazepam—Valium—which is *not* an opiate like oxycodone."

Both men agreed.

"The day nurse, Lorena Vivas, showed me Lucy Merchant's medicine chart. All she took were some vitamins and Benefiber in the morning and a five-milligram dose of diazepam oral suspension every night to prevent her from wandering and screaming out in her sleep. That's it. No narcotic. I have a photo of her chart. You with me so far?"

"So far," said Haggerty.

"So the question is, how did a narcotic get in that bottle? Someone had to put it there, but who?"

"Are there closed circuit cameras to check?" asked Muñoz.

Codella shook her head. "The patrons of Park Manor like their privacy too much."

"What is it with people and their need for privacy?" Haggerty grinned.

"So assuming our test kits are telling the truth," continued Codella, "then someone accidentally or purposefully added a lethal opiate to Lucy Merchant's diazepam."

"Technically it's an opioid," pointed out Muñoz. "Oxy isn't actually extracted from opium. It's synthetic. But go on."

Codella nodded. "Since her diazepam bottle was half empty yesterday, I'm thinking it's unlikely the oxy was in the bottle when it came to Park Manor from the pharmacy. Someone at Park Manor must have added it to the bottle."

"It makes sense, but you're stringing together a lot of *what ifs*, aren't you, Detective?" observed Haggerty. His tone was half teasing, half serious.

"Just follow my logic." She leaned forward and stared at both men across the table. "*If* the oxycodone was added to her bottle at Park Manor, and *if* the dosage was strong enough to kill her, then it must have been added the day she died. Sunday. Otherwise, she would have succumbed earlier."

"That makes sense." Haggerty nodded.

"And that means someone went into the dispensary and poured something into the bottle in the hours between her Saturday night dose and the one that killed her."

"Or they switched the bottles," suggested Muñoz.

"That would certainly be easier and faster," agreed Codella. "But that would require someone to interact with her pharmacy. I think someone added the drug, not switched the bottles."

"So we focus on anyone who was in Park Manor in the last twenty-four hours of her life," said Muñoz.

"The nurse on duty had the most opportunity," pointed out Haggerty.

"Agreed," said Codella, "and we have to check her out. But she would know all eyes would be on her."

"The caregiver who fed her the medicine," said Muñoz.

"We have to consider him too. But the oxy was added to the prescription bottle, and he doesn't have access to the dispensary. Someone else put the oxy in that bottle. I'm wondering about the Nostalgia care coordinator. A woman named Baiba Lielkaja. She's got keys to every door in there. She unlocked Lucy Merchant's suite for Brandon Johnson yesterday morning after Lucy Merchant died. And she called in sick today. I think something's up with her."

Haggerty frowned. "If you're going to go full steam ahead on this, Claire, you need to trace that oxycodone straight down her throat. You need an autopsy."

"I know. But the daughter's afraid to demand one, and the father doesn't want it."

"Get the DA involved. You need that body. Go see McGowan."

"He'll tell me I don't have enough evidence. Too many *what ifs*, as you say."

"Her body's going to be embalmed if you don't move fast."

"Actually, cremated, which is worse."

"So you maybe have two or three more days," said Haggerty.

"I have an idea."

Muñoz and Haggerty waited.

"I'm going to go see Merchant. Convince him to authorize an autopsy."

"Good luck with that!" Haggerty shook his head. "He's not exactly the world's nicest guy, from what I've read."

Codella shrugged. "Yeah, well, nice guys don't run banks, I suppose. But I have no choice." She looked into Haggerty's blue eyes. "Can I borrow Muñoz for a couple of hours?"

"You want to *borrow* my detective?"

"Just to do a little research on Merchant. I don't want to go in blind."

"Shit, Claire. That's not exactly standard procedure. Reilly's not going to be thrilled if I'm running a rent-a-cop operation while he's gone. You can't get a Manhattan North detective to do it?"

"You know the answer to that. McGowan won't give me shit. He wishes I was dead."

Haggerty gave her a skeptical look.

"No, I'm serious. I didn't tell you what he said when I came back from my scan yesterday. *Once cancer shows up on your doorstep, you can't ever really get rid of it, can you?*"

"He said that?" said Haggerty.

"With a big smile on his face."

Muñoz shook his head. "What an asshole."

"That son of a bitch," added Haggerty. "I'd like to throttle him."

"Do it indirectly, Brian. Help me. I need some backup."

Muñoz turned to Haggerty. "Reilly doesn't need to know. No one needs to know."

Haggerty shoved his hands in his pockets. "Shit, all right. Just to spite that bastard."

CHAPTER 27

Constance Hodges leaned on her desk and closed her eyes. The dull throb at her temples had turned into a gnawing headache. She wanted to go home, but it wasn't even two o'clock. She could still see that detective's face in her mind and hear her voice as she held up the medicine cup. *This is our way out.* But what if it wasn't? What if something other than diazepam showed up in the cup? *I should never have signed that authorization form. Why did I allow that detective to talk me into it?*

These thoughts expanded the oil spill of her panic. Her arms felt weightless. Her hands were vibrating. She could no longer keep Julia Merchant's accusations to herself. She would have to call the Foster Health Enterprises chief of operations, Michael Berger, and tell him what had happened yesterday. Berger would recognize the potential impact of the situation on the pending offer from Eldercare Elite. He would probably call a senior management team meeting with the corporate communications VP and the legal counsel, and she would be summoned to headquarters to give a full account. She would have to sit at the FHE conference room table with six Ivy League MBAs and summarize her conversations with the Merchants. She would be forced to tell them about Julia Merchant's surveillance video, and unless she could think of a very creative excuse, they would rake her over the coals for waiting twenty-four hours to give them a heads-up about it. And after she had spoken, they would discuss strategies for dealing with the situation, and all the while they would look past her as if she weren't even there.

She pictured Thomas Merchant. Where was he right this moment? He must know that she was in the hot seat because of his daughter. Why hadn't he shut Julia down the moment she opened her mouth? Had he known in advance that she was going to make that accusation in her office yesterday? BNA was financing Eldercare Elite's pending purchase of Park Manor. Did it serve his client's interests to see Park Manor's reputation besmirched? Was he planning to use the situation to demand a lower price for his client? Well, she had her own interests to serve and her own stories to tell, and she didn't intend to be the scapegoat in whatever financial gamesmanship was going on.

She studied her hands. Was it her imagination or were they trembling more than usual? Michael Berger would think she had Parkinson's if he saw her shake like this. Any observant person would think there was something wrong with her. She opened her bottom desk drawer and reached into the purse she kept there. Her fingers fumbled through the disorganized contents until they grasped the narrow neck of one of the miniature bottles she had been carrying around for a week. She'd spied the little bottles behind the register at the Murray Hill Wine and Liquor Shop the last time she had purchased a large bottle of Courvoisier. Something had propelled her to tell the proprietor, "Let me have a couple of those minis, too. They're so adorable." All week she had enjoyed knowing that the little bottles were with her. And now she realized that she'd purchased them for a reason. She had known—subconsciously, of course—that a time was coming when she wouldn't be able to get to the end of a day without them.

She pulled the miniature out of the purse and held it in her lap. The bottle's smooth contours comforted her in a way she knew they shouldn't. She unscrewed the cap, brought the bottle to her nose, and sniffed deeply. The aroma of vanilla and candied orange intensified her need. She closed her eyes and held the vapors in her lungs. *This is medicinal*, she told herself. *I've had a shock. A little sip would calm me down.* Memories contradicted her words—her mother cleverly stashing miniature bottles of vodka inside coffee mugs at the back of a kitchen cabinet, beneath sofa cushions, behind books in the bookshelves, under the box springs of her mattress—but Hodges dismissed those memories as soon as they surfaced. *No. I'm not like that.*

She put the bottle to her lips and tilted it up for just a tiny taste, and then she couldn't resist any longer. She raised the bottle again, tipped her head back, and sucked out the 80-proof liquid like mother's milk. She was guzzling the last drops when she suddenly registered that eyes were upon her, and she yanked the bottle from her mouth so quickly that a drop of the amber liquid dribbled down her chin.

Heather Granahan stood in the doorway. She had entered without knocking—or maybe she *had* knocked. Hodges wiped the droplet from her chin as casually as she could while she lowered her other hand, the one with the bottle, carefully below the horizon line of her desk. For several seconds, her eyes were locked with Heather's in a magnetic field of uncomfortable silence. How much had the assistant seen? Did she know what cognac bottles looked like? Was she standing there right now and thinking, *Constance Hodges is a secret drinker?*

It occurred to Hodges that if she were accused of drinking on the job, she would be fired and all her accomplishments would be overshadowed by this short interaction with the small vessel in her hand. At the same time, she realized that the thought did not alarm her. She was pleasantly disengaged from her own emotions. The cognac was already spreading warmth through her extremities. Her tremors were relaxing. She was beginning to float within a bubble of chemically induced calm. She said with confidence, "Yes, Heather. Is there something you need?"

"I can come back later," offered the redhead uncomfortably.

"No." Hodges tucked the empty bottle between her knees. "Come in now. I can spare a moment before my next call. Tell me what you need." And she watched Heather move to a chair. *I sound completely normal*, she assured herself. *Not defensive or overly solicitous. I could just as easily have been drinking ginseng from that little bottle. And Heather would never know the difference. Heather's not that bright.*

"I was wondering," Heather began timidly, "if I could take next Friday off. My mother is flying in and I'd like to spend the day with her."

The younger woman's needs and concerns were so trivial, Hodges thought, and suddenly she wanted to laugh out loud. Instead, she made a show of checking the Outlook calendar on her screen. She stared at the calendar for several seconds, not wanting to appear too unconcerned or too accommodating. And she felt Heather tense with anticipation and hope. Finally Hodges smiled and said, "I think that would be all right, but fill out the usual paperwork of course."

The young woman sighed with relief. "Thank you, Ms. Hodges. My mother will be so happy. We're going to go to Ellis Island."

"How lovely." Hodges watched Heather rise from her seat and close the office door behind her. Her assistant had seen without seeing, she concluded, like so many unobservant people in this world.

Hodges took the bottle from between her knees, screwed the top on, and returned it to her purse. Next time she would lock herself in the powder room at the end of the hall, she decided. And she ignored the small voice in the back of her mind that whispered, *There should never be a next time.* Her confidence had returned. She had done the right thing with Codella, she told herself. She *had* to work with the police. It had been smart to let the detective take those samples. If she hadn't, Park Manor would look very bad in the press. *She* would look bad.

CHAPTER 28

McGowan was in front of the men's room when Codella ran into him. "May I speak with you, sir?"

"What is it?" He turned to face her.

She told him what she had found at Park Manor and the results of the presumptive tests Muñoz had done. "Now we've established a chain of oxycodone from Lucy Merchant's prescription bottle to her medicine cup to the carpet in her bedroom. All I have to do now is prove that the trail leads into Lucy Merchant's body."

"That's shit, Codella. You and those fucking presumptive tests. Are you kidding me?"

"They're accurate more often than not," she told him, channeling Muñoz's words.

"But what does it prove? Old people take pain meds all the time."

"Lucy Merchant wasn't old. She was only fifty-six. And she wasn't on oxycodone or any other narcotic."

"So what are you proposing?"

"An autopsy."

"Jesus Christ." He poked his index finger into his ear. "You know, I skimmed her obit after you left my office, Codella. You need to read between the lines. The woman was a vegetable. She was locked in a dementia ward. Do you really want to waste your time on this?"

"You mean look the other way on a possible homicide?"

McGowan stuffed his hands deep in his pockets and leaned into her with his shoulders. "Do you know how many demented people get slipped a little something to end their misery? It's better for everyone, Codella. You'd be wasting taxpayer dollars on this. Let it go."

"Let it go?"

"You heard me."

"I'll pretend I didn't—for *your* sake," she said. "Can't you just see the *Post* headline? *NYPD Says 'Let It Go' After Broadway Legend Dies.*"

McGowan's face turned cold. He brought his hand up like a gun and aimed it at her. "You wonder why I don't throw you cases? You're a loose cannon, Codella. You see whatever the hell you want to see."

Codella shook her head. "You can't manufacture evidence, Lieutenant. I've got evidence. And I've got a couple of people over at that place that I'd like to ask some hard questions." She thought of Baiba Lielkaja. "All I need is your green light. You're going to regret it if you shut me down right now."

"You've got a lot of nerve, talking to me like that."

She watched the muscles in his jaw clench below the surface of his skin. She'd really pissed him off. She lowered her voice. "Just let me go see Merchant. It's his *wife* we're talking about. Let me ask him to authorize a postmortem."

McGowan shook his head and laughed. "Okay. Fine. Be my guest, Codella. Actually, nothing would give me greater pleasure than to see you commit career suicide."

"Shouldn't he want to know the truth? If he doesn't, he looks pretty bad, don't you think?"

McGowan jingled the keys in his pocket. "Don't ask me. Do whatever you want. You always do. And I'm going to sit back and watch you fuck yourself. Because all Merchant has to do is pick up the phone and call One Police Plaza and you're out the door. And the pain in my ass is gone."

"I'll take my chances." She smiled. "But if I get my autopsy and the ME confirms that the death isn't natural, I'm going to need an investigative team on this."

"*If.*" McGowan turned away, pushed on the men's room door, and disappeared.

CHAPTER 29

Brandon pushed himself up to his elbow to study Baiba's face. Sleep had replaced tension with calm. Everyone looked so trouble-free when they slept. Even old people looked like children, he thought.

He touched Baiba's hair lightly with his fingertips. He couldn't even count how many times he'd imagined lying close to her like this, but now that he was in her bed, he wished he were anywhere else. He didn't want to be here in the role of comforting friend. He didn't want to think about her underneath Thomas Merchant, moaning her desire, spreading her legs for him, letting him do those *different* things he liked to do.

Brandon shut his eyes for the fifth or sixth time and tried to clear his mind. He was tired, but he couldn't sleep. The metal support bar beneath the sleeper couch mattress dug into his shoulder blade. He climbed out as quietly as he could and sat at Baiba's small round table. To pass the time, he pulled his pharmacology textbook out of his backpack and reread chapter twelve for the test next Tuesday, but his mind kept wandering. Finally he closed the book and just stared at the motionless outline of Baiba's body under her comforter. He didn't even know her, he reflected. He only knew what she *wanted* him to know about her. Why did he even bother to stay here with her now? And why should he go back to Park Manor tonight and lie for her? Did she really want him to lie just to hide the fact that the drug dispensation rules had been violated? He studied Baiba's delicate eyebrows, long lashes, and flawless skin as if the answer were written on her sleeping face. Well, he would go back to Park Manor this evening, but not to protect Baiba, Hodges, or Cheryl O'Brien. He would go back there to find out what was really going on. Baiba wasn't concerned about him. He would have to protect himself.

He went over to the bed, bent down, and smelled the trace of her perfume. She had probably applied that perfume for Merchant before going to his place last night. "Good-bye, Baiba," he whispered, and he knew he wasn't just saying good-bye for now. He was saying good-bye to his feelings for her. Then he packed up his books and let himself out of her apartment, careful to lock the door behind him.

CHAPTER 30

In his peripheral vision, Muñoz saw Blackstone glance over at him every ten seconds or so. The bombastic prick was talking at the top of his lungs deliberately. He *wanted* to catch Muñoz's eye. He wanted an excuse to say, *What's the matter, Rainbow Dick? Am I interrupting your precious concentration?*

And he was, of course, but Muñoz wasn't going to give him the satisfaction of seeing his irritation. Muñoz kept his eyes on the computer screen. He had already accumulated three pages of notes on Merchant. His facility with the NYPD databases had improved exponentially in the last three months. Before then, he'd spent most of his time pounding pavement as a narc. He sat on park benches or strolled up and down St. Nicholas Avenue in ripped jeans and a hoodie buying twists of crack cocaine from low-level dealers and then busting them. And when he wasn't uptown, he was down on Centre Street reading voucher numbers into the records in front of grand juries so his lab reports could be entered into evidence. It was a grind that might have gone on indefinitely if he hadn't gotten shot in the shoulder and been promoted to Detective Grade 3.

He'd met Codella on his fourth day in the 171st. Captain Reilly got the call about a body and Muñoz was the only detective available. Reilly hadn't thought Muñoz was ready to handle a body on his own, so he'd called Manhattan North and McGowan had sent Codella. She had taken Muñoz under her wing and they'd worked the Sanchez case together for five non-stop days. Those had been his best days as a detective so far, and he was happy to be working with her again, even if it was unofficial.

Muñoz had already downloaded Merchant's history of traffic violations, the dates of his marriages and divorce, and his IRS case number on a tax evasion charge. None of that was going to help Codella very much when she faced Merchant in his executive suite. But now he had pulled up a three-year-old complaint in which Merchant was named. A twenty-four-year-old woman, Jackie Freimor, had accused him of sexually assaulting her at the Grand Hyatt Hotel. Unfortunately there were no details in the records, and the complaint had been dropped the next day.

Muñoz jotted the name and badge number of the Midtown police officer who had taken Freimor's statement. He picked up his phone, dialed Midtown, and got the desk sergeant. "You have an officer named Delibero? Nicholas Delibero?"

"*Had*," said the Sergeant. "Left last year."

"Where'd he go?"

"Don't know exactly. Out of state. Some guys aren't made for the city. They'd rather cruise the 'burbs in a cushy Crown Victoria, you know?" He chuckled at his own joke.

Muñoz thanked him and hung up. Freimor, he discovered with a little more digging, had married and now lived in the Westchester enclave of Pelham Manor. Her husband was Jack Hartley, who owned a food distribution company that serviced restaurants in the tristate area. Muñoz looked at his watch. There wasn't time to drive all the way to Pelham, get Jackie Freimor's story—*if* she was home and *if* she had a story worth getting—and be back in time to meet Codella at Edgar's Café in an hour.

He went on the Internet instead and started digging through the twenty pages of results that came up when he searched for Thomas Merchant, Bank of New Amsterdam.

CHAPTER 31

Codella pressed the buzzer. When no one responded, she pushed the square black button again and held it down for at least five seconds. Finally a woman's voice over the intercom said, "Who is it?"

"My name is Detective Codella. Is this Baiba Lielkaja?"

For several seconds, the only response was the hollow roar of the active intercom. Then the voice asked, "What is this about?"

"I'd like to speak to you, Ms. Lielkaja. May I come up? I have identification."

After a noticeable pause, the front door lock disengaged with a click. Codella pushed the door open and stepped into the parlor floor of a brownstone that had been converted into multiple apartments. She climbed the stairs to the third floor and came face-to-face with a blond woman leaning against the doorjamb in cotton drawstring sweatpants and an oversized sweater. A gray wool scarf was wrapped around her neck. Codella could see that she was striking, but puffy bloodshot eyes and pale skin blunted her beauty. "Ms. Lielkaja?"

The woman nodded.

Codella showed her shield. "May I come in?"

"Sure, but . . . I'm not well. And my place is a mess."

Codella shrugged. "Whose isn't?" She stepped through the door and immediately noticed the open pullout bed against the right wall of the room. On the opposite wall stood a laminate bookshelf filled with thick hardbound health care textbooks and paperback novels. Next to the bookshelf was a small desk that held a laptop and printer. There was no clutter. The studio apartment was anything but messy. The layout reminded Codella of her first rental in the city, an East Village one-room walk-up between Avenues B and C that she'd shared with too many cockroaches.

Lielkaja shut and bolted the door behind them. "What can I do for you, Detective? Has someone in the building been robbed?"

"I'm here to ask you some questions about Lucy Merchant's death."

Lielkaja raised her eyebrows. "Why?"

"You know how it is when a high-profile person dies," Codella answered casually. "This is just routine."

Lielkaja motioned to two chairs at a small round table near the kitchen. "What do you need to know?"

"Whatever you can tell me." Codella took a seat.

Lielkaja remained standing. "Can I get you something to drink?"

"No, thank you. Did Mrs. Merchant's death come as a surprise to you?"

Lielkaja frowned. "I suppose. A little."

"A little?"

"Well, she wasn't in hospice care. Usually when someone is near the end, hospice support gets involved."

"Was she frail?"

"I wouldn't say that. She was still ambulatory."

"When did you last see her?"

"Sunday evening. I don't usually work on Sundays but I did that night because we were down one caregiver, and Sunday night dinners are busy."

"Busy how?"

"A lot of families show up to eat with the residents. It gets pretty chaotic."

"And how did Mrs. Merchant seem at dinner that night?"

Lielkaja shrugged. "She seemed fine." Then she quickly added, "I mean, no different than usual. Why?"

"Tell me about Cheryl O'Brien."

"What about her? You're not thinking—"

Codella was used to people turning her questions back on her. Posing counterquestions could signal simple curiosity, but it was also a predictable technique of those who needed time to compose their thoughts. "I just need you to tell me about her."

"She's the night nurse." Lielkaja continued to stand. Codella noticed that her fingers gripped the top rail of the chair in front of her so firmly that the veins on the back of her hands stood out. "She works the seven to seven shift four nights a week. She's been with Park Manor for about six months. A very nice person. Very reliable and caring."

"And she gave Mrs. Merchant her medicine that night?"

Now Lielkaja's large, aquamarine eyes narrowed slightly. They did not shift away from Codella's in a telltale sign of obfuscation, but neither did they blink in a natural way. "That's right," she finally said.

Codella held her eyes. "Or did Brandon Johnson administer the diazepam that night?"

Lielkaja let go of the chair. She walked behind Codella and entered the tiny kitchen so that they were separated by a half-wall. "Julia Merchant told you that, didn't she?" Lielkaja turned on the faucet and poured water into a glass. "Well, she's wrong. That didn't happen. Cheryl gave the medicine. Only Cheryl. Brandon gave her water."

"You're sure about that?" asked Codella. "Absolutely sure?"

"Yes." Lielkaja raised the glass to her lips.

Codella nodded. "Why did you let Brandon into Mrs. Merchant's room after she was dead?"

Lielkaja set down her glass and sighed. "He wanted to say good-bye to her. I didn't think there was any harm."

Codella glanced around the apartment again. "Isn't it possible you also didn't think there was harm in him giving her medicine?"

"No," Lielkaja responded firmly. "That's different. That's a Park Manor rule. I don't violate rules."

A few minutes later, Codella stood on the steps in front of the brownstone. *I don't violate rules*, Lielkaja had said, but she had lied. Would Cheryl O'Brien tell the same lie? Would Brandon Johnson lie, too?

CHAPTER 32

Codella's favorite table at Edgar's Café—the one in the window on the downtown side of the door—was vacant, so Muñoz claimed it. He scanned the other tables. Benny, the owner of Edgar's, wasn't there. He usually didn't show up until the evening. Muñoz pulled out a chair and sat. As he stared out the window at Amsterdam Avenue, still slushy from yesterday's snow, he thought about the inevitable exchange he'd had with Detective Marty Blackstone fifteen minutes ago. Codella had called the squad room, and Blackstone had picked up the phone. "It's your lady boss, Muñoz," Blackstone had called to him. And after Muñoz hung up, Blackstone asked, "What's it like to be her boy? Do you enjoy jumping every time she says jump?"

Muñoz had ignored the comment, but then Blackstone leaned on the edge of his desk. "Are you giving me the silent treatment? Have I offended you?" His voice was dripping with mock sympathy. "Oh, you're just so sensitive, Muñoz. What's the matter? Is it that I'm not your type?"

Muñoz parked his feelings about Blackstone when Codella arrived five minutes later. Those feelings, he knew, were a ball of hard hatred he would have to dissolve if he was ever going to feel immune to the taunts, but he couldn't do it now. One of the waitresses Muñoz and Codella knew well took their order. Muñoz asked for an extra-thick vanilla shake, and Codella ordered tea and key lime pie. "He's eating at least half of it," she told the waitress.

Blackstone was right about one thing, Muñoz thought. He'd do almost anything for Codella, including eating half of her key lime pie. She was a better cop than Blackstone would ever be, and she had helped him when no one else would make the effort. On the Sanchez case, she had given him the chance to prove himself—and he had. And, he supposed, Marty Blackstone couldn't stand that.

Now he pulled out a small spiral notebook. "Ready for the Thomas Merchant saga?"

"Something tells me it's an interesting one." Codella leaned on the small marble-topped table.

He flipped to a page filled with notes. "Forbes put his wealth at three to four billion last year. I'd be happy with one percent of that. How about you?"

She shrugged. "I'd like to renovate my kitchen, but that's not going to happen any time soon."

"He's been chairman of BNA for eight years. Investors love him. But he's not very popular with the populists. In fact, he was summoned to Washington on Monday to testify about his high compensation. His base salary is ten million, but that's the tip of the iceberg. He gets a lot of stock options and bonuses. Apparently he makes four hundred times what the average BNA employee makes. The media is all over him right now."

"I know. It's a big show for the masses," Codella said. "But it won't change anything and he knows it."

"I'd feel like a prick if that were me."

"Which is why you're sitting here." She smiled. "What about his personal life?"

"Lucy Merchant is the third wife."

"Why doesn't that surprise me?"

"The first one was Eleanor Cutliff. She was from a wealthy Chapel Hill family."

"Old tobacco money?"

He nodded. "They married in 1980, and Merchant went to work for the father's hedge fund. He was twenty-five at the time and she was thirty-three."

"So he liked older women back then."

"Or he just liked them rich," suggested Muñoz. "Eleanor died two years later in a car crash. She left him a whopping inheritance. Her trust had matured when she was thirty-five."

"Sounds a little convenient."

Muñoz paused while the waitress set Codella's tea and his vanilla shake on the small table.

"I know," Muñoz said when the waitress was gone, "except that Merchant wasn't in the car when it happened. She was alone on a two-lane road, and the driver of the other car was grossly intoxicated."

The waitress returned and slid the key lime pie between them.

"Who was the second wife?"

"A popular Live at Five news anchor in the 1980s. Samantha Harris. They married four years after the first wife's accident." Muñoz checked his notes. "In 1987."

"Did she die, too?"

"No, they divorced after just a year."

"I bet she'd have some interesting insights."

"She moved to Chicago. She runs a popular syndicated talk show there."

"And Merchant moved from the D-list to the A-list by marrying Lucy Martinelli." Codella pushed a fork toward Muñoz. "Help me with this pie. I'm just going to have one bite."

He picked up his fork and speared the thickest part of the graham cracker crust. It occurred to him that he and Codella were like brother and sister; they didn't think twice about swapping germs. "He's been married to Lucy Merchant for almost twenty years."

"Happily, do you think?"

Muñoz leaned in and speared more pie. "Interestingly, his name came up in a complaint filed three years ago at Midtown. A woman named Jackie Freimor claimed he sexually assaulted her."

Codella lowered her fork.

"But the complaint was dropped the next day and there isn't much information. The cop who took her complaint left the NYPD last year."

"I want the details," said Codella. "Track down that woman." Muñoz nodded.

Codella lifted her fork for a second bite of pie. "What about his relationship to the daughter—Julia?"

Muñoz flipped to another page in his notebook. "They had a big fight at the Four Seasons just after Lucy Merchant went to Park Manor. It was on *Page Six*."

"What was it about?"

"I don't know. But I can tell you this: The daughter's a party girl. Goes to a lot of clubs. Vacations in Park City every winter. Last January she was out there and she wiped out on a slope and hit a tree. Fractured three vertebrae. Merchant hired a private jet to fly her back to New York for surgery at the Hospital for Special Surgery."

Codella sat back. "Only the best care for his little girl?"

"I wish I had more for you. He's had the same secretary for the past twenty-three years. She goes where he goes. Roberta Ruffalo. People call her his last line of defense."

"Well," said Codella, "let's see if I can get through her."

CHAPTER 33

Merchant watched Baiba's sleepy smile wither the instant she saw him. She started to shut the door, but he stopped it with his hand. "We need to talk. It's important."

"I don't want to talk to you." She pushed against the door.

He exerted an equal and opposing force. Now was not the time to *overpower* her. "You don't understand, Baiba. I—"

"I understand perfectly. You put something into that drink. You took advantage of me. I don't even know how I got home. And my neck—my body—now let go of my door."

He did not let go. He watched Baiba's delicate hand touch the scarf she had coiled around her neck, and he remembered his fingers around her neck last night. Just thinking about it made him want to fuck her again. With his free hand, he held up the small robin's-egg blue bag. "I brought you something."

"I don't want any more of your *gifts*."

But he saw her study the bag. She would know that the small box inside the bag held a gift more expensive than any of his previous offerings, and she would want to know how much he had been willing to spend to secure her "forgiveness" for last night. He knew the rules of the game he played. If you took, you had to give in return. "Go on." He smiled. "Open it. I think you're going to like it."

Still Baiba did not budge. She was playing *her* part, he thought. She didn't want to appear too willing to capitulate.

She wanted his moment of submission to last a little longer. Right now, she would be relishing his supplication. *Well, let her enjoy it,* he thought. He wasn't worried. Sooner or later she would look in the box. Women always opened the box. "I hope you like it," he whispered.

And true to his prediction, she took the bag from him. She reached inside, brought out the small, ribboned box, and then, in a fluid continuation of motion, she cocked her arm up and over her shoulder and pitched the box like a fastball. It narrowly missed his head and landed on the stairwell. "That's how much I like it."

Merchant turned to look behind him. The dented Tiffany box lay on its side against the wall at the foot of the stairs. Her little outburst made him want to drag her to the bed right now and spank—no, *throttle*—her, but now was not the time to punish her. Instead, he smirked appreciatively. "You just threw away five and a half karats."

"I don't care. I don't want your payoff."

"It's a gift."

"You're paying me off. You don't think I know what these *gifts* are all about?" She glared. "You want to keep me quiet. You think I don't know that? Well, guess what? I sold the last one. I cashed it in on Forty-Seventh Street for three thousand dollars."

His anger coagulated into cold fury at himself. Not only had he overestimated Baiba's sexual gameness, but he had underestimated her vindictiveness. He stared at the box and considered his next step. If he went to retrieve the box, she would probably slam her door on him. If, on the other hand, he entered her apartment, leaving the box where it was, someone might pocket a twenty-five thousand dollar pair of earrings. He shrugged. You didn't close deals with hesitation. He counted to three and pressed his weight into the door so suddenly that Baiba lost balance. As she stepped back to regain her footing, he moved inside and bolted the door behind him. "Let's talk. Just talk." He spoke calmly.

"I want you *out*."

"No you don't." He smiled. She liked his smile, he knew. He had felt her staring at his mouth that first night at the Four Seasons. She had wanted to kiss him even before they'd had wine. "But you're very angry with me," he added. "You probably want to hit me. Go ahead. I understand how you feel. I was wrong. I just wanted you so much, Baiba. It's hard to control myself with you. I went a little too far."

"A *little*?"

"I went too far." He held her deep blue eyes. A rush of blood was making him stiff. He saw her notice his erection. "No other woman has ever made me feel like this, Baiba. No one. Ever." Her arms were crossed, but he felt her resolve start to waver. "And I want to hear everything you have to say to me, Baiba." Wooing her back after such an egregious violation was an irresistible challenge. He made his voice sound perfectly sincere and convincing. The words he spoke didn't matter; it was all in the delivery. Baiba wanted to believe he cared about her. She was looking for the evidence. He just had to give it to her. He moved over to the small round table near her tiny pass-through kitchen, took off his gray suit jacket—no sense getting that wrinkled— and hung it on the back of a chair. "May I sit?" But he didn't wait for her answer.

She uncrossed her arms and moved them to her hips. "I have nothing to say to you." But he could hear her inner thoughts. *Make me feel better. Tell me I'm special to you. Be the daddy I never had.*

"You make me crazy when you're angry," he said. "I want you so much right now. I want you to sit on my lap."

She looked uncertain. "I think you should leave."

And then he called in the big guns. "I can't leave you, Baiba. I'm in love with you."

CHAPTER 34

Brandon punched in the five-digit Nostalgia Neighborhood code and went straight to the caregivers' room. He stuffed his backpack into one of the small lockers and sat on the couch. His shift didn't start for another hour. Should he go down to Ms. Hodges's office, he wondered, and demand to know what was going on? But why bother? She'd tell him lies just like Baiba had.

Maybelle entered the room and frowned. "What you doing here, Brandon?" She peeled out of her black wool coat.

"Baiba was shorthanded," he lied. "She asked me to come back—just until she finds a replacement."

"Hmmph. Well, *I* wouldn't do it if I was you. Not after Queen Hodges treat you that way yesterday." Maybelle plopped her substantial weight onto the next cushion. "I s'pose you hear the news?"

"What news?"

"A detective come today and look all around Lucy's suite. Josie tell me just now. She got it from one of the day girls. Chanelle. You not hear about it?"

Brandon shook his head. "What happened?"

"Nobody know for sure." Maybelle tugged off the shiny black Steve Madden boots she'd bought back in November. *Sixty percent off at Kings Plaza*, she had told him proudly the first time she'd worn them to work.

Josie came into the room as Maybelle leaned forward to put the boots into her locker. Josie's eyes met Brandon's and she said, "I thought I seen the last of you."

Brandon felt his hatred for her rise in his throat, but he said nothing.

Maybelle sat up and removed one of her big hoop earrings. "Brandon not hear about the police, Josie. Tell him what you know."

"I don't know nothing much." Josie snarled. "Only that some detective woman come here and look around. Supposedly she and Hodges go looking through the garbage."

"The garbage?" repeated Maybelle. "Why?"

"Nobody know," Josie answered.

Brandon watched Maybelle remove her second earring and set the pair at the bottom of her locker. He looked discreetly away as she pulled off her tight sweater and swapped it for a loose-fitting Park Manor polo shirt. Unlike him, Maybelle would never be caught dead wearing her uniform on the street.

Josie continued, "But I do know from Chanelle that the cop go into the dispensary and make Lorena answer all kind of questions."

"What questions?" asked Brandon.

"She not tell me." Josie opened a locker. Then she pointed toward the door and said, "Now get out of here. If you're a *man*, as you say, then you can't be watching me dress. Now go on."

Brandon stepped out of the caregivers' room. In the parlor, *Beauty and the Beast* was playing on the large flat-screen television over the fireplace mantle. A puffed-up, hypermasculine Gaston filled the screen. Brandon turned away, walked to the kitchen, and got himself a glass of water. Then he leaned against the long granite counter and thought about Baiba's words. *Tell anybody who asks that you gave Lucy water in that cup.* The memory triggered an electrical surge that traveled the length of his spine and made him slam down his glass. "Oh my God."

He rushed down the hall to Lucy's suite. He stared at the locked door while he replayed the events of Sunday night. He had followed Cheryl O'Brien into Lucy's bedroom at ten fifteen. They'd walked to the far side of her bed near the window and then Cheryl had handed him the medicine cup. He had lifted it to eye level—he was absolutely certain of this—and read Lucy's name on the cup. It was *her* cup and it held the same yellowish liquid she drank every night.

Lucy had been sitting on the edge of the bed, and he'd turned to her and smiled. "Okay, Lucy," he remembered saying. "Let's have a little drink." Then he pretended to drink from the cup. "*Mmmmm.* It's good. Have some, Lucy."

"*Mmmmm.*" Lucy echoed him. "*Mmmmm.*" It was a game they always played. And then, as he raised the cup to her mouth, her lips parted and she sipped agreeably. But after the first sip, she jerked her head back, squeezed her eyelids shut, and pressed her lips together in a sour expression. Then she slapped his hand so forcefully that a little of the diazepam spilled out.

Now Brandon leaned one shoulder against the wall where Lucy's nameplate had been removed. He punched his fist against the solid plaster and felt the pain throb in his knuckles as a hideous recognition dawned on him. Something bad was in that cup, and Lucy had tried to tell him about it. He had interpreted her nonverbal communication as an inconvenient symptom of her dementia, when in fact it had been the remnants of cognition. He closed his eyes and saw her sour face again. She might be alive right now if he'd paid more attention. He had let her down.

Dr. Evelyn Bruce rounded the corner in her white lab coat and shook her index finger at him. "You're needed in the ICU right now, Nurse!" Evelyn's bushy eyebrows made her look wild and severe.

"Yes, Dr. Bruce. I'm going now," Brandon assured her gently. He wondered if Evelyn had used this same condescending tone with the nurses at Sloan Kettering decades ago when she was a pioneering female surgeon. If he had worked for her then, he might have been offended by her high-handedness, but now he just felt sorry for her. She was stuck in a surreal Grey's Anatomy version of reality she would never get out of.

He watched her disappear into Arthur Lane's suite. Seconds later, Melissa Posen, Baiba's assistant care coordinator, followed her in, and Brandon heard Melissa gently saying, "You've already checked this patient's vitals, Doctor. He needs his rest now."

Brandon closed his eyes and pressed his fingers into his temples to help him think more clearly. If something other than diazepam was in Lucy's cup on Sunday night, how had it gotten there? Had Cheryl accidentally filled the cup with someone else's medicine? Was it conceivable that she had *purposefully* poured in the wrong medication? When she'd handed him the cup, had she deliberately weaponized him without his knowledge?

He shook his head. No. She wasn't capable of that. She had no reason to do that. But if she hadn't done it, who had? And then Brandon's mind called up an image of Baiba asleep on her pullout bed.

His heart pounded and he felt lightheaded. He returned to the caregivers' room. Maybelle and Josie were no longer there, thank God, and he grabbed his backpack, punched the combination code to let himself out of Nostalgia, and left Park Manor.

Madison Avenue was crowded with Upper East Siders returning home for the evening. Even after six inches of snow last night, the sidewalks in this zip code were perfectly clear. Brandon turned south. As he approached Seventy-Ninth Street, a woman with a newly groomed standard poodle charged directly at him, and he veered to avoid a collision. He turned to stare at the woman's back as she continued uptown. In her eyes, he realized, he wasn't even there.

He stopped in front of the diner Baiba had taken him to last Wednesday. He was, he realized, famished. The two slices of buttered whole wheat toast he'd eaten before his appointment with Judith had hours ago provided all the calories they could.

He entered the diner and slid into a booth along the wall. A ponytailed waitress deposited a sweating glass of ice water on his table, held out a menu, and said, "Coffee?"

His head was throbbing and he couldn't face the menu print. "Coffee, yes, and a bagel with cream cheese."

When she was gone, he sipped the water and stared across the restaurant at the booth where Baiba had pressed the envelope with three thousand dollars into his hands. Where, he wondered now, had she gotten that money?

CHAPTER 35

Codella showed her shield to the first floor security guards in the Bank of New Amsterdam main lobby. One of the guards made a call. Then he walked her to a private elevator, swiped a card, and sent her express to the top floor. When the doors opened, a well-dressed, mature woman was waiting to receive her. "I'm Roberta Ruffalo," she said. "Mr. Merchant's executive assistant."

Ruffalo had a short haircut that made her look younger than she probably was. She stared appraisingly through horn-rimmed Prada eyeglasses. Codella shook her hand and gave her an NYPD card.

"I wish you had called before coming all this way, Detective." Ruffalo smiled with cool cordiality. "I could have saved you the trip. Mr. Merchant is not in the building. He's been in meetings all afternoon. Is there something I can do for you?"

Codella smiled back. "You can call him for me, Ms. Ruffalo. You can tell him I'm here and that I need to speak with him in person. Tell him it's very important."

Ruffalo frowned. "His schedule is incredibly tight, Detective—as you can imagine."

Codella nodded. "Which is why I didn't ask him to come all the way uptown to my office. But I need to speak to him."

Ruffalo stared at her silver wristwatch. "I'm not even sure I can get in touch with him. He may be on an investor call right now."

"Why don't you try?" Codella smiled again. "Tell him I'm here and that I'll wait for him."

"If I do get him, he'll want to know what this is in reference to."

"It's about his wife."

"Then maybe I can help you. I'm handling all the arrangements."

"This has nothing to do with arrangements, Ms. Ruffalo. Call him, please. Now."

The woman still didn't oblige. "If he's with clients, it could be hours before he's able to return."

Codella stepped past the woman into the sleek and spacious waiting room outside Merchant's office. The wall across from the elevator was floor-to-ceiling glass and provided a dramatic view of Lower Manhattan and New York Harbor. The rich and powerful of New York City saw a very different skyline than the average soul on the street, she reflected. She turned to face Ruffalo. "I hope you're wrong." She sat on a couch. "Because NYPD detectives don't like to be kept waiting any more than bank chairmen do, and I don't intend to leave this office until I speak to him face to face."

CHAPTER 36

Muñoz summoned a thick Spanish accent. It wasn't hard. He'd listened to thick accents all his life. "I speak with Jackie Hartley?"

"Who's calling please?"

"You are Mrs. Hartley?"

"What do you want?"

"I calling from Westchester Children Fund."

Click.

Muñoz returned the phone to its cradle, pushed his chair out from his desk, and stood. She was home. He signed out a car, and five minutes later he was on the West Side Highway heading to Pelham Manor.

Jackie Freimor, now Jackie Hartley, lived in what looked like a hundred-year-old brick Tudor on Ely Avenue. He rang her front bell and stood under the glow of a bright porch light. The door opened, and the woman who answered looked startled to see his tall, dark figure. He held up his shield quickly and stated in perfect English, "Mrs. Hartley?"

"That's right."

"I'm with the NYPD. My name is Detective Muñoz."

Her shoulders relaxed. "What can I do for you, Detective?"

"May I step inside?"

She let him into a spacious vestibule. A vintage cast-iron coat rack stood in the corner beside the door. It held a man's worn parka, several hats, and a child's blue snow jacket with clip-on mittens. Beyond the vestibule was a corridor that led to the back of the house. Three toy trucks were parked at the side of this corridor. A small child—a little boy, Muñoz guessed—lived in this home. To the right of Muñoz, a staircase ascended to a second floor, and to his left was an elegant living room. Would Mrs. Hartley invite him to sit in there, he wondered, as she locked the door behind them.

But she only faced him and crossed her arms. "What can I do for you, Detective?" she repeated.

"Three years ago, you lived on Twenty-Third Street in Manhattan, correct?"

"Yes," she said in a cautious tone.

"And your name then was Jackie Freimor?"

"What are you getting at, Detective?"

"In March of that year, you attended a party at the Grand Hyatt."

Her expression instantly hardened and she shook her head. "I have nothing to say about that." She moved toward the door.

"You filed a complaint against a man named Thomas Merchant."

"No comment," she said.

"Which you dropped a day later. I'm curious about that."

"People change their minds about things, Detective. Now you really have to go."

"Or did he change your mind, Mrs. Hartley?"

She stared at him with eyes that looked simultaneously frightened and angry.

"Did he take out a checkbook and change your mind, Mrs. Hartley?"

"I can't talk about this. I want you to leave my home."

"Why can't you talk about it?"

"Please, you have to go."

Muñoz gazed into the expensively furnished living room, up the carpeted steps, and down the long hall. "He paid you enough money to take you all the way to Pelham, didn't he?"

She gave no response.

"Does your husband know?" And now tears brimmed in her eyes. "No, of course he doesn't. You weren't married then. You were—"

"I was a naïve young woman just out of college, Detective. I let myself be talked into going somewhere I shouldn't have gone. That's it. Now please, you have to leave."

"I'm sorry." Muñoz shook his head. "But I can't go without answers." He looked at his watch. "What time does your husband get home, Mrs. Hartley?"

"Why are you doing this to me?"

"I need to know what happened at the Grand Hyatt."

"I signed a contract, Detective. I—"

"You could have put him in jail."

Hartley walked into the living room and sat on the couch. Her body folded into itself. She covered her face in her hands.

Muñoz followed her into the room. "You can talk to me now," he said gently but firmly, "or you can still be telling me why you can't talk to me when your husband gets home. Which is it going to be?"

She wiped at the tears on her face. "If Merchant finds out I violated—"

"He will *not* find out. I give you my word."

She sighed what sounded like years' worth of anxiety. A long moment of silence passed. Finally she cleared her throat and sniffled back her tears. "A friend of mine called me up that night and said she was in a suite at the Grand Hyatt and there were some bankers. She said I should come over and have a drink with them."

Muñoz nodded. *Keep talking,* he thought. *Keep talking.*

"So I went over." She looked up at him. "Don't judge me, Detective. I was young."

Muñoz sat beside her on the couch and put his hand on hers. "You don't think I've done things I regret, Mrs. Hartley." It wasn't a lie.

"Most of them were older guys. In their forties. Probably married." She laughed ruefully, a reminder that hindsight usually revealed your blind spots. "I wish I had turned right around and gone home. But then he came over to me—"

"Thomas Merchant?"

She nodded. "I didn't know who he was until he introduced himself. He was holding a drink for me. Champagne. He was very charming, very attentive. He didn't come on to me. He just asked me questions about myself as I sipped the champagne. And then I started to feel a little dizzy. I thought the champagne was going to my head. He offered to walk me to a chair. He led me into another room—to sit down, he said. There was a bed in that room, and the next thing I remember, I was waking up and my clothes were off and I knew someone had had sex with me."

"What happened after you filed the complaint?"

"A lawyer called. She wanted to cut a deal."

"What happened?"

Hartley looked at her watch. "My husband and son will be home any minute, Detective. If I tell you this, you have to get out of here and never come back."

"I promise."

"I got a lawyer. My girlfriend's brother. We met with Merchant's attorney. What a hard act she was. She asked how much it would take to make the problem go away. My lawyer asked for one million dollars. She laughed in our faces and countered with a hundred thousand. I felt like a piece of real estate. In the end, she bought my silence for five hundred thousand. She wrote the check right then and there, and I signed a confidentiality agreement and dropped the charges. I was young, Detective. I felt responsible for what had happened. I shouldn't have been at that party in the first place. I suppose I felt as if I'd gotten what I deserved. Believe me, I've regretted the decision a thousand times, but what's done is done. I met my husband six months later, and he doesn't know about it and he never will. He thinks we bought this place with a nice inheritance from my deceased aunt."

"And you don't need to tell him otherwise," assured Muñoz as car headlights flooded the living room picture window.

"That's my husband. Oh, God!"

"Let me handle this," said Muñoz.

A moment later, the front door opened and a child called out, "Mommy?"

Jackie Hartley shot up from the couch and smoothed her skirt. "In here, honey."

Muñoz got to his feet as Jackie Hartley reach down to lift her young son into her arms. Then a bald man in a black wool coat entered the room. "What's this?"

"Are you Mr. Hartley—Jack Hartley?" asked Muñoz.

"That's right." Hartley dropped his briefcase. "Who the hell are you?"

The man was like a vicious tomcat with his fur up, Muñoz thought. Muñoz pulled out his NYPD identification card and shield. "I've been waiting for you, Mr. Hartley." He smiled. "Your wife assured me you'd be home very soon, and she was kind enough to let me wait."

Hartley relaxed marginally. "Oh."

"I just need a moment of your time." Muñoz reached into his wallet slowly, figuring out what to say. He brought out his nephew's high school graduation photo. "We're looking for this man. He's dangerous. We received a tip that he was employed by your company."

Hartley looked at the photo and shook his head. "No. I've never seen this guy in my life."

"You're certain of that?" persisted Muñoz. "Just look at it one more time."

"I don't need to look at it one more time," said Hartley.

Muñoz returned the photo to his wallet. "Then I'm sorry to have interrupted your evening." He nodded at Jackie Hartley, turned his back to her, and left. As he pulled the car away from the curb, he called Codella. "Where are you?"

"In Merchant's office. Waiting for him to show up."

"Well, here's a little something you'll find interesting."

CHAPTER 37

The diner booth was comfortable, the coffee was hot and brac-
ing, and the bagel was warm and crisp, but as hungry as Brandon
was, he could hardly get it down. Had he inadvertently killed
Lucy Merchant? How would he live with himself if he had?
Should he go straight to the police?

A heavy anchor was dragging him down into a place with
which he was all too familiar. His arms and legs felt numb. The
sensation, he knew, was depression invading his body, taking
hold, supplanting all the happy and hopeful feelings he'd felt this
morning after leaving Judith Greenwald's office.

He signaled the waitress to bring his check, still trying to
make sense of what was happening. Why had Baiba really asked
him to lie about the contents of that cup? Had she known that
something bad was in it? Had Hodges known, too? Were they
trying to set him up, to make it look as if he had killed Lucy?
If that were so, then running away from Park Manor tonight
would only make him look guiltier.

He paid his check and left the diner. He stood on the street,
not knowing where to go. If he got on a train and went home
right now, the anchor would drag him all the way to the bottom.
Voices in that blackness would speak to him, and he knew what
they would say. *You're all alone. You have no one. You don't even have
a job. Give up. It's too hard.*

Instead he turned west and walked toward Fifth Avenue. He sat on a bench a block north of the Metropolitan Museum. His hands were cold and his ears burned. He fished in his backpack for his knit cap. The lanterns along the edge of Central Park were lit, and the sky in front of him, facing east, was charcoal. Behind him, on the west side of the park, the final rays of setting sun would be casting a deep purple hue across the sky. In the Nostalgia Neighborhood, Mr. Lane would be wandering—he always wandered at this hour. Maybelle would be saying *Where Brandon gone to?* and Josie would be saying *We better off without him.* Or *her*, he thought. She would probably say *We better off without her.*

Then Baiba's bloodshot eyes stared out at him from his mind. Baiba had pretended to care about him all these months. She was always touching his arm, winking at him, telling him how good he looked. And she had given him the three thousand dollars. Her act of generosity—what he *thought* had been generosity— had given him so much hope and confidence. She had made him feel special. It wasn't the cold hard cash she had placed in his palms; it was the fact that this beautiful woman, who would never in her life have to apologize for who or what she was, had accepted who he wanted to be and was helping him on his journey. But it was all an act. He had never been special to her. And for all he knew, the money she'd given him had come straight from her banker boyfriend.

Tears burned in his eyes. Well, he didn't want that money. He certainly wasn't going to use it to pay for his operation. He didn't want to have to think about Baiba having sex with Thomas Merchant every time he looked at his new chest in the mirror. *Goddamn you, Baiba*, he thought. *Why did you do this to me?*

And then he remembered Baiba telling him why she kept going back to Merchant. *He brought flowers. He gave me another little Tiffany bag.* If she really hadn't liked what he did to her, would she have gone back to him just for flowers and jewelry?

He told me he had to see me or he would go crazy. Had she really fallen for that?

Brandon rubbed his palms together to get the blood flowing to his numb fingers. What if Baiba *wasn't* an innocent victim? There was no denying she'd had choke marks around her neck today, but what if she'd *enjoyed* getting those marks as much as Merchant had enjoyed putting them there?

Brandon closed his eyes, and all these thought fragments shifted together like tangrams into one monstrous picture in his mind. Baiba had set him up. She had murdered Lucy Merchant. She hadn't called him over this morning because she'd needed him—her whole rape story was a big lie. *He took me to the Four Seasons*, she had said. *It was so romantic.* Baiba was mesmerized by Merchant's wealth and attention. And she was afraid it would all go away. She knew better than anyone that Lucy Merchant could easily live five more years in her Nostalgia cocoon and that Merchant couldn't possibly divorce Lucy without looking like a scoundrel. And she probably knew that sooner or later, he would tire of her and move on to a different attractive blond—that all the Tiffany gifts and meals at the Four Seasons would become a thing of the past—unless she seized her opportunity and became the new Mrs. Merchant. And so she had planned a murder using Brandon as her devoted pawn.

He rocketed off the bench. How would Baiba answer to *those* charges, he wondered. He stepped off the curb and waited for an opening in the downtown traffic. Then he jaywalked across Fifth Avenue and headed back in the direction of her apartment. What other lies would she tell him?

CHAPTER 38

Codella watched Thomas Merchant fly out of the elevator and beeline into his office as if she weren't there. Ruffalo followed him in, and the door closed. Codella counted the minutes and imagined the back-and-forth they were having about her. *Why is she here?* Merchant would demand. And Ruffalo would say, *Something about your wife. She wouldn't tell me. She refused to leave. I tried my best to get her out of here.*

When Ruffalo emerged from the inner office, she wore a smile that was only skin-deep. "Mr. Merchant will see you now, Detective," she announced as if he were a head of state generously granting an audience to a pathetic supplicant.

"Thank you." Codella played along.

Merchant was tall and thin. He had the good kind of gray hair, the kind that made you look distinguished without looking old. Even from twenty feet away, she could tell his black suit was probably worth more than the entire wardrobe in her bedroom closet. And the instant their eyes met, she realized that she'd never leave here with what she wanted unless she allowed him to feel like the winner of the encounter. She thought of McGowan saying, *Nothing would give me greater pleasure than to see you commit career suicide.* She couldn't let that happen. Somehow she had to make Merchant believe he was in control. But how?

She approached his massive glass desk, held out her hand, and said, "My condolences on your wife's death."

"Spare the bullshit, Detective." He sat in his Herman Miller executive throne. "What's so important that you had to interrupt my schedule?"

He was hardly a man softened by mourning, she thought. Her instinct was to lash back, but she swallowed the impulse. "I apologize for the interruption. I'll make this as brief as I can." She sat across from him, although he had not offered a seat. "Your daughter came to see me yesterday afternoon—"

"My daughter came to *you*?"

"That's right. To my office at Manhattan North. She asked specifically for me."

"Why?"

"She has some concerns about the circumstances surrounding Mrs. Merchant's death."

"Let me guess," he said. "She told you about a videotape."

"She played it for me, in fact."

Merchant shook his head and wagged an accusing index finger at her. "You should have called me right then, Detective. You should have picked up the phone and dialed my office then. I could have put things into perspective for you."

"Why don't you do that right now."

"I don't have time for this, Detective."

"But your daughter—"

"My daughter is—" He paused to consider his words. "She's understandably upset by her mother's death, and quite frankly, she is imagining things."

Codella crossed her legs and took her time before speaking. "You know, I thought so too at first. But now I'm not so sure."

His eyes narrowed. "What do you mean?"

"There are a few irregular circumstances surrounding Mrs. Merchant's death. They warrant a closer look."

"What irregular circumstances?"

"I'm not at liberty to disclose those right now."

"Look, I'm her husband." His forefinger stabbed his desktop with so much force that the thick glass vibrated. "You have to tell me."

"I'm sorry." She watched the anger percolate on his face. "But I can't. You just have to trust me on this. The evidence is circumstantial, but it's compelling."

"What are you suggesting, Detective? That someone killed my wife?"

"I'm not ready to make a definitive statement quite yet," Codella said.

"Then why are you here?"

"Because I need your help."

"You won't tell me anything, but you *need my help*?"

"To put some questions to rest. An autopsy would do that. I'd like you to request one."

Merchant leaned back and brushed at his lapel. "Absolutely not. Now get out of here." He pointed to his door.

Codella didn't move. "A postmortem could put everyone's mind at ease."

"Julia's, perhaps. But not mine. I have enough problems with the press. I don't need them speculating on whether I killed my wife. I'm not naïve, Detective. I know what's in your head. You won't tell me the details because the husband is always the suspect. Right? You know what would put my mind at ease? If the NYPD had the decency to send an *experienced* detective to see me, not one who swallowed my daughter's paranoia hook, line, and sinker."

Codella willed herself not to respond to the insult. Merchant was just one more angry man—like McGowan, like her father— who needed to flaunt his supremacy. But in the aftermath of cancer, she didn't fear the threats she could see coming at her, and she calmed herself with the comforting reminder of what Dr. Abrams had said this morning. *You're boring. Don't come back for six months.*

"How long have you even been on the job?" Merchant asked.

"Long enough."

He leaned over his desk in a way she knew was meant to unnerve her. "How long?" he demanded. "I want to know."

He wanted her to cower. But she wouldn't do that. Maybe she was about to commit "career suicide," but she was suddenly done letting him have the upper hand. She placed her elbows on her side of the desk and leaned toward him instead of away. "If you're that interested in the trajectory of my career, Mr. Merchant, why don't you have Ms. Ruffalo Google me. You'll get all the answers you want. But let me clarify one thing: I don't swallow people's stories hook, line, and sinker. I follow a chain of evidence. That's my job. And I came here because I thought you'd want to know what happened to your wife. I think the press will be more interested in the fact that you *don't* want an autopsy than they would be if you did. I think your analysis of the situation is entirely foolhardy. But then, what do I know?"

Merchant leaned back. "I did not kill my wife."

She thought of Muñoz's phone call five minutes ago from a street in Pelham Manor. She was tempted to say, *And I suppose you didn't rape Jackie Freimor, either?* Instead, she said, "If you didn't kill your wife, then you have nothing to fear."

"Bullshit," he said again. "The media doesn't care about the truth. They'll use anything they can to eat me alive."

"Including the fact that you turned me down." Codella took an autopsy authorization form out of her jacket pocket and placed it on his desk. "Don't you want to be on the right side of this investigation?" She stared at him. "I'm going to get an autopsy one way or another. You can sign this form and make it easy or I can go to the DA and show them what I've got." She pitched her bluff with as much casual confidence as she could muster. She felt him watch her closely. She blinked naturally. She didn't look away. When enough time had passed, she said, "Sign the form, Mr. Merchant. And call the Office of the Medical Examiner. Your wife is an icon of the musical theater world, and you are a man of influence. A call from you would expedite things. And then we could put this issue to rest."

She slid the paperwork across the glass without looking away from him. He stared at the form for several seconds. Finally the hardness in his eyes gave way. He picked up his pen and scrawled his signature next to the X she'd drawn. "Satisfied?" He pushed the form back. "I didn't kill my wife."

CHAPTER 39

Julia Merchant's phone rang. She paused her Netflix movie and waited for the ringing to stop. When were they going to quit harassing her? She'd spoken to at least five of them, and they all asked the same questions. *Which of your mother's shows was her favorite? Who were the performers she admired most? Is it true Gordon Kahn helped her get her first audition? Are there any backstage anecdotes you can share with us? Who did she consider her best choreographer?*

Julia had obliged each reporter with the sound bites they sought when what she really wanted to do was tell them, *Leave me the fuck alone!* They were all piranhas feeding off the scraps of her mother's life. They never even pretended to care about what Julia was going through.

And then one reporter had dared to broach her most painful subject. "Your mother acknowledged that she was a carrier of a presenilin mutation that caused her early onset Alzheimer's. Have you been tested for the mutations? Are you concerned that you'll share her fate one day?"

"Oh my God, you fucking asshole!" she'd screamed into the phone before ending the call. She didn't intend to speak to any more reporters.

The ringing stopped and her answering machine switched on. She waited for the hang up—reporters never left messages; they liked to catch you off guard—but her father's voice blared through the speaker instead. "Pick it up, Julia. Now."

She lifted the phone from its charging station.

"What the hell is wrong with you?" he snapped.

"What are you talking about?"

"You went to the police and didn't tell me?"

Julia closed her eyes and cringed. For an instant, she felt only fear of his explosive temper. Then she took a deep breath and reminded herself that *she* was in the right—not him. "You didn't pay attention to my concerns. You didn't believe me."

"Because it's nonsense."

"How do you know it's nonsense?"

"Because no one would kill your mother. I'm sorry, but what would be the point? I hope you're happy that you're going to get your autopsy, but do you have any idea what my life will be like when the press gets their hands on this little tidbit? I'm already getting butchered in the *Business Times*. Now I have to be in the tabloids, too?"

"Why? You're afraid of what they'll find when they comb through your closet?" Julia couldn't resist the taunt.

"Is that why you're doing this, Julia? To embarrass me?"

"I did it because something happened to my mother."

"You're right. Something did happen to her. But it wasn't murder, honey."

"She should never have married you."

"Maybe not." He laughed. "But you'd still be my daughter."

"I wish I weren't." She knew she sounded like a five-year-old.

"Does that mean I should stop those transfers into your account every month?"

"Those transfers barely pay my expenses anymore," she blurted out angrily.

"Well that's too bad, because I'm no longer going to pay for your clubbing and your trips. You almost got yourself killed last year. You need to get a job and do something with your life."

Now he sounded like Pamela, she thought. "You don't know what it's like to be your daughter."

He sighed. "Well, you don't know what it's like to be your father, either. Get yourself a therapist, Julia. I'll pay for that." He hung up.

CHAPTER 40

Haggerty was there when she arrived, and he'd brought them takeout Indian.

"How did you get in?"

"Your doorman gave me the key." He smiled. "How was your day?"

She pushed back her annoyance. "Muñoz was really helpful. He dug up some pretty damaging dirt on Merchant. Can I borrow him again tomorrow?"

He came up behind her. "You're abusing your personal relationship with me, Detective."

"Maybe." She pulled away and turned to face him. "But we're making progress. Merchant signed the autopsy authorization. McGowan is pissed, of course. He knows he'll have to give me a team."

"Grab some plates," said Haggerty.

She reached into the cupboard. And then it occurred to her: What if she hadn't wanted to eat Indian? What if she hadn't wanted him to be here at all tonight? Was he going to show up like this whenever he wanted to? "The only way I could get on his good side is to get another round of cancer."

"Don't say that."

"Why not? It's the truth."

"Well, I don't want to think about it."

"Maybe you should," she said.

His hand was pulling a white cardboard carton of rice from the takeout bag. He stopped and faced her. "Why are you saying that?"

"Well, I'm not exactly a good risk, now am I?"

"Did you get bad results from the scan, Claire?" His expression looked suddenly alarmed.

"No. I'm fine. I don't have to go back for six months, but . . ." She shrugged.

He sighed his relief. "But what?" He set the rice carton on the counter. "What's with you tonight?"

"Nothing," she lied. "I'm just tired. I'm not good company right now."

He moved closer. "Are you trying to say that you want me to go?"

She shrugged. "I don't know." She peeled out of her jacket and hung it on a stool by the counter across from the sink.

"You're not being honest."

"Okay," she admitted. "I just wasn't expecting you to be here right now. I—look, this—us—it's all just happening a little fast for me."

He crossed his arms. "You're scared."

Codella combed her fingers through her hair. "I'm not scared. I just know how these things end."

"*These things?*" he repeated. "What *things?*"

"Relationships." She pictured her father and mother fighting in the kitchen on Pleasant Street. She thought about McGowan always flirting with female uniforms fresh from the academy and Fisk bitching about how much his wife was taking him for in their divorce. Where would she and Haggerty end up if this went any further?

"You know as well as I do that we would never last."

"How can you know that? I don't know that."

"Trust me. We'd be happy for a couple months. Maybe even a couple years. And then you'd get bored or I'd get bored or you'd start drinking too much or I'd get too wrapped up in a case and before you know it, one of us would end up wishing the other one wasn't there. We'd fight or ignore each other or cheat on each other, and all the good things we ever had as partners and friends would be gone. History. Just because we got greedy and tried to make us into something we were never meant to be."

Haggerty threw up his hands. "Jesus, Claire. I'm not the other asshole men in your life! I'm not your father. I'm not McGowan."

"I know that."

"I don't think you do." He shook his head. "You know, I'll always remember the time you shoved me up against the inter-rogation room wall because you were so pissed that I didn't trust you to keep my secret. You remember that?"

She nodded.

"Well, now it's my turn. Now I'm pissed. Because you don't trust me. You're looking right at me, and you're seeing someone else. So why don't you take some time and think things over." He walked out of the kitchen, and the next thing she heard was the front door opening and slamming shut.

Let him go, she told herself. *It's better this way.* But was it? She imagined him not in her kitchen, not in her bed, not in her life anymore, and she realized—with uncomfortable jolts of regret and trepidation—that she had changed in some funda-mental way and that being with him might now feel more natu-ral, more right, than being alone.

She moved quickly to the door. When she opened it, he was still standing on the landing waiting for the elevator. He could have disappeared down the fire stairs, she reflected. He had cho-sen to give her time to come after him. He had *wanted* her to come after him. "I'm sorry." She grabbed his arm. "Come back inside."

"I don't think so."

"Please," she said.

"Why?" he demanded.

"Because you got all that good food. We should eat it."

He squinted. "You know that's not the answer I want."

He was going to make her say it. "Okay. Because I'd miss you."

He shook his head. "That's not a good enough reason, either."

The elevator doors opened. He stepped forward. She pulled him back to her. "No!" She almost never cried, but now she started to.

He let the doors close behind him, and he clasped her tightly against him, kissed her mouth, and whispered, "I love you, Claire. And you love me. Just deal with it, okay?"

WEDNESDAY

CHAPTER 41

Rudolph Gambarin was a workaholic, and he liked to start cutting bodies early in the day. Lucy Merchant's examination had begun by the time Codella got there. From outside the room, she heard the whirr of a precision saw. She could almost feel the high-speed blade grinding into her own sternum. She waited for the sound to stop. Then she opened the door, stepped inside, and silently worked her arms into a gown and tied on a mask. She positioned herself at the foot of the stainless table, opposite Gambarin. She'd been in his exam room enough times to know that he didn't like to talk while he worked.

As usual, the ubiquitous odor of decay was unpleasant. Codella always avoided taking deep breaths during postmortems. When she inhaled the smell of putrefaction, it felt as if someone else's death were infesting her lungs. She had never been repulsed by the clinical dissection of a body, but as she watched Gambarin pull the chest flap up, exposing blood-red tissue and organs, she felt the familiar heaviness that always invaded her arms and legs in an autopsy room. The sensation was like an unearthly gravity pulling her right into the ground.

She focused on Gambarin's delicate gloved fingers severing arteries and ligaments, and then in her mind she was back at the side window of Joanie Carlucci's house, staring through the glass at her father's fat gloved hands gripping the handle of the baseball bat. And for the first time, she realized why she always felt this strange paralysis during autopsies. Here in this room of stainless steel and cold tile, her muscles and tendons remembered that first time she had met death. Now she pictured Joanie Carlucci holding her arms in front of her face as her father adjusted his grip like a designated hitter heading to the plate. If Claire had fled from the window in that moment, she would not have seen his act of violence. He might have gotten away with murder. But she hadn't been able to move. Her legs had felt glued to the driveway of that house the same way they felt fixed to Gambarin's autopsy room floor right now.

The precise, methodical medical examiner detached Lucy Merchant's organ set. One at a time, he cradled each organ like a newborn and transported it to a scale where his assistant weighed it, recorded its measurement, and took tissue samples. And all the while, Codella gripped the edge of the table the way she had grasped the ledge below Joanie Carlucci's window, and she reflected on the consequences of her father's violent act. At the age of ten, she had become a foster child to a jewelry manufacturer's rep and his wife in Meshanicut. Throughout her father's trial, the couple devoured the local news coverage at night when they assumed she was asleep, but she hardly ever slept in those weeks and months, and she heard the live reports from her bedroom at the back of the first floor. Organized crime experts described her father's ties to Rhode Island mob families, panels of forensic psychologists diagnosed his abnormal psychology, and notable child psychologists predicted her fate in brashly clinical terms. She would suffer paralyzing post-traumatic stress disorder, severe depression, attachment issues, and sleep disorders. "That monster didn't just murder a woman; he murdered his child's future," one expert concluded.

When Gambarin and his assistant finished with the organs, they placed a body block behind Lucy Merchant's head. Codella watched as Gambarin picked up his saw. Had she been psychologically damaged? Was she depressed? Did she have attachment issues? She thought of Haggerty and his own family of alcoholics and how the two of them had finally, after so many years, stumbled their way into cautious intimacy. Well, wasn't everyone in some way or other fucked up by their childhood?

The procedure was over in two hours. When Gambarin pulled off his mask and wiped his forehead with a towel, Codella held her breath, trying not to betray her deep impatience for information. He might or might not weigh in on the cause of death before he finalized his report, and if she left without confirmation of her theory, she would be very disappointed.

She watched him stare at the fruits of his labor. "The external exam yielded nothing out of the ordinary," he finally announced as he rubbed his eyes. "No scratches. No bruises. Certainly no knife wounds or bullet holes. She did have one little basal carcinoma spot on the dorsal side of the left hand but nothing to indicate a cause or manner of death."

"And internally?" Codella asked in a carefully neutral voice calibrated to Gambarin's perpetually blunted affect.

He reached for a water bottle on a stainless counter. "She was a physically fit woman with the musculature of someone still in her prime. There is no plaque in her arteries. The blood vessels around her heart look perfectly normal. The valves appear healthy. I saw no thickening of the pericardium. Heart disease did not cause her death."

"So do you know what did?"

He pointed to her lungs and nodded. "Noncardiogenic pulmonary edema."

"Fluid in her lungs?"

He nodded. "She basically drowned to death." He picked up a pen and pointed it at Lucy Merchant's mouth. "That's why her lips turned bluish. You see? She wasn't getting enough oxygen."

"But how? Why?"

"Usually pulmonary edema results from congestive heart failure. But as I've said, this victim's heart was completely healthy when death occurred. Something else caused her edema."

"What?"

Gambarin lifted Lucy Merchant's left eyelid, exposing a milky-white cornea. "It's difficult to see, but there's miosis of the pupils."

"Miosis," she repeated. "Constriction?"

"That's right."

She couldn't contain her impatience any longer. "So what are you saying?"

"The autopsy results are consistent with toxin-related non-cardiogenic pulmonary edema."

"A drug overdose?"

"Yes."

Codella let out a huge sigh. "Her medicine cup tested presumptively for oxycodone."

He nodded thoughtfully. "An opioid overdose could certainly explain this, depending on the concentration, of course. We won't know for certain until we get the toxicology back."

"Which could take weeks."

"More like a month," he said. "Things have been very slow coming back. They really need to do something about that. But based on my observations, I'm willing to go out on a limb and state that there's probable cause of an overdose. And that should be sufficient for you to move your investigation forward."

When Codella got back to her car on First Avenue, she called Muñoz and gave him the news. "I'm going up to Manhattan North to fill McGowan in. I've got to get a team looking into the Park Manor staff. Can you swing over there, get a contact list of employees and residents, and e-mail it to me before ten o'clock? I'll let Hodges know you're coming."

CHAPTER 42

Merchant rode downstairs in his private elevator, stood in the lobby, and peered out the door of his Fifth Avenue building. Since he'd been subpoenaed to testify in front of the senate subcommittee, reporters had tried to ambush him every morning as he walked to the Escalade. They waited in idling cars and jumped out the moment they saw him. He didn't intend to get ambushed today about his Lucy's death. He scanned the cars along the street. The coast looked clear, thank God, and he dialed Felipe and said, "Swing around. Right now."

A minute later, the Escalade pulled in front of the entrance. Tony, Merchant's tall Yugoslavian doorman, walked outside in front of Merchant like a human shield. When they reached the curb, Tony opened the back door of the Escalade and moved aside at the last possible instant so that Merchant could scoot in before anyone could snap a photo of him. Tony said, "Have a good day, Mr. Merchant," and the door slammed shut.

The car left the curb. *So far, so good*, Merchant thought, but with the police investigating Lucy's death and the autopsy happening today, he would be prime meat for the media. He pulled out his phone, scrolled through his contacts, and called Park Manor.

Constance answered on the second ring.

"You're at your desk very early," he said.

"What can I do for you, Thomas?" Her voice sounded cool.

"I'd like to take you to lunch."

"Oh?"

"For all you've done," he added quickly. "The Four Seasons, twelve thirty?"

"I can't. I've got a detective on the way over here. I don't know what my day is going to hold."

"But I need to talk to you."

"And I'd like a word with you, too," she said ominously. "But it's not a good time. In fact, it's a terrible time, and you should know that. I'll just say two words: Julia. Videotape."

Merchant sighed. "I know. I'm sorry. How about tomorrow?"

"I don't know. Let's see what tomorrow brings."

CHAPTER 43

Codella stared at the faces around the conference room table. McGowan had assigned her a team, but he'd hardly given her the best members of the squad. The only other homicide detective in the room was Paul Novotny, a bald, angular cop who had announced he would retire at the end of April. He spent most of his time these days surfing between Expedia and Travelocity looking for hotel and airfare deals for the big trip to Prague he planned to take with his wife. The other five faces consisted of Matthew Swain, a brand-new detective with no homicide experience, and four uniformed officers who would run the background checks under Novotny's supervision. She hadn't brought Muñoz into the meeting. McGowan, who was leaning in the doorway, would have called her on that. Muñoz would just have to be her secret weapon.

She held up yesterday's *New York Times*, *Daily News*, and *Post*. "Lucy Merchant's obit is in the *Times*. Read it if you haven't already. The *Post* and *Daily News* will give you the lowdown on Park Manor. I'll leave these on the table. You should know who the victim is. This isn't your run-of-the-mill drug deal gone bad. We're investigating the death of a Broadway legend who was given a drug overdose."

Swain, the young detective, was taking notes—a good sign. Novotny was blowing his nose, and the three male uniformed cops looked more interested in their coffee cups than anything she was saying. The only other female cop in the room, Jane Young, had her eyes on McGowan.

"Come on," said Codella. "Has anybody in here even seen a Broadway show lately?"

"*Lion King* with my daughter, seven years ago," said one of the uniforms as if Codella had actually wanted an answer.

"Wife took me to *Beautiful* for our anniversary. Carole King. It wasn't bad," said another cop.

"All right, all right. You may or may not give a shit about Broadway legends, but believe me, plenty of people in this town loved Lucy Merchant. A candlelight vigil in Times Square last night drew more than three thousand people, and when they find out she didn't die a nice, natural death in her sleep, they're not going to like it."

Codella paused until Jane Young—who McGowan had been spending a lot of time "mentoring" lately—stopped looking at McGowan and focused on her. "Listen up, everyone, because I only intend to say this once: Memorize the faces around the table. This is your team. If you mention details about the case to anyone not at this table—I don't care how insignificant those details seem to you—you're violating my direct order and I'll make sure you never work a homicide with me again. You got that?" She glanced at McGowan. *If* she ever had another homicide case, she thought. She saw heads nod. "Okay, so let's start with a little background."

Codella told them about Lucy Merchant's early onset Alzheimer's diagnosis. "She moved to Park Manor eighteen months ago. She lived in a special dementia care unit called the Nostalgia Neighborhood."

Novotny slapped the table. "That sounds like the place for my father-in-law."

"Yeah, but you can't afford it, Novotny," she said. "None of us can afford it. We couldn't even afford a closet there with our combined salaries."

Novotny shrugged. Codella continued, "You'll be vetting the entire staff at Park Manor along with the residents and their families. Lucy Merchant's primary caregiver was a young man named Brandon Johnson. The care coordinator of the Nostalgia Neighborhood is a woman named Baiba Lielkaja. Lucy Merchant's Nostalgia neighbors are a who's who of New York business, culture, and society names. The families of these residents come and go from the facility. You're going to look into them, too. You're searching for any past or present connections between them and Lucy Merchant, anything at all that might suggest a motive for murder."

McGowan cleared his throat. *Don't forget I'm here. Don't forget I'm watching you,* he reminded her. He still didn't buy her murder theory even after Gambarin's autopsy results. He wanted her to be wrong as much as she wanted to be right. "Lucy Merchant's husband is Thomas A. Merchant," she continued. "Chairman of BNA—that's Bank of New Amsterdam for anyone who still keeps his cash in a mattress."

Matt Swain, the young detective, laughed. At least someone in the room had a sense of humor.

"The freezer's a lot safer than the mattress," said a cop named Fenton.

"Merchant's been all over the financial pages lately because a Senate banking subcommittee made him testify about his obscenely high compensation," Codella continued. "He doesn't like the idea of us digging into his wife's death. No surprise there. And he certainly won't like it if his name turns up in the papers. In fact, he'll go for our throats." *Her* throat, she meant. "That's why you're not going to pound the pavement and talk to just anyone." She and Muñoz would do that, she thought. "You're going to discreetly research him and all the other people on the list using our databases. You are *not* to contact them. Let me say that again: do *not* contact anyone directly. I hope that's perfectly clear. Nobody plays the Lone Ranger. You got that?"

The last thing she wanted was some glory-seeking detective-wannabe fucking up the case. Again she waited for heads to nod.

"Detective Novotny will make your individual assignments at the end of this meeting. Work fast. I need you to get through these names by tomorrow—yes, it'll be a late night—and if in the course of your research you come across anything that seems remotely important, share it with Detective Novotny. He'll decide whether or not to pass it up to me right away. That's all. Now let's get to work."

CHAPTER 44

Constance Hodges dialed the number on the detective's business card. She counted four rings before the voice on the other end answered, "Codella."

"Detective, it's Constance Hodges." She made a conscious effort to sound confident, like one professional speaking to another. It was the same way she tried to sound whenever she called Michael Berger to update him on Park Manor's daily operations. "I've been trying to reach you."

"What can I do for you, Ms. Hodges?" came the equally professional response.

"Detective Muñoz was here earlier this morning. He asked for a list of names. I thought you were going to run those tests yesterday and put this all to rest."

"I did run the tests, Ms. Hodges." The detective's voice was matter of fact. "And I'm afraid the results won't allow us to abandon the investigation after all."

"Does that mean you found something?"

"I really can't tell you more than that."

Hodges heard finality tucked inside Codella's politeness. She leaned her elbows on the desk and pressed her lips against the phone's receiver as if she were speaking directly into Codella's ear. "We need to talk, Detective."

"Why?" asked Codella bluntly. "Is there something you haven't told me?"

"No, but I know this place," answered Hodges. "I know the people—their habits, personalities, backstories. I can be a resource to you."

"I appreciate your willingness to cooperate, Ms. Hodges. Thank you. I'll keep that in mind."

Hodges recognized the dismissal but was not deterred by it. She routinely survived the insouciance of Park Manor residents and family members. She had withstood the condescension of the puffed-up MBAs at Foster headquarters. And what did she really have to lose by pressing on? Park Manor would be injured by this investigation, and that meant she would be injured. She had to at least try to shield the institution—and herself—from culpability in whatever had happened. If she let the detective shut her out, then she couldn't hope to influence the information Codella received, the interpretations she would make, the conclusions she might draw. "If Lucy Merchant's death was—God forbid—murder, then there are some things you need to know, Detective, and I can save you a lot of time."

In the pause, Hodges knew that Codella was assessing her motives. Could she be trusted? Did she really have information? She waited, and finally Codella said, "I'm on my way to an interview right now, but I'll come as soon as I can." And then the connection was broken.

Hodges's felt her heart pounding. She took a deep breath and dialed the next name on her mental list.

Michael Berger never sounded friendly. He didn't like her, she knew, but then he didn't like anyone who wasn't a fellow member of the Harvard Club. She ignored his surly tone and got to her point. "The bad news is that Lucy Merchant's death is probably not of natural causes. The police are continuing their investigation."

"You mean she was murdered?"

"That word has not been used—yet."

"Shit! This is bad timing, Constance. Really bad timing."

Berger, of course, was thinking about the pending sale to Eldercare Elite. If Park Manor's reputation was tarnished, Eldercare would either come back to the table with a lowball offer or walk away completely, and if that happened, Berger wouldn't reap the rewards he was hoping for. "Could Merchant be behind this?"

"Are you honestly asking me if he killed his wife? That would be going a little far out on the limb for a bank client, don't you think?"

"He's a fucking bastard. I don't trust him. Why didn't he stick his wife in his own client's facility?"

"Because ours is better," said Hodges, but she knew that was only one of the reasons. "Let's just work very closely with the police on this," she said. "Now is the time to look cooperative. Assuming it was murder, we have to make sure whoever is responsible doesn't make Park Manor look negligent."

"And how are we supposed to do that, Constance?"

"I'm not sure yet, but I have a few ideas."

"I hope you do, because Renee wants this sale to go through, and if it doesn't, it's *your* head."

Hodges didn't grace his threat with an answer.

"Give me regular updates," he demanded, and then he hung up. She took a deep breath and stared at the phone. *You fucking pompous asshole*, she thought. *I hope you die a hideous death.* She didn't care how many Ivy League diplomas he had on his corner office wall. He wasn't half as intelligent as she was. How did people like him end up making twenty times what people like her made? If Eldercare Elite bought Park Manor, he would pocket millions while she would face the loss of her position and purpose. Despite his assurances to the contrary, she knew very well that after the sale she would be replaced by an Eldercare Elite insider. And now she couldn't even take solace in the fact that Lucy Merchant's death might disrupt the deal, because if Park Manor's reputation was damaged, she would take the fall for that as well.

She picked up the phone and dialed Thomas. Maybe she should have lunch with him and get things on the table. As she listened to the rings, her anger mushroomed. Then Roberta Ruffalo's voice warbled, "Mr. Merchant's office," and Hodges realized she wasn't ready to talk to him—she needed to think things through a little more—so she slammed the phone down.

She opened her bottom drawer and grabbed her purse. Then she walked past Heather's desk to the powder room at the end of the hall, locked the door, set her purse on the marble sink, and plunged her fingers deep inside to find the treasure within. When she had swallowed all the liquid and could feel warmth spreading through her chest and releasing the tension in her neck, she returned the empty vessel to her purse, flushed the toilet, and ran the faucet for several moments before she opened the door and walked back to her office. Merchant might be a *fucking bastard*, she thought, but at least with Merchant, she knew whom she was dealing with.

CHAPTER 45

Cheryl O'Brien's curly hair was just a shade away from black. Her skin was ruddy and her lips were too thin for the bright-red lipstick she'd applied. Her pale-blue dress was an inexpensive wraparound from a season or two ago, and her shoes were scuffed black flats with worn-out heels. "I need to ask you some questions," said Codella.

O'Brien glared at her with exasperation. "Are you kidding me? What's going on? I just got grilled by some other detective."

Codella squinted into the woman's small eyes. "What? Who did you just speak to, Ms. O'Brien?"

"Some Detective. Novotny or something like that. Look, I've got to leave pretty soon."

Codella barely managed to contain her rage. "I'm sorry that you need to speak to both of us," she said. "I won't take up much of your time. May I come in, Ms. O'Brien?"

"It's *Mrs.*" The woman was gaunt, and her shoulders curved inward although she was no more than forty. She hugged her door and seemed to debate her next move. Finally she swung it open. Her Stuyvesant Town apartment was on a low floor, and the living room windows faced another red brick tower within the large postwar residential complex. The room was somber. "You can come in for a minute or two, but—"

"Thank you." Codella stepped in.

The woman gestured to a plaid couch—an ancient Jennifer Convertible, Codella guessed. She would have preferred to remain standing, but sitting on dilapidated and uninviting furniture was often a requirement of her trade, and she duly committed to a cushion and thanked the woman.

"You were one of the two last people to see Lucy Merchant alive."

"I suppose so," agreed O'Brien.

"You and her caregiver."

"Yes. Brandon. Brandon Johnson."

"You gave Mrs. Merchant her evening medications." Codella stated this rather than asked, and the woman dropped her eyes guiltily.

"Yes. Her valium. Diazepam."

"You prepared it in the dispensary?"

"That's right."

"Tell me when and how you prepared that medication, Ms. O'Brien."

"*Mrs.*," O'Brien corrected her again. "I have to go to work very soon, my other job."

Codella leaned forward. "This is important, Mrs. O'Brien."

"Are you saying I did something wrong? That other detective kept asking me about where I used to work. What was that all about? I didn't do anything."

"No one thinks you did," Codella assured her quickly. That fucking Novotny. Now she couldn't put any hard questions to O'Brien. She had to tread lightly. Novotny had spooked her. "I just need to know how you prepared the medication."

"I always prepare the meds the same way. In the dispensary. I wear an orange vest. That tells everyone I'm not to be disturbed. The medications are in a locked cabinet. I prepare each resident's medications one at a time."

"Could you describe that procedure?" Codella asked in a calm voice she wouldn't have had to use if Novotny had followed her orders and stayed on the databases.

"First I label the cup. I put the resident's dosage into the cup—sometimes it's liquid, sometimes it's a pill or several pills—and I check off the box on the medication checklist. Then I put the cup on a tray and move on to the next resident's meds. When they're all prepared, I start my rounds."

"Did you notice anything unusual about Lucy Merchant's medicine bottle that night?"

"What do you mean?"

"Well, was it in its usual position? Did it look out of place in any way?"

O'Brien squinted. "No, I don't think so."

"Did the medicine itself look any different than usual?"

She shook her head.

"How long did Mrs. Merchant take diazepam?"

"Since October or November, I think."

"And why did she take it?"

"She got very anxious at night. She had trouble settling down. Dr. Fisher tried her on Atavan—that's what most of the residents take—but it didn't work for her."

"How did she behave at night before she took the diazepam?"

"She'd get out of bed and wander around. She would scream at anyone she passed."

"What did she scream?"

"Oh, crazy stuff, you know. *Stop it. Get away from me. You can't make me do that.* Nothing rational. Sometimes she called me Daddy. She was having delusions. Dementia is a terrible thing, you know."

"You said Detective Novotny asked about your work history. Forgive me if I'm repeating something he already asked you. How long have you worked at Park Manor?"

"Going on six months."

"And before that?"

"Eldercare Elite," she said. "And I was a visiting home nurse." She looked at her watch. "I still am, and I'm supposed to be with a patient in half an hour."

"Can you tell me why you left Eldercare Elite to come to Park Manor?"

"More money," O'Brien said. "They offered me the night shift. It pays more and I can be a visiting home nurse during the day. And we need the money."

Codella nodded. "I just have one more question. The night Mrs. Merchant died, did you allow her caregiver, Brandon Johnson, to administer the medication?"

O'Brien looked into her lap. She didn't move or speak.

Codella waited. She had to know if the nurse would lie the way Baiba Lielkaja had lied or whether she would tell the truth like Hodges. The silence answered the question long before O'Brien opened her mouth.

"How did you know?" the nurse finally asked.

"Why did you do it?" Codella countered.

"Because whenever I came into her suite, she turned belligerent." Now O'Brien spoke in a steady stream, as if she were relieved to have the truth out. "I don't know why. No one else caused her to act that way. Maybe I reminded her of someone? All I know is that I would have been fired if Brandon didn't help me. And my husband lost his job last year."

"I'm so sorry."

"He sold software. He didn't make his quota. I need this job."

Codella heard the terror in O'Brien's voice. She was a woman trying to provide for her family against the odds. "Who do you think Lucy Merchant could have mistaken you for?"

"I don't know. As I said, she called me Daddy sometimes." She laughed. "Not that I look like a daddy—I hope."

"Did she call you by any other names?"

O'Brien shook her head. "She couldn't remember names, not even her daughter's."

Codella nodded. "All right, Mrs. O'Brien. That's it for now. Thank you for your time."

Codella returned to her car and sped up First Avenue with her hands gripping the wheel the way she wanted to wring

Novotny's neck. She crossed the park at Ninety-Sixth Street and pulled behind Manhattan North. Novotny was sitting at his desk and staring at the computer when she barged in his office.

He looked up. "What's eating you, Codella?"

"I gave the team direct orders not to contact anyone from Park Manor, and you went right to the phone. You called up one of the last two people to see Lucy Merchant alive."

"Cheryl O'Brien." He smiled. "That's right. She worked for Eldercare Elite until six months ago," he said. "You didn't know that, did you? Eldercare is trying to buy Park Manor, Codella. It was in that *New York Times* article. Something's going on there. She's part of something bigger. It's an important connection."

"An important connection? How the fuck do you know it's important?"

"She could be a plant. Don't you see?"

"You don't want to know what I see, Novotny." She leaned across his chair as if she were going to tear him to shreds. "Did it ever occur to you that if you're a nurse at Eldercare, then Park Manor is the next logical step in your career? It's the pinnacle of care facilities in Manhattan. People have all kinds of reasons for making a move, Novotny. You were supposed to come to *me* with your *connections*. Cheryl O'Brien is not our killer. I spoke to her. She didn't hide anything. If you ask me, she's just busting her ass to keep her family afloat. You're a fucking moron."

Novotny pointed a finger at her. "Don't use that tone with me, Codella. I don't work for you."

"You do on this case. You report to me. And as of right now, you're off the team." She grabbed the Merchant files off his desk.

He pulled them back. "You can't do that."

"Oh, yeah?"

"I'll go to McGowan," he threatened. "We'll see who wins that one."

"We'll see right now." Codella turned and stomped down the hall to the lieutenant's office. "Am I running the Merchant case or aren't I?"

McGowan looked up from a precinct map on his desk. "What's your problem, Codella? I gave you a team, didn't I?"

"Good. And as of this moment, Novotny's off it. If he contacts one more person involved in the case, I'm writing him up."

CHAPTER 46

Hodges watched Heather's thin fingers set the cup and saucer in front of Codella. "Thank you, Heather," she said, but her kindly tone and benevolent smile were *not* for her assistant's benefit. Detectives, she supposed, were like psychotherapists. They registered far more than the words you uttered. In the minuscule movements of hands or mouth, they read your fear or anxiety. In the rise and fall of your voice, they detected amiability or animosity. In the angle of your gaze, they distinguished between veracity and deception. Hodges did not intend to provide any windows into her soul, but she would certainly watch for Codella's unconscious revelations.

As soon as Heather left the room, Hodges said, "Thank you for coming, Detective."

Codella sipped her tea but said nothing.

Hodges sensed that a hard, protective shell surrounded Codella. But if she could just crack that shell, the two of them would be on equal footing. "I imagine you haven't had time for lunch, Detective. Let me get you a sandwich from our Manor Bistro." She picked up her phone.

Codella shook her head. "Please. Don't trouble yourself. I'm fine. Thank you."

"It's no trouble at all," Hodges insisted. "How does turkey and brie on a baguette sound?"

"Really, I'm fine."

"Our chef does a very nice sandwich. Let me order you one." Hodges gave the order to Heather. When she hung up, she said, "I can only imagine how demanding your job is on a daily basis."

"We all have demanding jobs," said Codella.

"Maybe so, but I suspect yours is a bit more demanding than most—and you're a little too modest. I confess. I Googled you yesterday after you left my office."

Codella shrugged. "Yes? Well, I suppose we all Google each other these days, don't we?"

"But we're not all NYPD celebrities."

"I just do my job."

Here was a skillful deflector, thought Hodges, a woman who would make an interesting and challenging patient. Yesterday Hodges had been too unnerved by the detective's surprise visit to observe her closely, but now she scrutinized her face. She was not beautiful in the "classic" sense—not like Baiba with her long blond hair, large eyes, and voluptuous lips—but her coal black hair, ice-blue eyes, and cerebral intensity made her compelling. Hodges leaned forward. "You've been through a lot, Detective. It must be difficult for you, coming back after the terrible health scare you've been through."

Was it irritation or suspicion that caused Codella to frown for an instant? The detective was sensitive about her illness, Hodges observed as she sipped coffee from her clear glass mug. "I trained as a clinical psychologist," she explained, "and I've worked with a number of patients who went through cancer treatment. I know how debilitating it is, and I know how hard it is to come back. I admire your stamina."

"I'm fine now," was all Codella said in return. "Why did you ask to see me, Ms. Hodges?"

Hodges folded her hands on her desk. "I want to discuss a staff member I think you should look into."

"That wasn't necessary. We're looking into *all* your staff members."

"I realize that," said Hodges. "But your background checks won't turn up any criminal records. We have a very rigorous employee review process at Park Manor." She reached for her coffee again and watched her hand ascend to her lips. There was no tremble, she assured herself. "We use a private investigative firm staffed by former NYPD detectives like yourself. They run criminal checks on all prospective staff members. They finger-print. They speak directly to friends and neighbors of applicants. We also administer a personality test to future employees."

"Even caregivers?"

Hodges smiled. "I like to know who I'm working with. And we update our background checks on a yearly basis—no exceptions."

"That's impressive," Codella acknowledged.

"But we've had someone on our staff for the last few years who failed to meet some of our employment criteria. Please bear with me while I give you a little history on this. About two and a half years ago, Park Manor denied employment to a male caregiver. He happened to be a gay man. And let me say right up front that I personally have nothing against gay people. I have many gay friends and acquaintances. It's of no concern to me. But this young man was—well, let's just say that his effeminate gestures were quite pronounced."

"And you felt he wouldn't go over so well with the Park Manor clientele?"

"I *knew* he wouldn't go over well here, but that's not why we denied him employment," said Hodges. "He'd been treated for depression, and we don't hire people with known emotional instability. Remember, these caregivers are making life and death decisions for people who can't make those decisions for themselves. We serve a wealthy and litigious clientele. We have to protect them and ourselves." Hodges paused.

Codella nodded. "Long story short?"

Hodges opened the file she had pulled for this meeting. "Long story short. He filed a complaint with the Civil Rights Bureau of the New York State Attorney General's Office. He claimed Park Manor had violated his protections under New York State's Sexual Orientation Non-Discrimination Act, SONDA."

"I see," said Codella. "And what happened?"

"We settled out of court and paid a hefty fine. Since then, we've made a few hiring decisions that I would prefer not to have made. And one of them happens to have been Lucy Merchant's primary caregiver, Brandon Johnson."

"The caregiver who held her last medicine cup to her lips."

"That's right."

"He is also gay?"

"No. He's a transgender man."

Codella sipped her tea. "And that disqualified him for employment?"

"No. What disqualified him was the fact that he was under a psychologist's treatment."

Codella shrugged. "But you were a psychotherapist. You know that half the people in Manhattan have seen a therapist. If we disqualified them all from jobs on the basis of that, we'd have a severe workforce shortage on this island, Ms. Hodges."

"Please, call me Constance. And I agree with you, Detective. All of us have moments when we need to tell our story to someone, don't we?" She gave Codella a penetrating look that said, *Yes, I know about your past. I put my investigative team to work on you.* Although Codella did not move a muscle, Hodges could feel her register the unspoken message. "But I think this young man has *serious* issues," she continued. "They wouldn't have concerned me if I were running a restaurant and he were my waiter. But as I said previously, he makes daily life and death decisions for our residents. And I hired him against my better judgment because I felt pressured to do so by the Foster Health Enterprises counsel. You see, Brandon applied for his position right after the case I just mentioned, and although transgender individuals are not explicitly protected under SONDA, he could have argued that we turned him down because of his *perceived* sexual orientation.

Our legal counsel strongly encouraged me *not* to decline him employment given his credentials."

"What credentials did he have?"

"He was a certified nurse's aide in New York State, and he'd worked as an emergency medical technician in the state of Michigan."

"In other words, he looked impeccable on paper."

"That's right."

"What serious issues did you think he had?" asked Codella.

"Gender dysphoria. Clinical depression. And after observing him for the past two years, I would also characterize him as someone suffering the long-term effects of emotional abandonment."

"How so?"

"He shows a desperate need to feel connected to someone. And whom does he choose to connect with? A woman who can't even remember his name. He treated Lucy Merchant like the mother he wished he'd had. He was more doting than her real daughter was, and he wanted her all to himself. He wouldn't let anyone else near her. He boasted about how she smiled when he came into her room. He bragged about all the things only he could coax her to do." Hodges sipped her coffee again before summing up. "He met Lucy's physical needs, Detective, but Lucy sustained him emotionally. He had a fantasy relationship with her. He used her to fill the huge gulf in his life."

"Then why would he kill her?"

Hodges felt herself in complete command of the interview now. "I can think of at least two reasons, Detective. For one thing, he might have sensed her slipping away from him. Recently Mrs. Merchant's memory has been deteriorating rapidly, and perhaps he couldn't stand the prospect of another parental abandonment. Julia Merchant told me a gold charm was missing from her mother's room the morning she died. The charm was a dancer—like Lucy Merchant—and it wouldn't surprise me at all if Brandon Johnson took that charm as a symbol of her to hold onto."

Codella was quiet for a moment. Then she said, "You mentioned there were two possible reasons?"

Hodges nodded. "The other very real possibility is that he conflated Lucy Merchant with the *bad* mother from his past. He might have lashed out at her the way he wanted to punish the biological mother who emotionally abandoned him."

Hodges paused while Codella typed notes into her iPhone. Then the detective looked up at her. "Have you ever seen his temper flare? Has he ever acted violently here?"

"No," Hodges acknowledged. "But I've seen evidence that he has violent impulses. On Monday morning, I brought him into my office along with two other caregivers who worked the shift when Lucy—Mrs. Merchant—died. I was debriefing them, and he got very defensive. At the time, of course, I didn't realize that the death might be suspicious. In the course of the conversation, I found out he had violated Mrs. Merchant's care plan. He gave her ice cream before he got her ready for bed. Mrs. Merchant is on a strict no-sugar diet. I was not happy with him, and he gave me a look that let me know he felt nothing but contempt and rage."

"How old is Brandon Johnson?"

Hodges stared at his employment application. "Almost twenty-three," she said.

There was a knock at the door and Hodges called out, "Come in."

Heather set a plate and cloth napkin on Hodges's desk in front of Codella's seat. Codella thanked her. When the young woman was gone, she asked, "Is there anyone else on your short list of people with motive and opportunity?"

Hodges shook her head. "Not that I can think of right now, Detective."

"What about Baiba Lielkaja?"

"Baiba?" Hodges glanced down and readjusted her chair. Where the hell was Baiba, anyway? She hadn't even bothered to call in this morning, and she wasn't answering her phone.

It was *her* fault that Brandon Johnson had dispensed medications against protocol. It was *her* fault that he had been in Lucy Merchant's suite after she died. If Baiba had been doing her job, enforcing the policies of Park Manor, Julia Merchant would not have had a suspicious video to take to the police, and *none* of this would be happening.

"She was on duty the night Lucy Merchant died," pointed out Codella. "And she has keys to the dispensary."

Hodges shook her head. "Yes, but she doesn't prepare or dispense medications. I just don't see that, Detective." The fact that she didn't *want* to see it was more to the point, of course. Whoever had ended Lucy Merchant's life was going to end up on the front cover of national news magazines and go down in the annals of crime history. It would be far better for Hodges if the killer was Brandon Johnson. At least Hodges could defend herself against him. She had been coerced into hiring him. The laws of the land had left her powerless to exercise her better judgment. Sometimes good sense should be allowed to trump political correctness, she could argue.

"What about the Merchants?" asked Codella.

"What about them?"

"Could either of them be involved, in your opinion?"

Hodges thought immediately of Michael Berger's comment. *Could Merchant be behind this?* She knew Merchant well enough to know he was capable of many things, but she didn't think murder was one of them. And although Julia had surprised her by initiating this whole inconvenient investigation, she didn't see her hand in murder, either. "The question is why?" she said. "What would be in it for them?"

"An end to Lucy Merchant's misery? The elimination of expense?"

"But you must know that expense is of no concern to the Merchants." Hodges shrugged. "And Mrs. Merchant has been very comfortable here. Her quality of life was as good as it could possibly be."

Codella looked at her watch and stood. "I'll think about what you've told me," she said. "I appreciate your insights."

Hodges had the distinct impression the words were intended merely to placate her.

"I do have a request," Codella added.

"Of course. Whatever you need."

"We're going to need to speak with several people on your staff. It would be helpful if you could designate a room in which Detective Muñoz or I could conduct interviews here, on site. Otherwise, we'll be forced to bring your staff members to a precinct."

Hodges concealed her dread with a smile. "We'll make arrangements, Detective."

Then Codella was gone, and Hodges stared at the turkey and brie sandwich on her desk. The detective had not even touched it.

CHAPTER 47

"To what do I owe this *pleasure*, Thomas?"

"Can we suspend the sarcasm for now?" said Merchant. "I called Pamela Martinelli the *attorney*, not my bitchy sister-in-law."

Pamela's verbal claws did not retract one bit. "*Both* Pamelas are bitchy. What's going on?"

"A detective came to see me yesterday."

"What detective?"

Merchant reached for the card on his desk. "Codella. Claire Codella, NYPD. Have you heard of her?"

"I only deal with the feds."

"Well, she camped out in my office and refused to leave until I spoke to her."

"About what?"

"Lucy's death. She seems to think it wasn't natural. She wouldn't tell me why, but I know this is Julia's handiwork, god-damn her."

"What did this detective want from you?"

"She wanted me to request an autopsy."

"And what did you do?"

"I signed her form and made a call. What the hell else could I do? I'd look guilty if I didn't. I've got enough public relations problems right now. Jesus!"

"Well, if I were your lawyer—which I'm not, and I don't intend to be ever again—I would advise you not to speak to anyone else or sign any more papers without legal representation."

"No shit! But I don't want to use a BNA lawyer for this, and I don't want anyone else involved in my personal affairs. I want you."

Merchant heard the smirk in Pamela's voice as she said, "You want me to provide cover for you, is that it? Lucy Merchant's sister gets behind her beleaguered brother-in-law, the grieving widower who makes four hundred times more than his janitor?"

"Don't worry. I'm not expecting you to do it pro bono."

"I don't handle murder cases, Thomas," she told him in a snotty tone that betrayed her enjoyment of his predicament. "I limit my work to unethical financial thieves. Who knew you were both."

"I'll take that to mean you're officially my counsel should I need it?"

"I'll think about it," she said. "In the meantime, don't say another word to anyone. Don't even utter a syllable in front of the police."

CHAPTER 48

He was waiting in the lobby of the Borough of Manhattan Community College. He was only inches taller than she was—five-foot-five or six, Codella guessed. His gray eyes, pensive and alert, studied her closely. He had a sensuous mouth, solid cheekbones, and a strong, symmetrical nose. He was handsome, she decided, though his good looks were somewhat obscured by a bad case of acne. He combed his fingers nervously through spiky blond highlights. There were whiskers below his sideburns where he obviously shaved. But the facial hair faded away at the jaw line. He had no hair above his upper lip and only patchy whiskers on his chin. His Adam's apple was convincingly male. But his arms and shoulders still had not been altered dramatically by testosterone. He was a work in progress, she thought. "You're Brandon Johnson?"

"I am." His voice was low but gentle. "And you're Detective Codella?"

"That's right." She shook his hand. "Is there a place we can sit? Can I buy you a cup of coffee or tea?"

He led her to a small student café, and they sat at a table. "How old are you, Brandon?" she asked, although she already knew.

"I'll be twenty-three next month. Why?" He removed the tea bag from his cup.

"And you're a student here at BMCC?"

"That's right. I'm studying to be a respiratory therapist." He straightened his posture as he said this. "I graduate next fall."

"So you work at Park Manor to pay for school?"

"I did. I quit on Monday."

"You quit?" Codella wondered why Hodges had not mentioned this fact. "Why did you quit?"

He shrugged.

"Well, you must have had a reason."

He stared at the table.

She needed him to drop his shields. "How long have you been transitioning, Brandon?"

His head shot up.

"You're on testosterone, aren't you?" she asked in a matter-of-fact voice.

He nodded.

"How long?"

"About a year and a half. Why? What does that have to do with anything?"

"Maybe nothing," she answered casually.

"Then why did you ask me?"

Codella leaned forward. "I'll cut right to the chase, Brandon. I know you administered Lucy Merchant's medication on Monday night. I saw the videotape and I've spoken to Constance Hodges. She admitted it."

Brandon shrugged. "Well, good for her for telling the truth. I never tried to hide it. I don't see why it was such a big deal. You do what you need to do to get the job done. Lucy didn't respond to Cheryl so I helped her. Big deal. Hodges should never have lied about it in the first place."

Codella found herself impressed by the unpolished but articulate young man. "You don't like Constance Hodges, I take it?"

"What's to like about her? All she cares about are her rich clients and covering her own ass."

"What do you think of the other staff members?"

"They're okay. Most of them."

Codella watched him crack his knuckles. She leaned forward and stared into his eyes. "Did you put something into Lucy Merchant's medicine cup Sunday night?"

"No!" Brandon slammed his fist against the table so loudly that students at surrounding tables jumped. "No," he said with more control.

"Because it's very likely that whatever she drank from that cup killed her."

His face contorted with obvious distress. "I knew it. Oh, God. I just knew it."

Codella remained silent as he described how he had helped Lucy drink her medicine that night, how she had made a face after the first sip and slapped the cup away.

"And spilled some of the contents?"

He nodded. "But I *made* her finish it." The tears welling up in his eyes reflected the harsh fluorescent light shining down from the ceiling. "I killed her. Oh, God!" He put his elbows on the table and buried his head in his palms. "I didn't know I was doing that. You have to believe me."

If he was acting, he was a very convincing actor, Codella decided, but she wasn't ready to buy anyone's act just yet. "If you didn't put something in the cup," she asked, "then who did—and why?"

"I have no idea! Why would anybody want to kill Lucy Merchant?"

"I wish I knew." Codella sipped her tea.

As Brandon looked around the room, Codella studied him closely. His gray Abercrombie & Fitch henley was threadbare. His wristwatch was a cheap Timex, and his Converses were coming apart at the toes. People had all kinds of reasons for doing unspeakable things, she reflected. And then, of course, there were the people who didn't even need a reason to do them. She crossed her arms and wondered if Brandon was capable of unspeakable acts. When he returned his gaze to her she said, "You're in a difficult position, you know."

"What do you mean?"

"I mean, all eyes are going to turn in your direction."

"But I told you, it wasn't me. I cared about Lucy."

"It doesn't matter what you say. No grand jury ever takes someone at their word. The circumstances aren't in your favor. You were in the room. You weren't supposed to handle her medication. You gave her the cup even after she tried to slap it away. You're a respiratory therapy student, so you probably know about medications that cause breathing problems. You got that liquid down her throat despite her protests. And you're on testosterone. Some expert will get on the stand and talk about your mental instability and aggression." She paused. "And on top of all that, you returned to the scene of her death in the morning. You kissed her good-bye. What would you think if you were on a jury?"

In the silence, Codella saw a tear fall from his eyes.

She handed him a napkin. "Did you take anything from Lucy Merchant's room when you went in there that morning to say good-bye?"

"Take something? What would I have taken?"

"A little gold charm, a dancer."

"Lucy used to wear that charm around her neck when she first came to Park Manor. But then she started to tug at the chain, and she broke it one night. I put it into her bedside table. It's been there ever since."

"Apparently it wasn't there on Monday. Julia Merchant noticed that it was missing that morning. She mentioned it to Constance Hodges."

"I swear to you, I didn't take it. What more can I say to convince you?"

"Tell me whatever it is you're holding back."

"I'm not holding anything back."

And now in his tone she did sense him protesting a little too much. "I can't take the heat off you, Brandon, unless you're honest with me."

He glanced over his shoulders.

"Right now. One chance," she said. "No bullshit."

"Okay, but not here. Let's walk."

Codella followed him down a long corridor. They went outside and crossed the West Side Highway. Brandon stopped on the snow-covered bike path and leaned on the railing overlooking the Hudson River. The still-bitter wind from Monday night's nor'easter invaded every opening in Codella's jacket. She raised her collar and stuffed her hands in her pockets. Her ears were already cold. Brandon wasn't wearing a coat. He zipped his gray sweatshirt, pulled the hood over his head, and brought his hands inside the sleeves. Codella watched his eyes follow a floating chunk of ice bobbing uptown with the strong current. "Why are we out here? You must be freezing," she said.

"I'm fine," he snapped, but his chin was trembling. "I could feel all those people listening to us."

"Start talking," she said. "I need answers."

Then he turned to her. "It's Baiba. I think she's involved."

"Baiba Lielkaja?"

"She's having an affair with Thomas Merchant."

"How do you know this?"

"Because she told me."

"When?"

"Yesterday. She asked me to come over and see her. She told me she'd been to his place the night before. She's been there other times, too. She looked really bad. She had marks around her neck."

Codella remembered her own visit to Lielkaja yesterday. She remembered the wool scarf coiled around the care coordinator's neck. "Go on."

"She told me that he'd put something into her drink Monday night and that he had sex with her, rough sex . . ." His eyes pleaded. "You can't say you learned this from me. I promised I wouldn't tell."

Codella held up her hands to signal stop. "Go back, Brandon. He gave her *what*?"

"I don't know. Like a date rape drug, I guess. In her drink. She drank it, and then she didn't remember anything else."

Codella thought of Jackie Freimor in her big Pelham Manor home bought with Merchant's payoff. Was Baiba Lielkaja another Jackie Freimor? How many were there in the banker's past?

"He made her feel special," said Brandon. "And she liked what he did to her. She *liked* it. She admitted that to me."

From his contorted expression, Codella sensed he found it hard to say these things and even harder to imagine Baiba Lielkaja doing them. And it occurred to her that Brandon Johnson might have his own deep and complicated feelings about Baiba Lielkaja.

"Merchant had his personal driver, Felipe, pick her up," he continued. "And he gave her presents—Tiffany jewelry, flowers— and he took her to nice restaurants like the Four Seasons."

"What are you suggesting, Brandon?"

He shook his head. "I don't know."

"Yes you do."

He kicked the railing with his worn-out Converse. "What if she liked him so much that she—" Then he stopped. "Never mind." He bent down, picked up a clump of snow, and flung it into the river.

"Say it, Brandon. Go on."

"What if she liked him so much that she wanted to be the new Mrs. Thomas Merchant? What if she used me to kill Lucy?"

And then they were both silent. The theory fit with Codella's existing suspicions about Lielkaja. But the new facts suggested other possibilities, too. If Thomas Merchant were capable of drugging and raping women, was he also capable of murdering his wife? Had he and Baiba plotted murder together? She took Brandon's arm and pulled him away from the railing. "Come on. Let's go back inside. It's easy to get ahead of ourselves. We don't have all the facts yet. We need more."

He was silent as they returned to the lobby of BMCC. Then he turned to her and said, "I didn't kill Lucy. She was a beautiful, sad woman with lots of bad memories. But she lit up whenever I came near her, and I cared about her. Not because she was famous. It was because we connected. She communicated with me in her own limited way. I was the only one."

Codella watched him disappear down the corridor. He had definitely fed Lucy Merchant the oxycodone that killed her, but she doubted he had done it deliberately. The question was: Whose guileless instrument had he been? Baiba's? Merchant's? Or someone else's?

CHAPTER 49

Lorena Vivas's long dark hair was pulled into a ponytail. Her soft brown eyes gave her face a compassionate and reassuring aspect. Her expression was sober. When she sat across from Muñoz at a table in the Park Manor library, he instantly judged that she could not have murdered anyone. Codella would caution him, *Don't rush to judgment like that. Just gather the facts.* She believed he had a tendency to be too trusting and that he relied too heavily on his gut reactions to suspects and witnesses. But he didn't think that he was naïve. Even as he formed a rapport with someone like Lorena Vivas, another part of him stood outside of the interaction, watching it, evaluating it. Years of hiding his own identify as a gay man beneath a straight façade had taught him how to be simultaneously inside and outside each human interaction. "You're the day nurse," he said now. "Is that correct, Ms. Vivas?"

"Lorena." She nodded.

"And you—and only you—dispense medications during your shift?"

"That's correct."

"Let me guess—a lot of Tylenol, baby aspirin, and Benefiber?"

"You've got it." She laughed appreciatively. "And a few residents are on statins. A few take SSRIs. And then, of course, there's morphine for the hospice patients who are in pain."

"What about oxycodone?"

She nodded. "But usually only when a resident has had a knee or hip replacement."

"Is anyone in Nostalgia taking oxycodone right now?"

She shook her head.

"Other than you, who has access to the dispensary in Nostalgia?"

"It's locked at all times, and the only people who have a key are the nurse on duty and Baiba, the Nostalgia care coordinator. I suppose Ms. Hodges has a key, too, but she hardly ever comes up."

"Did she come upstairs on Sunday during your shift, Lorena?"

Vivas's smooth forehead wrinkled in concentration. "I don't think so."

"Where do you keep your key while you're working? Is it with you at all times—like my service revolver is?" He smiled.

"Yes. Always." She tapped the pocket of her burgundy Park Manor scrubs. "I never put it down. One of our residents, Dr. Evelyn Bruce, thinks she still does rounds at Sloan Kettering. Last year she got into the dispensary—not on my shift—and carted out bottles of medicine. She's a little crazy. Well, they're all a little crazy, to be honest," she acknowledged conspiratorially.

"Like in that book I read once. The one with Nurse Ratched?"

"*One Flew over the Cuckoo's Nest.*"

"That's it. Not that you're a Nurse Ratched."

"I hope not," she laughed.

"At any time on Sunday, did you leave the dispensary unlocked?"

Vivas opened her mouth to say no and then stopped. Her forehead wrinkled again. Her eyes squinted. Then her whole face cringed. "There was an accident in the dining room at dinner time that evening. A resident fell over a chair and took a pretty hard fall."

"Who was that?"

"Mrs. Lautner. Dottie Lautner. She has very poor balance."

"What time did this happen?"

"It must have been between six and six thirty. I was in the dispensary. Mrs. Knight is on antibiotics—she has a UTI—and she takes a pill with dinner. I was preparing that. Baiba called me, so I dropped what I was doing and ran out. I didn't lock the meds cabinet or the dispensary door."

"You went to the dining room?"

Vivas nodded.

"How many minutes would you say you were away from the dispensary?"

The day nurse considered. "Somewhere between five and ten minutes, I guess. Probably closer to ten."

Muñoz jotted notes on his pad. "Was anyone standing near the dispensary when you ran out of it?"

"I don't think so. Everyone was in the dining room. Residents. Caregivers. Visitors."

"Visitors? What visitors?"

"Family members. They show up to eat with their loved ones."

"Which family members were there?"

"I don't know all their names. I'm sorry. I don't interact with them that much. But Baiba knows them. And the caregivers, of course. They could definitely tell you."

"Did you notice anyone in or near the dispensary while you were in the dining room?"

Vivas shook her head. "I wouldn't have seen. I was on the floor with Mrs. Lautner. She landed on her elbow. It swelled immediately. I was concerned that she might have an olecranon fracture." Vivas bent her arm and rubbed her own elbow. "That kind of fracture happens when you come down hard on your elbow. As it turned out, she did fracture it. She ended up in surgery yesterday. She's still in the hospital."

"Did you notice anyone near the dispensary when you returned there?"

Again, Vivas shook her head. "Just Baiba. Baiba had gone back to her office to call Mrs. Lautner's daughter—no, niece, I think. Baiba might have seen someone. You should ask her."

"Thank you, Lorena." Muñoz stood and handed her his card. "If you think of anything else, please call me immediately."

Ten minutes later, he got more details from Maybelle Holder. "Mrs. Lautner fall over a chair that wasn't pushed in."

"Why wasn't it pushed in?"

"Same reason as always, I suppose. Somebody pull it out. The visitors, they don't think about the consequences. They don't see how hard it is for the residents."

"Who was near that chair? Who could have pulled it out?"

Holder rubbed her eyes. "Well, let's see. Charlene were with her, of course. Charlene Sullivan. She's assigned to Mrs. Lautner. And Julia Merchant was there. But she were sitting. She were feeding Lucy Merchant at the table over. She the one who call out for help."

"Who else was there?"

"Mrs. Knight's husband. He come for dinner. First time in a month! He were standing right there snapping his fingers to get Josie's attention. He want her to get him another coffee."

"Who else?"

"Mr. Lane. I see him wandering. He always wander during supper. The man don't know how to sit still. Usually that's when he go into people's rooms. He's a kleptomaniac, you see. But he were in the dining room that night."

Maybelle Holder was hard to keep focused. "Anyone else?" Muñoz asked patiently.

"Senator Prinz's granddaughter. She get all upset trying to find a table."

"And where were you?"

"In the kitchen. I hear the crash and come running."

Muñoz tried to visualize the scene, but Holder's details were not coalescing. He tore a piece of paper off his pad and pushed it toward her. "Can you draw me the layout?" He held out his pen, but Holder said she wasn't good at drawing.

Muñoz made a rectangle. "Let's say this is the table where Lucy and Julia Merchant were sitting. Where was Lucy?"

Holder tapped her elaborate nail extension on one side of the rectangle. "Lucy always sit here. Julia were kitty corner, there."

Muñoz jotted their initials where Holder had pointed. "And where was Mrs. Lautner?"

"She were standing in the aisle between them." Holder pointed, and Muñoz drew a star to represent her.

"And the man who asked for coffee?"

"Mr. Knight. He were standing right by the chair she trip over. Here."

Muñoz drew another rectangle and wrote the word *Knight* where Holder indicated. "And the granddaughter you mentioned?"

"Somewhere here." Holder tapped a spot beside the star. "And Charlene were right behind Mrs. Lautner."

"So it's unlikely Charlene could have pulled out the chair before Mrs. Lautner tripped on it."

"That's true."

"So, assuming someone pulled it out, it would have been one of the others—the senator's granddaughter, Mr. Knight, or Mr. Lane."

"I put any money on Mr. Knight," said Holder. "All he care about was his coffee."

CHAPTER 50

Julia Merchant swallowed the dregs of her Starbucks latte and massaged her neck where the healed fracture was aching again. Carlos and Susana would be in Park City again next week, but this time she wouldn't be with them. She didn't know where she would be. Nothing felt right anymore. There was no normal now. It was already two o'clock, and she hadn't done anything. If this were an ordinary day, she would be walking to her physical therapy appointment right now, and from there she'd go straight to Park Manor and have dinner with her mother. But she would never do that again, and she hadn't anticipated how untethered she would feel in the absence of that small daily ritual.

She stripped out of her T-shirt and pajama bottoms and got into the shower. Under the steaming water, she thought of Pamela's unkind remark about her mother yesterday at lunch. *You know what my therapist called her? A malignant narcissist.* Maybe her mother had been a little narcissistic—most performers were—but that remark was awful and very poorly timed. Pamela had been jealous of her sister, Julia concluded.

When she finished showering, she got dressed and left the apartment, walked to the florist on Lexington Avenue, and had them construct a bouquet of pink orchids. Then she walked to Maison du Chocolat and charged a one-hundred-piece Boîte Maison to her father's account. And then she walked up Madison to Park Manor.

Hodges was at her computer screen when Julia entered her office. The director stood and came around her desk immediately. "How are you doing, Julia?"

"I don't know, Constance. I don't know what to feel or think. I don't know what's happening. Do you?"

"The police are here, in the second floor library. They're interviewing members of the staff."

"Detective Codella?"

"No. A different detective. A man named Muñoz."

"Well, that's good, isn't it? They need to find out what happened."

"Yes. Absolutely," Hodges agreed, and for once Julia felt comforted by the woman's presence.

"I brought some flowers and chocolates for the caregivers." She shrugged. "I know I haven't always been the nicest person here, but—"

"That's very thoughtful of you, Julia. And I know the staff will be very thankful. Everyone is feeling the loss. They'll be happy to see you, I'm sure."

"I'll just go up then." Julia backed out of the office. In the elevator, she impulsively pushed the second floor button instead of the third. When the doors opened, she stepped off and turned toward the library. The detective was sitting by himself at a table near the back of the room, in front of the window that faced the Park Manor courtyard below. He was writing in a small spiral notebook and didn't look up until she was almost to his table. "I'm Julia Merchant."

He stood and held out his hand. "Detective Muñoz."

She shook it. He was handsome, she thought. *Her* kind of handsome. "You're part of the team investigating my mother's death?"

"That's right," he said.

"Are you making any progress?"

"These things take time."

"But you'll find out what happened?"

"That's our goal," he said, and she heard reassurance in his voice.

"Because it's hard, you know, thinking that she was healthy one day and dead the next. It's not easy to accept her death under those circumstances."

Muñoz pulled out a chair for her. "Why don't you sit for a moment?"

When she was seated, he said, "Do you mind if I ask you a question or two?"

"Of course not. Anything to help."

"I understand you had dinner with your mother the night before she died."

"That's right. She was very happy. At least I have that memory."

Muñoz returned to his seat and set a sketch in front of her. "There was an incident in the dining room that night. A woman fell. Do you remember?"

"Yes, I remember. I saw her go down. It was pretty bad. I heard a pop when she hit the floor."

"Can you tell me what happened after that?"

"I called out. I don't remember exactly what I said. *We need help here*, or something like that."

"What happened next?"

"Baiba called the nurse—Lorena—and she came over. The resident who fell was crying and moaning. Lorena sat her up and looked at her arm. And then she told Baiba that the woman might have broken her arm and that Baiba needed to call the ambulance team."

Julia watched Muñoz take notes in his spiral notebook.

"Then what happened?" he asked.

"Baiba made the call, and the ambulance guys were up there almost immediately."

"Was the nurse with Mrs. Lautner the whole time this was happening?"

"I think so. Yes."

"Were you there the whole time?"

"Except when I went to the restroom."

"When was that?"

"While the ambulance crew was lifting her onto the stretcher. I asked my mother's caregiver to sit with her while I took a quick break."

She watched Muñoz take more notes. He was left handed, and he wrote in a jerky scrawl. He said, "The dispensary is next to Baiba Lielkaja's office. Did you pass it on your way to the restroom?"

"No. I went through the kitchen so I wouldn't get in the way of the ambulance guys. But I came back that way."

"Did you happen to look in the dispensary?" he asked, and she felt his full attention on her now.

"Oh my God," she said. "You're thinking that's when someone could have put something into my mother's sedative, aren't you?"

"Just answer the question, Ms. Merchant. Did you see anyone in the dispensary?"

"I saw Baiba, but—"

"You saw Baiba Lielkaja?"

Julia nodded.

"She was *in* the dispensary?"

"Yes."

"Did you mention this to Detective Codella when you went to see her on Monday?"

Julia Merchant shook her head.

"Don't you think you should have?"

Her hand went her mouth. "I didn't think—I was so focused on the video. On the nurse and the caregiver in her room. It never occurred to me that—"

"What was Lielkaja doing in there?"

"She was at the counter, opening a bottle."

"What bottle?"

"I don't know. It was white. Tylenol, maybe."

"And you're absolutely sure it was Baiba? You could swear to that?"

"Of course I'm sure. I know Baiba well, Detective. I've seen her almost every day for the past eighteen months. I don't think I'd confuse her with anyone else."

Julia watched Muñoz sit back and nod. "Of course," he said apologetically.

"Is there anything else I can tell you?"

He shook his head. His mind was somewhere else, she thought.

Julia pushed out her chair and stood. "Well, let me know if there is."

Then she went upstairs and let herself into Nostalgia. Baiba was not in her office, but Melissa Posen was right outside it, standing on a stepstool in front of a framed cork bulletin board. Julia watched Melissa use blue pushpins to mount a long strip of text at the top of the board. Below the text, the young woman pinned a recent photo of Julia's mother sitting in the Nostalgia dining room. Julia studied her mother's vacant eyes. As Melissa mounted a second snapshot, Julia realized she wasn't breathing and that she didn't want to see any more images. She turned, walked into the kitchen, and set the flowers and chocolates on the counter. And then she let herself out of the Nostalgia Neighborhood as fast as she could.

CHAPTER 51

Codella answered the call from Muñoz as she sped up the West Side Highway. "I'll meet you at Lielkaja's apartment in fifteen minutes," she told him.

He was standing at the bottom of the care coordinator's brownstone steps when she pulled up and got out. Halfway up the block, men were unloading a crate from a double-parked truck. "I just spoke to Brandon Johnson," she shouted over angry horn blasts from cars having trouble squeezing through. "According to him, Lielkaja and Merchant were sleeping together. Apparently Merchant liked it rough."

"No surprise considering Jackie Freimor," said Muñoz. "I just saw Julia Merchant. According to her, Lielkaja was in the dispensary Sunday night."

"She told you that just now?"

He nodded. "She saw Lielkaja standing at the counter with a white bottle in her hand."

Codella frowned. "Why didn't she mention that to me on Monday?"

"I asked her that. She said it never occurred to her to think of Baiba being involved."

"Maybe because all along she's been convinced it's someone else."

"Who?"

"Her father." Codella remembered her instant dislike of Julia when they'd first met, and she felt her annoyance at the young woman flaring up again. She climbed the steps and Muñoz followed. "It's time to put some hard questions to Baiba."

She pressed the care coordinator's buzzer, but there was no response. She held it down a second time for several seconds. There was still no answer. "I want to speak to that woman." She pressed the superintendent's buzzer. When his voice came over the intercom, she said, "NYPD. Let us in."

A minute later, the super appeared and opened the front door for them. Codella showed her identification, and she and Muñoz headed for the stairs. The super started to follow, but Codella turned on the steps and held up her hand. "No. You stay down here."

Muñoz banged on Lielkaja's door. "Police!" he called. "Open up."

When Lielkaja failed to answer, Codella pounded the door with her fist. Then she took out her iPhone and dialed the care coordinator's cell phone number. She listened to the ringing through her phone, and then she realized she could also hear the ring on the other side of the door. She looked at Muñoz. "Get that super up here," she said.

Muñoz descended to the first floor and she waited in silence. How many times had she stood in front of someone's locked door like this? Were they going to find an empty, unremarkable room on the other side, or were they about to enter yet another scene of terrible violence?

A minute later, she and Muñoz watched the super insert a key into Lielkaja's lock. He swung the door open and moved to step forward, but Muñoz grabbed his arm and pulled him back into the stairwell.

Codella had seen what he saw. "Put your hands in your pockets right now," she instructed him. "Go back to your apartment and stay there. Don't speak to anyone you see. Don't touch anything. Nothing. If you do, you're tampering with a potential crime scene and I'll make sure there are consequences. Do you understand?"

He nodded, but his eyes kept darting into the room. "Go," she said. "Now. We'll speak to you later."

When he was gone, she and Muñoz moved carefully into the room. They stopped at the foot of the bed. Lielkaja lay on her back with one arm dangling off the mattress. The scarf Codella had seen coiled around her neck yesterday now lay on the mattress along with her big sweater. Codella stared at Lielkaja's flawless skin and clouded sea-blue eyes. She wore a gray T-shirt and the same cotton sweats Codella had seen her in yesterday. Her full breasts pressed against the thin fabric of the shirt. Her body was firm and shapely. A few strands of her butter-blond hair were in her face. She was like a reclining starlet who might rise from sleep at any moment to electrify the room. But Lielkaja was never going to rise. Her lips were bluish. Her pupils were tiny pinpoints. And her skin was cold and lifeless when Codella checked for a pulse.

"I'd say she's been dead since yesterday." Codella moved to the side of the bed. Lielkaja's fingernails were clean and unbroken. No blood stained her body or the bed. Her throat was red, just as Brandon had described it, and yellowish, thumb-sized bruises dappled her upper arms.

"Note the time, Muñoz. And call it in."

Muñoz fished in his jacket pocket for the small spiral notebook he always carried. As he recorded the time and got on his phone, Codella lifted her iPhone and photographed the body. Then she turned to survey the room. Fifteen feet away, a clear plastic Juice Generation cup sat on the round blond-wood table where she had interviewed Baiba yesterday. The lid was on the cup, and a straw was sticking through the lid. The inch of liquid still in the cup was dark red.

Codella walked over to the table. Only then did she notice the single sheet of folded paper resting beneath the cup. She was staring at the two typed lines of text on the paper when Muñoz came behind her. They read the words together. *I'm sorry Thomas. I can't live with what we did.*

"What do you think?" asked Muñoz.

Codella didn't move or speak. In her mind, she heard Thomas Merchant's voice yesterday in his office. *I did not kill my wife.* She pictured Brandon Johnson shivering in front of the Hudson River today as he told her, *What if she liked him so much that she wanted to be the new Mrs. Merchant? What if she used me to kill Lucy?*

Codella could feel Muñoz waiting for her interpretation, but she wasn't ready to give one. She walked to the bathroom. Nothing looked out of place. She pulled a tissue out of a box and used it to carefully open the bathroom medicine cabinet. The shelves were filled with perfumes, face creams, and a solid rack of nail polish bottles in various shades of red, pink, and purple. The only medications were Claritin and Advil. If she'd drugged herself, where was the drug?

She walked into the kitchen. It was spotless—not a dirty glass or plate on the counter or in the sink. She looked into the garbage can. It was empty except for a yogurt container. She glanced over at Lielkaja's desk. Finally she returned to the table. "We're supposed to believe that Baiba and Merchant killed his wife and then she committed suicide out of guilt. It doesn't feel right to me."

Codella pointed to the laptop and printer on the desk. "Why would you bother to type out a two-line suicide note?" she asked. "I mean, I could see if she were leaving a long letter, but—two lines? Why not just grab a pen?"

"Maybe she's used to typing things out? Maybe she's a little compulsive?" Muñoz didn't sound convinced.

"And here's another thing," said Codella. "Does she look like someone who just got back from Juice Generation? Are we supposed to believe she got dressed—remember, it's thirty degrees outside—went to the smoothie store, came back, and put on her sweats and T-shirt to drink up and say farewell to life?"

"You think someone brought her the smoothie and printed out the note."

Codella nodded. "If she mixed her own death potion, Muñoz, then where did she get it? I don't see any drugs lying around here. Do you? This place is immaculate."

"So who are you thinking?"

"Well, that's the million dollar question."

Sirens were sounding on the street below. "Stay here. Guard the scene," she told him. "I'll go down and meet them."

Three NYPD squad cars had pulled up, and six uniformed officers from this Upper East Side precinct were standing on the street when she stepped outside. Codella approached the one wearing sergeant's stripes. She filled him in and then the sergeant started issuing orders. Soon the building was surrounded by yellow tape. One officer with a notepad recorded the license plate numbers of parked cars up and down the street. Two other officers guarded the crime scene perimeter, holding back pedestrians who arrived to do their own little investigations. An officer named García was stationed at the building entrance to sign people in, and another officer was inside the building making sure no one left their apartments.

A precinct detective Codella didn't recognize showed up twenty minutes later and flipped her his shield in the stairwell outside Lielkaja's door. His name was Cooper. He was tall, about forty, with curly towhead hair you'd expect to see in Norway, not Manhattan. "What the fuck are you doing at my crime scene?" he asked.

Codella would have asked the same thing if she were in his shoes. This was his precinct, after all, and precinct detectives were territorial. As far as he was concerned, she didn't belong. She pulled out her identification. Whenever she had to do this, it felt like comparing the size of their dicks. "Manhattan North Homicide," she said in case he couldn't read. "This body is part of an ongoing investigation, and we're going to have to work this scene together. It's going to be a long afternoon and evening, Detective. I don't want to have to pull rank, but I will."

"Hey, I know you," said Cooper. "You're the one who solved the Elaine DeFarge murder, aren't you? You caught that Wainright Blake guy who cut off locks of hair." His tone turned almost reverential. Codella shrugged. Attention to her achievements always made her uncomfortable, but reverence was infinitely preferable to antagonism. "What's your investigation?" he asked.

There was no reason not to share the details with him. This body was going to make the news. In fact, the satellite uplink trucks would probably arrive any minute. Too many dispatch calls guaranteed that the media was on to this. And they would quickly learn that Lielkaja was connected to Park Manor. It wouldn't take a genius to draw the connection to Lucy Merchant.

Codella introduced Cooper to Muñoz. "From the looks of it, someone paid her a visit, and we need to know who. We need as much information as we can get from the neighbors. Can I count on you to work with Muñoz on this?"

Cooper looked at Muñoz. "Yeah. You can count on me."

"Good." She checked the time on her iPhone. In a few hours, she hoped, she would be sitting across from Thomas Merchant in a Manhattan North interview room, and there was something she needed before that happened. "Get as much as you can out of the neighbors. I'll be back here in half an hour."

She went downstairs and climbed in her car. She was staring at the reddish-brown façade of Lielkaja's building as the crime scene unit van pulled up. She watched the team take their equipment out of the van in a carefully choreographed routine they performed every time they were called to a body. She watched them climb the front steps and sign in with García. Then she started the car engine and checked her messages. Constance Hodges had left two voicemails, but she didn't want to talk to Hodges right now. She dialed Merchant's office at Bank of New Amsterdam and waited for Roberta Ruffalo's crisp voice to answer.

CHAPTER 52

"Where are you right now, Pamela?"

"Centre Street. I just got out of court. What is it?"

Merchant looked out his window as he spoke. The cloud cover was dramatically low this afternoon. The spire of the Freedom Tower was barely visible, and the water reflecting the clouds in New York Harbor looked gray and murky. The water surrounding St. Bart's would be emerald green right now, he thought, and he wished he were there with no press to hound him, no police to question him. He'd been there last New Year's, he remembered, with a brunette named Claudia. She had been more adventurous than Baiba, but not nearly as beautiful or irresistibly vulnerable. "That detective called me two minutes ago. She wants me to meet her at her precinct this evening."

"Why?"

"To update me, she says."

"Update you on what?"

"The autopsy."

"She can't do that over the phone?"

"Exactly. What if she really wants to interrogate me?"

"About Lucy's death?"

"Julia put ideas into her head." There was a long silence, and he knew what Pamela was thinking. Why was he nervous unless he had a reason to be? "I'm just not sure I trust her."

"You should never trust a cop who wants to talk to you. You know that," said Pamela. "Put her off. Tell her you'll come in tomorrow."

"I *can't* just put her off, Pamela. It's my wife we're talking about. She knows I'll have to come. The autopsy was this morning. She said she'd call me back in a couple of hours and tell me when to get there. And I want you there with me, as my attorney, just in case."

"Aren't you making a pretty big assumption—that I trust you?"

"You've seen my worst, Pamela. I admit I'm no angel, but—"
He waited.

Pamela sighed into his ear. "All right. But if this goes south for you, you'll need someone else to represent you. I don't do murders, and even if I did, I certainly wouldn't defend the person accused of killing my sister—no matter how pissed I am at her. Got it?"

"Fine," he said. "I'll call you as soon as I hear from her."

"Not so fast," Pamela said. "What do I need to know before I get in there?"

"How can I answer that," he said, "when I don't know what she's going to ask?"

"Don't be evasive with me, Thomas. You know what I mean."

"Look," he said, swiveling his chair away from the window, "your job is to protect my interests, Pamela. Not probe for information you don't need. Just keep your phone nearby." He hung up.

CHAPTER 53

Codella sped to the 171st and filled in Haggerty.

"So what are you doing here?" he asked.

"I need you to print out some photos for me."

"Sure." He sat at his desk.

Codella selected two photos from her iPhone collection and forwarded them to Haggerty's email. He downloaded the images to his desktop and sent them to the printer across the room. She stared at the enlarged photos. They were a bit grainy, but all the pertinent details were still dramatically visible.

"Thanks." She stuffed them into a manila folder. "I've got to go now." She touched his two-day-old beard and kissed his cheek.

On the way back to Lielkaja's, she made her obligatory call to McGowan. "There's another body," she said. "A woman named Baiba Lielkaja. The Nostalgia care coordinator from Park Manor. There was a suicide note at the scene, but it's bullshit. She was murdered."

His silence told her he was reserving judgment.

"CSU is there, and we've got a canvass going. I'm bringing Thomas Merchant up to the station tonight. I'll brief him on the autopsy results and see what I get out of him."

The sun had set, streetlamps were on, and reporters were clustered outside the crime scene tape when Codella returned to Lielkaja's building. A wind-blown brunette holding a microphone came at her as she emerged from her car, but Codella held up a hand and said "No comment" in a voice that stopped her cold.

She signed in with García and found Cooper and Muñoz on the second floor. "Tell me you've got something," she said.

"Yeah. We're catching residents as they come home from work. There's only twelve units in the building and we've accounted for eight so far." Cooper seemed eager to be the spokesman. He read off his pad. "A widow lives alone in 2B—Mrs. Pagonis—and she saw a silver-haired man in an overcoat leave the building just after four PM yesterday. She was coming in as he was going out."

Codella looked from Cooper to Muñoz. "Merchant has gray hair."

"I know, and it's him," Muñoz pronounced with certainty. "It's got to be him. After Cooper spoke to her, I went back up and asked her for more details. She described a tall, thin, distinguished-looking man. He was wearing an *elegant* black overcoat, she said, and when the outside door closed behind him, she watched him walk down the steps and duck into a black SUV."

Merchant had his personal driver, Felipe, pick her up, Codella remembered Brandon saying. "I was with Lielkaja at three thirty," she said. "Merchant must have come right after me. Was he carrying anything as he left?"

"You mean like a Tiffany bag?" Muñoz shook his head. "Not that she saw."

Codella shrugged. "Anything else?"

"Yeah," said Cooper. "A couple in 4A was returning home around eight PM and a young man, early twenties, came in through the front door right behind them. Didn't use a key. Wasn't a resident. Said he was going to a friend's."

"Description?"

"Green parka. Gray sweatshirt. Blond streaks in the hair."

"Shit!" Codella said.

"What?" asked Muñoz.

"That description matches Brandon Johnson. I saw him early this afternoon. He was wearing the gray sweatshirt. He's got the blond streaks. But he told me he'd been here in the *middle* of the day, not at night." She reached in her pocket for dry-mouth gum and stuffed a piece in her mouth. Dr. Abrams had told her she might want to invest in the company that made this gum or else try acupuncture, which seemed to help some people get rid of this lingering and annoying chemo side effect. When she'd left Brandon Johnson this morning, she reflected now, she had trusted his veracity. But how could this data not rekindle her suspicions? "Did you find Lielkaja's phone in there?"

"On the floor under the bed," said Cooper. "Lots of calls unanswered. I had them checked out as soon as the CSU guys lifted prints."

"And?"

He read off his notes. "Three calls from Park Manor—two this morning, one around noon."

Those calls, Codella guessed, would have been from Hodges, wondering why her Nostalgia care coordinator hadn't shown up to work. "And the others?"

"Two from the guy you just named—Brandon Johnson."

"When did he call?"

Cooper checked his notes. "Just after six PM last night and again at seven."

"Find out where he was when he made those calls."

Cooper jotted a note. "And there were three calls from a cell phone that belongs to Thomas Merchant."

"Ahh. You saved me the best for last."

Cooper smiled.

"You're absolutely sure?"

"Verizon doesn't lie, and his name's right in her directory."

"What time did he call her?"

"Ten PM last night and nine AM this morning."

Codella turned to Muñoz. "Those were after she was dead."

"Which suggests he didn't know she was dead."

"Unless he's the one who killed her and he placed the calls to throw us off." She looked back to Cooper. "Find out where he was when he made those calls."

She climbed one flight up to Lielkaja's apartment with Muñoz and Cooper behind her. The body had been removed. As she watched from the door, a crime scene investigator wearing a white Tyvek jumpsuit leaned over the pullout couch and picked up a hair or fiber with tweezers.

The lead investigator—it wasn't Banks or anyone else she knew—came to speak with her. His combed-back hair accentuated his severe widow's peak. His placid expression and foreshortened neck made him look tortoise-like. "What can you tell me?" she asked.

"There was no forced entry."

She nodded. She knew that already.

"And no struggle."

"What about prints? How many sets did you lift off the laptop?"

"There were no prints on the keys," he said.

"How about on the suicide note?"

"Nothing."

She pointed to the Juice Generation cup. "Whatever's in that cup killed her, and I need to know what it is."

Muñoz had come up behind her. "Can you get your hands on a Raman analyzer?" he asked the CSU detective.

"Sure. I can do that."

"Can you do it as quickly as possible?" Muñoz asked politely. Then he turned to Codella. "Raman Spectroscopy," he explained. "You just point and scan. I wish I'd had one of those when I was a narc."

"You're no narc anymore." Codella squeezed his arm gratefully. "I need you to find me Brandon Johnson. Bring him to Manhattan North. He's got some explaining to do."

CHAPTER 54

Merchant stared out the plate glass windows in the lobby of the BNA building. All he saw were network news vans, prop cameras, and reporters gripping mics. Where was the Escalade? The vans were usurping the curb in front of the revolving doors. The reporters reminded him of a lynch mob; they all wanted a piece of him. Even if Felipe could get in front of the doors, Merchant couldn't get to the car without running that gauntlet. He turned to Chester, the senior security officer he'd known for almost a decade. "Take me the back way."

"Yes, sir." Chester nodded.

Merchant called Felipe as Chester led him through labyrinthine passageways to an unmarked set of doors at the back of the building where trucks made deliveries. A few minutes later, the Escalade pulled up. Chester checked the alleyway, gave the all clear, and Merchant ducked out into the darkness. Just before Chester closed his car door, Merchant pressed a Ulysses S. Grant in his palm. "Thanks, buddy."

Twenty minutes later, he walked into Manhattan North and approached the desk sergeant. "Detective Codella is expecting me."

"Take a seat," said the sergeant in a gruff, unimpressed tone that Merchant wasn't used to hearing from people. The bench was hard, and he didn't like to be kept waiting.

Ten minutes later, Codella appeared. "Let's go upstairs."

They entered a small, windowless room, and Merchant said, "My attorney will be here shortly."

"Your attorney?"

"Safety precautions, Detective."

"Whatever makes you feel comfortable, Mr. Merchant." She gestured to a chair. "Would you like some coffee?"

"Black."

She left and returned a few minutes later with a white mug for him and a water bottle for her. She sat across from him and folded her hands. "I appreciate your coming up here. I thought it would be best to tell you about your wife's autopsy results in person."

"Go on," he said.

"Mrs. Merchant died of a condition called noncardiogenic pulmonary edema. That means her lungs filled with fluid and she couldn't breathe. Usually pulmonary edema results from a heart condition, but in the case of your wife, the medical examiner believes the cause was a drug overdose."

"In other words, Park Manor fucked up?"

"Or someone wanted her dead." She paused. He could feel her watching him. "We need toxicology to confirm the ME's findings, but it does appear that someone added a concentrated dose of oxycodone to her nightly sedative."

CHAPTER 55

The door opened and a woman barged into the interrogation room as if it were *her* private chamber. Codella watched the woman set an elegant briefcase on the table and pull out the chair next to Thomas Merchant. She sat, rested her hands on the table, and announced, "Pamela Martinelli, Mr. Merchant's counsel."

"And Lucy Merchant's sister," observed Codella.

"That's beside the point right now, Detective." Martinelli's voice had a crisp, antagonistic edge. She wore a gray suit jacket and matching skirt, and her dark hair was short but elegantly cut. Judging from the crow's feet around her eyes, Codella guessed she was in her late forties. "I'd like to know why my client is here."

"Why don't I let your *client* explain." Codella shifted her gaze to Merchant.

He turned to Martinelli. "According to the detective, Lucy died of a drug overdose."

Martinelli turned to Codella. "A drug overdose?"

"It needs to be confirmed by toxicology," said Codella, "but that is the *probable* cause of death based on the postmortem exam performed this morning. The drug in question, oxycodone, was not being administered to any residents in the Park Manor dementia care unit. Therefore, it's unlikely Mrs. Merchant's death resulted from an accidental overdose. We're treating this as a probable homicide."

"And why did you need to bring my client all the way up here to tell him that?"

"I thought it best to speak in person."

Martinelli crossed her arms. "In an interrogation room?"

"For the sake of *privacy*, Ms. Martinelli. Mr. Merchant came here voluntarily. This is not an interrogation, so I would appreciate if you didn't try to interrogate me, either."

"Do you have any suspects?"

"We have persons of interest."

"And should I assume that my client is one of them?"

Codella watched the woman remove a legal pad from her briefcase. Martinelli had just learned that her sister's death was a homicide—murder—and yet she expressed no emotion. Neither she nor Merchant evidenced any of the emotions she usually observed in the immediate family members of a victim—unbridled sorrow, denial, outrage, or angry demands for retribution.

"Everyone is under investigation until this case is solved. I'm sure you understand that, Ms. Martinelli."

Martinelli cast a cool, dismissive look across the table. "Is there any other news you want to share before we leave?"

Codella said, "Yes. There is one other thing."

"And that is?" Martinelli demanded impatiently.

Codella leaned forward and kept her eyes squarely on Merchant. His was the only face she wanted to study when she spoke her next words. "Baiba Lielkaja, the Nostalgia Neighborhood care coordinator, is dead."

Merchant sat back and inhaled sharply.

Pamela Martinelli gripped his arm.

Codella stared at Merchant. "And you were having an affair with her," she said as if it were a proven fact.

Now Martinelli was out of her seat. "Stop right there, Detective, I want to speak to my client alone. Leave us. *Now.*"

Codella pushed out her chair and stood. "I'll give you five minutes. Figure out your next move, because I know what mine will be if you're not honest with me. Your personal driver's cell phone number is sitting on my desk. So are the names and numbers of your doormen. And I look forward to a nice, long coffee klatch in here with Roberta Ruffalo."

"Cut the intimidation routine, Detective."

"It's no routine, Ms. Martinelli. Mr. Merchant knows who he's been with and what he's done. And he knows I can find out on my own just like that." She snapped her fingers, and then she stepped out of the room and closed the door.

CHAPTER 56

Merchant took a deep breath. Baiba was dead. She was *dead*. He shook his head.

"That bitch," Pamela muttered.

"Tell me about it." Merchant stood and paced back and forth. He could still see Baiba yesterday afternoon pitching the Tiffany box into the stairwell. He could feel the box whizzing by his face. He could smell the citrus shampoo in Baiba's hair when she finally calmed down and sat on his lap. He could taste her salty tears when she told him he had hurt her. He could hear himself saying, "Daddy wants you so much."

"Jesus Christ, Thomas. Focus!"

Thomas looked Pamela in the eye. Thank God he'd summoned her. Codella might know how to deal with lawyers, but his lesbian sister-in-law was a whole other story. She'd gotten him through the Grand Hyatt thing, and if anyone could get him through this, it was her.

"Tell me right now what I'm dealing with, Thomas. Is this another Jackie Freimor?"

"I was seeing her," he admitted.

"*Seeing* her?"

"You don't want the gritty details."

"You're right. I know you too well." Pamela combed her fingers through her short hair. "Just tell me you didn't kill her."

"Of course I didn't kill her." He loosened his tie.

"You know this looks incriminating for you."

"Don't tell me the obvious. Just get me out of this."

Pamela tapped her fingers on the table. He watched her think for several seconds. "You had consensual sex," she finally announced. "That's it. No details. You're a married man with an incapacitated wife, and you were trying to have a discreet relationship under difficult circumstances. A jury would sympathize with that. Got it?"

"Got it."

"Is there any curveball she could throw at us?"

Merchant remembered the Tiffany box he'd left at Baiba's apartment. Even if the police found it, how could they prove he'd given it to her on the day she died? If they traced it back to the flagship store, they would find that Roberta Ruffalo had charged the earrings to his credit card a week ago.

"Well? Is there?"

Merchant considered Baiba's Monday night visit to his apartment. If Codella questioned Felipe or the doorman, they would acknowledge they had seen Baiba. But that was no crime. Codella could never know he'd given Baiba something in her drink. It wouldn't be in her system now. That drug couldn't be traced after four to six hours. "No," he finally said. "Not that I know of."

"Well, if she does throw a curve, do us both a favor. *Don't* try to catch it. Remember, anything you say in here can be used against you later, so let me do the talking. I'll tell you when to speak and when *not* to. Understood?"

She was a control freak like him, he thought. She probably controlled things in bed, too. It wasn't at all hard to imagine his sister-in-law taking someone like Baiba over her knees for a little spanking. The question was, could she get Codella over her metaphorical knee right now?

Two minutes later, Codella was back in the room staring at him with her penetrating blue eyes. Pamela broke the silence. "Look,

Detective. My client admits he had a consensual sexual relationship with Baiba Lielkaja. There's nothing illegal about that."

"How many times did you see her, Mr. Merchant?"

Pamela nodded for Merchant to speak.

"Only four times."

"When?" Codella asked.

"I don't remember the dates."

"Do you remember if you had *consensual sex* with her on Monday night?"

"*Yes.*" He returned her sarcasm with his own.

"Is that yes, you remember, or yes you did have sex with her on Monday night?"

"My client answered the question, Detective," snarled Pamela.

"Where did you have sex on Monday night?"

"Where are you going with this, Detective?" Pamela demanded. "This Baiba person died yesterday, not Monday. She didn't die as a result of her relationship with Mr. Merchant."

Codella seemed neither impressed nor intimidated by Pamela's pronouncement, Merchant noticed. "Where did the two of you have sex that night?" she asked.

"In my apartment," he answered.

"And how did she get there?"

"My driver picked her up."

"Felipe, you mean?"

She knew his driver's name. She was letting him know she'd done her research. He might have underestimated her, he thought. "That's correct," he said, barely controlling his fury.

"What time did she arrive?"

"Around nine thirty."

"And how long did she stay?"

"Felipe drove her home around one AM."

"And how would you characterize the sex you had?"

Pamela broke in. "Enough, Detective. That's a gratuitous question." She leaned across the table. "He already told you the sex was consensual. That's all you need to know."

Merchant watched Codella lean forward in response to this statement. "I was at her apartment today, Ms. Martinelli. I saw her body." Then she opened the manila folder in front of her, pulled out two photos, and slid them across the table so they faced him. "Take a good look at your *consensual* handiwork." She watched him closely. "Are you telling me she liked having your hands around her neck, cutting off her oxygen supply?"

Pamela slammed her hand on the table. "That's enough!"

Codella completely disregarded her display of outrage. Her eyes remained on him like a relentless cameraman's lens. "At what time exactly did you go to Ms. Lielkaja's apartment yesterday?"

There it was, Merchant thought. The curveball Pamela had anticipated. Pamela recognized it too and gripped his arm to keep him from speaking. "Quit fishing, Detective," she said.

Codella reached in her pocket and cracked open a fresh piece of Biotene gum. She slid it into her mouth and chewed. "Don't get cancer," she said casually. "The chemo gives you dry-mouth, and it never goes away."

"Cut the bullshit," said Pamela. "Come on, Thomas. You've cooperated enough."

Codella spoke as he pushed out his chair. "The crime scene unit has been all over that apartment. We've got a cell phone, fingerprints, and neighbors who saw things, Mr. Merchant. We know who's been there and who hasn't. What time were you there?"

Pamela tugged at his arm. "Let's go, Thomas."

He got to his feet. His mind felt immobilized. Inert. *Baiba is dead.* He pictured her again, on his lap yesterday in her apartment, just before he left her. He could still feel her arms around his shoulders as if she would never let him go. "Why do I want you so much?" she had whispered as she moved on top of his thighs, her desire already erasing her memory of the pain he'd caused her the night before. Maybe it wasn't desire that kept her coming back to him, he thought now. Maybe it was a terrible need—a need as deep as his own—that had nothing to do with him.

Pamela put on her coat. "My client has been frank with you, Detective. In return, we expect you to respect his privacy. His wife has been incapacitated for a number of years. He's a man trying to have some semblance of a life. We don't expect to read about his sex life in the *New York Post*. Are we clear?"

"*You* are," answered Codella. "But I don't know about your client."

Martinelli moved to the door.

"I still want the answer to my last question," said Codella. "What time did he go to her apartment. And I'll talk to everyone until I get my answer."

Merchant opened his mouth again, but Pamela said, "Shut up, Thomas. She's bullshitting you."

CHAPTER 57

Novotny grabbed her arm before she could follow Muñoz into interview room A. "What's that tall dick doing here?"

She faced him. "He's with me."

"He's not one of us."

"No, but I can trust him. He doesn't go rogue." She yanked her arm free.

"Fuck you, Codella."

"Not in a million years, Novotny." She went in and closed the door in his face.

Brandon was slumped in a straight-backed chair, and he didn't look at her. A navy knit cap was on his head. His cheeks were red from the cold. He jiggled his legs like a small boy who needs the bathroom. "Do you want something to drink?" she asked. "Something hot?"

"I'm fine." He shook his head. "I just don't like police stations, okay? Let's just get this over with."

Codella and Muñoz sat across from him. "So you've been to police stations before?" she asked.

"Once or twice."

Codella remembered what Hodges had said: *Your background checks won't turn up any criminal records on our employees.* "When have you been to a police station?"

"When I was a kid."

"What took you there?"

"I don't see how that's important," he said.

"Why don't you let us decide that?"

He glanced from her to Muñoz and back. "My father beat me up. Okay? I had to give a statement."

"How old were you?"

"Fourteen."

"That must have been difficult for you." As soon as she said it, she realized she was projecting her own emotions onto him. *She* was the one who'd found it difficult to tell a police officer the truth about a murderous father and a physically abusive mother.

"It wasn't so bad," Brandon said. "He was a fucking bastard."

Codella studied him again. Outwardly he looked so vulnerable, but he was tough, too, it occurred to her now. There was really no telling what he was capable of, and it would be wrong to underestimate him. "Do you know why I asked Detective Muñoz to bring you here?"

"I suppose you plan to blame Lucy's death on me, right?"

"When we spoke this morning, Brandon, you didn't tell me everything."

He fiddled with the zipper of his green parka. "What do you mean?"

"You told me you were at Baiba's apartment yesterday during the day. You didn't tell me that you went back there at night."

Brandon stopped playing with the zipper. He didn't move or speak.

"Someone matching your description entered Baiba's building last night at eight o'clock. That person went in behind a couple that lives in the building. They gave a detailed description, Brandon. They described *you*."

She watched his face closely. It remained impassive.

"What do you have to say?" she asked.

He shrugged. "So I went back. So what?"

"Why did you go there?"

"Because—" He shook his head. "I don't know. It's complicated."

"Try me."

"You brought me all the way up here for this?"

Codella glanced at Muñoz. Either Brandon didn't know Baiba was dead or he was pretending not to.

"I left her apartment around two thirty," he said. "I went to Park Manor. When I got there, I found out you'd been over there asking questions. I got scared. So I left. I went to a diner and started thinking about Baiba and Merchant and how Baiba gave me three thousand dollars a week ago. I got thinking that maybe she set me up—like I told you—that she used me to kill Lucy so she could be with Merchant. I wanted to talk to her. I wanted to look her in the eyes and ask her some questions." He paused.

"And did you ask her those questions?"

"No. She wasn't home. So I left."

Codella leaned in to him. "Brandon, Baiba is dead."

She and Muñoz watched his reaction. At first just his brow furrowed. Then his head started to shake slowly. His eyes narrowed as if he were confused. And then he started to cry. "No," he whispered. "No."

"I'm afraid it's true," said Codella.

"How?" Tears streaked his face now. Were they tears of sorrow or the tears of someone guilty and repentant?

"We're waiting for forensics."

"And you think I did it?"

"Put yourself in my position, Brandon. You didn't tell me the truth."

"How can you say that? You didn't ask me about last night. I didn't think it mattered. I omitted one little piece of information. I never lied to you. I've been more truthful than anyone else has been about the things that matter!" He folded his arms on the table and buried his face in them. And now he was sobbing openly.

Codella silently signaled for Muñoz to step out of the room. When he was gone, she reached across the table and laid her hand on Brandon's arm. "Were you in love with Baiba?" she asked very softly.

His hands tightened into fists, but he didn't lift his head. "She was my *friend*. That's all. Or I *thought* she was my friend."

Codella kept her hand on his arm. "Were you in *love* with her, Brandon?"

He jerked his arm away, pushed out his chair, and knocked it over as he stood. "Quit asking me that!"

Codella pressed on. "You loved her. You were in love with her."

"No!" he said, but the protest sounded hollow. She knew she was right. And she knew that she needed to act just like the detective who'd interviewed her the night her father murdered Joanie Carlucci twenty-six years ago. She hadn't wanted to admit anything, either, and he'd known that. In the end, he'd had to say all the terrible truths she didn't want to acknowledge. *Just shake your head if I'm right. He picked up the bat. He hit the woman with the bat. He hit her many times.*

Now Codella said all the things Brandon couldn't bring himself to say. "Baiba disappointed you deeply yesterday when she told you about Merchant. She broke your heart, didn't she?"

He kicked the toppled-over chair with his left foot. "Stop!"

"She broke your heart. Admit it. It's not a crime."

He punched his fist into the plaster wall and let out a loud angry cry of pain that wasn't purely physical. She stood and went around the table and put her hand on his shoulder. He turned from her and pressed his forehead against the wall.

"You knew she'd never want you the way she wanted him. She wanted things that you couldn't give her, didn't she?"

His head shot up. "I wouldn't want to give her those things. I would never mistreat her like he did. I would never tie her up or hit her or choke her like he did."

"You were angry. You felt betrayed."

He didn't speak.

"Did you kill her, Brandon?"

He whipped his body around to face her. "*No!*" And there was nothing hollow about that denial.

CHAPTER 58

Haggerty had already claimed a corner table when she and Muñoz arrived. He stood and kissed her cheek. She turned her face to touch his lips with hers, and in that instant she imagined Brandon wanting to kiss Baiba that way, and she felt a little sad for him—for what he'd wanted but never received. Muñoz was staring at them so she asked, "What?"

"Nothing. I'm just getting used to this new development."

She rolled her eyes. "Yeah, well, when do we get to meet your new *development*?"

She took a seat against the wall so she could look out. Haggerty and Muñoz ordered beers, and she asked for Perrier. While they studied the menus, Haggerty said, "You'll be interested to know that the local news now has a name for your case. The Park Manor Murders."

"That's not very creative," she said. "We could put our heads together and do a lot better than that."

She pulled off her jacket as Haggerty asked, "So are the deaths are related?"

Codella scanned the other tables in the dimly lit room. The music was loud and no one was sitting close enough to hear their conversation. She leaned in and told him about the interviews at Manhattan North. "Brandon, Merchant, and Baiba Lielkaja were part of one very unhappy love triangle. Before Lielkaja turned up dead, I wondered if she might have been responsible for Lucy

Merchant's murder. I was starting to buy Brandon's theory that she murdered Lucy so she could have Thomas Merchant all to herself. Now this so-called suicide note suggests that she and Thomas *conspired* to kill his wife. But if they worked together, then why was Lielkaja murdered—because I'm telling you, she didn't kill herself."

"Maybe Merchant didn't conspire with her out of love," suggested Haggerty. "Maybe he was just sick and tired of being chained to a woman with dementia. Think about it. He wants his freedom. He wants her out of the picture, but he can't get the job done alone. So he wines and dines Lielkaja. Makes her feel special. Promises she'll be the next Mrs. Merchant. And as soon as Lielkaja does her part, he gets rid of her, too."

"And types the suicide note," finished Muñoz.

"Right." Haggerty sipped his beer.

Codella pictured Merchant in the interview room hours ago. Was he a murderer? "We know they were having an affair," she said. "We know he sexually assaulted at least one woman in the past. And we know he went to Lielkaja's apartment yesterday because a neighbor saw someone leaving the building who matched his description perfectly. Assuming Brandon told me the truth, then Merchant is the last person we know of who entered that apartment. The question is, would he really go to all that trouble to get rid of his wife? What's in it for him to take a chance like that?"

"Maybe he really did love Lielkaja," Muñoz suggested, "and they killed the wife together, but then Baiba got cold feet and threatened to go to the police."

They considered this for a moment. Then Haggerty said, "And there's the other possibility, of course." He was warming up to his favorite game of *what if*, Codella observed. How many times had she and Haggerty played that game over the years? His mind was agile, and he could spin scenarios faster than anyone she knew. "Let's still assume Baiba killed Lucy Merchant. Let's say she acted alone, that she wanted Lucy out of the way so she could seduce Merchant and marry him. There's plenty of motivation for that—billions of dollars' worth. But then Brandon Johnson finds out about her affair with Merchant, and he murders her out of jealousy."

"But Baiba's the one who told Brandon about the affair," Codella countered.

"According to Brandon," Haggerty replied. "But maybe that's just what Brandon told you. What if it didn't really happen that way? What if he found out on his own, went over there, and took his revenge."

Codella stared across the restaurant and remembered Brandon's forceful denial just an hour ago. Was he a far more calculating individual than she had assumed him to be? She remembered Constance Hodges's merciless deconstruction of his psyche. She reviewed the simple and damning facts: He had loved Baiba. He had felt crushed by her betrayal. He had gone back to her apartment last night and told no one about it.

She shook her head. "No. It didn't happen that way."

"What makes you so sure?" Haggerty asked.

"Think about it. Would he let himself be seen by residents of the building if he were on his way to kill her?"

"Maybe he didn't know he was going to kill her until he got up there. Maybe he lost control."

Codella couldn't think of any way to counter this. She sat in silence for several seconds. Why was she so determined to believe he was innocent? Why did she find herself rooting for him? What if he had lied to her about everything? What if her instincts about him were dead wrong?

"I need to know a lot more about that kid. I just wish there were someone other than Constance Hodges to talk to."

"There is," said Muñoz. "There's a personal reference in his employment file."

THURSDAY

CHAPTER 59

Merchant scanned the *Wall Street Journal* first. *BNA Banker Requests Postmortem on Wife.* Well, that story was in his favor. The *New York Times* had the headline *NYPD Probes Broadway Legend's Death.* That was neutral enough, and Baiba wasn't even mentioned. Then he saw the cover of the *Daily News* on the car seat, and his heart sank. There he was walking down the front steps of Manhattan North after his meeting with Codella last evening. And in the photo right next to his was a thin, hooded figure exiting the same Manhattan North door. Someone had tipped off the press.

He picked up the tabloid and stared at the headline. *Banker and Trans Caregiver Questioned in Park Manor Murders.* He threw the paper across the back seat of the Escalade and shouted, "God-dammit!" His worst fear was happening. The tabloids were going to butcher him.

Merchant pulled out his phone and made the call.

"Park Manor." Constance's voice was steady and professional.

"Good morning, Constance. How are you holding up?"

"Better than you, I imagine." Her voice had a little edge. She had read the headlines, too. She was enjoying his discomfort as much as his daughter probably was, he thought. He spoke in a low voice into his phone.

"They're going to slaughter me, Constance. You know I had nothing to do with these deaths. I need your help."

She was silent for several seconds. Then she said, "I need some help, too."

He knew what she meant. "Okay, let's talk," he said. "Let's help each other. Have lunch with me today."

She didn't answer right away, and he could hear the thoughts running through her mind. Was he really innocent? Should she help him or should she let him dangle in the wind? Could she trust him? "Noon," she finally said.

"Four Seasons," he responded.

He sat back and felt the vibrations of the Escalade's wheels as the car sped down the West Side Highway. He stared at the lights of Hoboken across the river. On September 11 of 2001, he had taken a ferry to New Jersey hours after the World Trade Towers fell. He had weathered so many crises in the past, and he would weather this one as well, he assured himself, but he felt very alone. Lucy was gone. Baiba was gone. His daughter had caused this trouble with her anger and paranoia. He was going to have to look impervious all day while people watched him for signs of weakness and guilt. He did not look forward to walking through the revolving doors of BNA ten minutes from now, but to hide would be much worse.

He took a deep breath and mentally slipped into his invisible armor.

CHAPTER 60

Codella had gone to sleep thinking about Brandon Johnson, and he was still on her mind as she made her way to Manhattan North at seven thirty AM. She felt sympathy for the young man. She didn't want him to be guilty. She wanted to believe that he was like her, someone who had defied the odds and not succumbed to the dire expectations of norms and statistics. She knew there was the danger of letting her feelings cloud her judgment, but she wasn't going to rush a verdict against him. When she got to her office, she left a voicemail message for Judith Greenwald, the reference Brandon Johnson had listed on his Park Manor job application. Not until Ms. Greenwald called her back did she realize that the woman was his clinical psychologist. "I'd like to speak with you in person," Codella said.

"I'm sorry," Greenwald replied. "But I don't discuss my clients."

"You've seen the papers, I'm sure," said Codella. "Your client is in trouble. Let me come and see you."

There was silence at the other end.

"Please. When can we talk?"

"I can fit you in for fifteen minutes at eleven o'clock," Greenwald said. "But don't expect me to violate my oath of confidentiality. It's not going to happen."

Greenwald's office was below sidewalk level in a building on Christopher Street between Seventh Avenue and Waverly Place.

She buzzed Codella inside, and the detective followed a narrow corridor that led to a small waiting room where the only window was near the low ceiling and she could see feet and legs passing by on the sidewalk above.

Greenwald appeared and invited Codella into her office. As Codella sat on the olive couch, she had the eerie impression she was about to become the patient in a therapy session. Greenwald occupied what was obviously her usual chair. Then she watched Codella and waited.

Codella got straight to the point. "Two homicides have occurred, Ms. Greenwald—or should I call you doctor?"

The psychologist shrugged. "Take your pick. It's not important to me."

"Two people are dead, and your client has been placed at the scene of both deaths. He is currently the most compelling person of interest we have."

The other woman did not hide her concern.

"I'm here because I need more insight into him."

"You're asking me to share information that was given in confidence. I already told you I'm not going to do that. I have a responsibility to Brandon, not to you." She said this without any rancor.

"Can you tell me anything that would help me eliminate him as a suspect?"

Greenwald leaned forward. "The American Psychological Association code of ethics would compel me to report any child or elder abuse I had learned about in my sessions. That is an exception to my confidentiality that I tell my clients about when we begin our therapeutic relationship." She crossed her legs and stared at Codella with soft, intensely brown eyes. "I have not reported any information about child or elder abuse in relation to my client."

Codella nodded gratefully. "So I can assume he never confessed to Lucy Merchant's murder in front of you."

"That would be an accurate deduction," she said.

"Can you tell me anything about him? Just give me some insights."

"No," she said bluntly. "But I will speak in general terms about the transgender community, if that would help."

Codella nodded.

"As a whole, they are as diverse in their interests, ambitions, and emotions as members of the cisgender community."

"The what?"

"The community of people whose biological gender matches their self-identity. It's the opposite of transgender. But transgender individuals do have some greater challenges."

"For instance?"

"They're more prone to depression. That is a fact corroborated by many studies. And they have a much higher suicide rate—more than forty percent by some estimates. They are routinely harassed on the job. They're denied employment, often rejected by their families, and often subjected to domestic violence from family members, too. That is the world Brandon Johnson is part of." Greenwald stared into Codella's eyes, and Codella understood her unspoken message. Brandon Johnson had suffered these challenges.

"You said they're more prone to suicide. Are they also more prone to homicide?" Codella asked.

Greenwald shook her head. "People like Brandon feel self-hatred and hopelessness. They lash inward, they punish themselves—even when they deserve to punish others."

"Did Brandon ever talk to you about a love interest?"

Greenwald looked at her watch. "That question falls into the category of information I will not share."

"I think he was in love with a young Park Manor administrator who we found dead yesterday. Baiba Lielkaja. I think he was in love with her and became very upset when he found out she was sexually involved with someone else. I need to know if he felt enough anger toward her to harm her."

"I only have a few more minutes, Detective," Greenwald said. "Let me be clear about this: If I knew any of my clients had the *intent* to harm others before they acted on it, I would be obliged to inform the police. I did not do that. If, on the other hand, I learned about something illegal that my client had done *after* he did it, I would be bound by confidentiality *not* to tell you."

Codella knew this, too, but she had hoped Greenwald wouldn't be so rigid. Brandon had chosen an excellent advocate, but in this case, she wasn't sure whether his advocate was helping or hurting him. Codella made one more effort. "If your client confessed to murder, you couldn't tell me, but if he didn't confess, you could tell me that, couldn't you, and put my mind at ease?"

Greenwald stared at Codella for a long time before she said, "Answering yes might put your mind at ease, Detective, but it would be a violation. My clients need to know that I live up to my part of the bargain in here. I'm working with a very vulnerable clientele. It would ruin my work with them if they didn't trust me. I will only say this: I have had no conversations with Brandon since he left my office on Tuesday morning, and that is before this death occurred. Brandon has worked hard in here. He has been through a lot. I respect him tremendously. And I am more than confident he has done nothing to harm anyone."

She had come as close to answering the question as she would, Codella knew. She stood. "Thank you very much, Dr. Greenwald. I appreciate your time."

CHAPTER 61

Julia Merchant lifted her phone from the bedside table and scrolled through the dozens of private Facebook messages she had received. Most of them were texting acronyms and emoticons expressing her friends' shock and disbelief about what was happening. The senders, she realized, had beaten her to the morning papers.

She reached for her laptop on the floor beside her bed and went from website to website reading the stories about her father, her mother, and Baiba Lielkaja. She stopped when she got to the *Daily News* headline. This one, she knew, would enrage her father. She stared at the side-by-side photos of him and Brandon Johnson. Her father would not be amused by the juxtaposition.

She closed the laptop and returned it to the floor, thinking of her father's words on the phone yesterday. *Do you have any idea what my life will be like when the press gets their hands on this?* She imagined him now, sitting in his executive suite. He always got to his office by seven AM, so he would have read the articles hours ago in the backseat of the Escalade while Felipe drove. For a split second, she felt sorry for him. He was alone and under siege. And she had the impulse to pick up the phone and say something kind. But what? I believe in you? I know you didn't do this? I'm sorry I started all this? But she *wasn't* sorry. He *deserved* whatever embarrassment and discomfort he was feeling right now. He had earned it so many times in the past. He undoubtedly assumed she did not remember that past or that her memories of it were so impressionistic that she could not grasp their significance. Otherwise, how could he look her in the eyes now? But she remembered all too well.

She pulled the fluffy duvet up to her chin and pressed her head into her soft down pillow. She thought of him offering to pay for her to see a therapist—maybe she should take him up on his offer. She could talk out the disturbing memories, exorcize them from her brain, and move on with her life. But wasn't it too late for that? Wasn't the damage done?

She pulled the covers right over her head. She did not want to get out of bed. Maybe she would stay right here until Detective Codella made an arrest and this was all over.

CHAPTER 62

Brandon could feel all their eyes staring at him. They had seen his picture in the paper. They were probably texting about him right now or surreptitiously taking his photo and Snapchatting it to their friends. They would be wondering if he was mentally ill. They would be watching for signs that he might pull a gun and start shooting at them. And he felt like doing just that.

When the instructor dismissed them, he rushed out of the lab, flew down the stairs, and burst through the doors to the street. He crossed the highway and stood in his usual spot overlooking the river and New Jersey beyond. How many times had he stood here eating his lunch and staring into the churning waters? Had he known on some level that these waters would be his eventual escape route? Had he always known that he was supposed to leap into these waters on one of the coldest days of February and end his misery?

He gripped the railing and extended his head forward so that all he saw in his peripheral vision was the gray water below. The current was strong. His eyes locked on little whirlpools until he followed a decomposing tree branch carried by the current. The water would be frigid. The moment he jumped in, it would saturate his parka, shirt, pants, and shoes and awaken all his senses. He would feel more alive in that split second than he had felt at any other time in his life. But in the very next instant, he would probably regret his decision and cry out for help as he struggled against the current and the weight of his water-soaked clothes. Drivers on the West Side Highway would whizz by without any awareness of his emergency. And soon he would understand that his struggle was useless, his decision was irrevocable. And then he would search his memory for one last image to hold onto. And what would that image be? Baiba smiling at him? Judith Greenwald telling him, *You've done hard work in here.* Singing "Cell Block Tango" with Lucy? All of those moments in time were so ethereal—they only existed in his mind—and when he had sunk below the surface of life, they would be gone forever.

Brandon pulled his head up and stepped back from the railing. He didn't have the courage to take his life that way. He started walking uptown on the bike path that bordered the length of the highway. Cars drove by him in the opposite direction, heading toward Battery Park, and he imagined stepping headlong into traffic. He stared up at the Empire State Building rising above the other Midtown skyscrapers and imagined hurtling himself from the top floor. And then he thought of all the jumpers who leaped to their death in front of an oncoming train. He could go to the Chambers Street Station right now and stand at the end of the platform where the Number 2 emerged from its tunnel. The train would still be moving fast, and if you leapt in front of it right there, the conductor couldn't possibly see you in time to brake.

He continued to walk. He imagined his fractured body on the rails, people staring down at him from the platform. They wouldn't really care about him. They would just want to see what a mangled body looked like. And they would carry his image home in their short-term memories, describe him to their friends and family, and quickly forget about him.

He began to cry. He was giving in to self-pity, he knew. Judith would say, *You have a choice, Brandon. You always have a choice how you respond to things.* He turned onto Pier 46. No one was there, and he screamed at the top of his lungs, "I hate you all!

I hate everyone! Fuck you, fuck you, fuck you!" His words were swallowed up in the frigid winter wind. But when they were out of him he felt calmer. He didn't want to disappear from this world or give up his dreams. Yes, they were modest, but they were real. He would become a respiratory therapist and work in a hospital one day. He would intubate people and save their lives. They wouldn't know him, but they would know what he'd done for them in their moment of need, and he would feel a sense of accomplishment in that. Maybe he would earn enough money to buy a little apartment in Queens or the Bronx—he'd never be able to afford Brooklyn. And if he was very lucky, he might find someone to love—not someone like Baiba, but someone who would love him back.

He left the pier and continued to walk.

CHAPTER 63

Codella had taken no chances this time. She presented a search warrant to Constance Hodges. "I've come to examine Ms. Lielkaja's office. There's the outside chance I'll find information in there that will help us with the case."

Hodges stared at the warrant and nodded. "Shall I take you up?"

"You can, if you prefer," said Codella, "but it's not necessary. I remember the Nostalgia code. I'll just be in her office. I won't disrupt any activities."

Hodges remained downstairs, and Codella was relieved not to have her company.

The first thing she noticed when she switched on the light in Lielkaja's office was the empty Juice Generation cup sitting on the right side of her desk. Codella stared at it for several seconds, remembering the identical cup she and Muñoz had found in Lielkaja's apartment. Then she got to the business at hand. The desk looked cluttered, as if Lielkaja had left her work with every intention of picking up exactly where she'd left off. An events calendar was open to the month of February, and a ballpoint pen lay next to the calendar. Lielkaja had scribbled notes on a pad next to it.

A cream colored sweater hung off the back of her desk chair. A computer sat at the far end of the desk. It was turned off. A coffee mug next to the computer served as a pen and pencil holder. The message on the mug read *Make Someone Smile Today!* There were other inspirational messages in the room, too. *We Inspire, We Connect, We Are Caregivers* was the affirmation on a poster taped to the wall behind the desk chair. A poster on the wall across from the door featured a quote from Maya Angelou: *If you find it in your heart to care for someone else, you will have succeeded.* Had Lielkaja personally believed in these inspirational words, or were they simply motivational tools for her staff?

Codella opened the left desk drawer. Lielkaja was apparently an Earl Grey tea drinker, and she had a plastic sandwich bag filled with dark Dove chocolates. Her right hand drawer held a stapler, three hole punch, paper clips, and tube of Origin's lip gloss.

Codella powered on the computer. While she waited for it to boot up, she stepped into the corridor. From this vantage, she could see into the parlor, the dining room, and the kitchen. Breakfast had been served and was now being cleared from the tables. Several residents sat in the parlor in front of the large flat-screen television. Few, if any, eyes were focused on the screen, however. Some of the residents slept sitting up. Others pulled at their garments or stared at their hands as if their limbs didn't really belong to them. They were like cars, Codella thought— luxury cars, to be sure—warehoused in long-term parking on the lowest level of an exclusive Rapid Park garage.

In the kitchen, a caregiver was wiping off the counter. At one table in the dining room, a professional-looking staff member held up cards in front of a smiling resident. "What color is this?" Codella heard the woman ask.

The resident squinted at the card for several seconds as she considered her answer. "Blue," she finally said.

"Blue?" The staff member pointed. "Look again, Mrs. Knight. Are you sure that's blue?"

"Yes," the resident insisted. "Are you trying to trick me?"

Codella turned back to Lielkaja's office and noticed a cork bulletin board on the wall between the office and the small staff room. Large typed letters at the top of the board spelled out *Farewell to a Beautiful Neighbor*, and below these words was a collage of photos mounted with green, white, red, and blue pushpins. There were glossy date-stamped photos as well as pixelated digital printouts from a color copier. Together, the photos were a hastily made tribute to Lucy Merchant's eighteen months at Park Manor.

Codella moved closer. In one photo, Lucy stood in the parlor in front of a Christmas tree next to Brandon Johnson, who was dressed like one of Santa's elves. In another, she sat at a dining room table in front of a birthday cake. Baiba Lielkaja was hugging her and smiling at the camera in another photograph. A big black caregiver danced with her in another. Thomas Merchant appeared in just one photo, sitting uncomfortably next to his wife at a Thanksgiving table filled with other dementia sufferers. Codella scanned the photos for Julia, but didn't find her image.

Her eyes kept returning to one photo in particular, a glossy colored one with a date stamp that indicated it had been taken only weeks after Lucy Merchant had moved into the Nostalgia Neighborhood. There was something haunting about this photo. Lucy Merchant stood in her bedroom next to the window, arms folded, mouth closed, eyes staring into the camera. They were sentient eyes, Codella thought, eyes that seemed to say, *I know why I am here. I know what is happening to me.* But the detail that was even more compelling than those eyes was located on the windowsill of the bedroom. What Codella saw there made everything fall into place. She heard her own voice whispering, "Oh my fucking God. Why didn't I see it?" But she already knew the answer. Her desire to see one thing had blinded her to what was actually in front of her. She'd violated her own rule of the game and allowed her personal history to impose a narrative on the present—the *wrong* narrative.

She removed the blue pushpin holding the photo in place, pocketed the photo, and rushed out of Park Manor. There was no need to search Baiba Lielkaja's office now.

CHAPTER 64

"Well, here we are alone again—just like old times." Merchant smiled.

Constance Hodges knew that smile so well. Flirtatious. Insincere. Manipulative. "Not exactly alone." She gestured to the lunch crowd in the Four Seasons Pool Room.

"Would you rather be alone in my apartment?"

"No, thank you." But that wasn't entirely true, and he probably knew it, too, she thought. "Why did you ask to see me, Thomas?"

Merchant laughed. "Don't play my therapist, Constance."

"But it's what I am." She shrugged. "Even after all these years."

He sipped the dry white wine in his sweating glass. She waited. He had never been able to outwait her.

"I hate the media," he finally said.

"They're not very nice to high-paid financiers or cheating husbands, are they?"

He sipped again. She craved a drink, but she wasn't going to have one. She was the therapist right now, and she wouldn't show her vulnerabilities, although Merchant would test her sorely. She would go back to Park Manor after this lunch and calm her nerves in private.

"You could help me, Constance."

"Help you how?" She sipped her ice water.

"We could hold a press conference at Park Manor. You could tell them how I supported my wife."

"I'd rather tell them all the things I can't tell them about your past."

"Why are you being so hostile, Constance?"

"You know the answer to that perfectly well. Your bank is financing the end of my career."

"What are you talking about?"

"Don't pretend with me, Thomas. BNA is behind Eldercare Elite's bid, and when the deal goes through, my job goes away. You know that as well as I do."

He laughed. "Come on. They'll still need an executive director."

"An *Eldercare Elite* director. Not me."

"What are you saying?" he asked. "What do you want from me?"

"I want that deal to go away. Permanently."

"And how am I supposed to make that happen?"

"I don't care how you do it."

"And that's your price for saying a few nice things about me to the press?"

She let her silence be her answer.

"They're going to crucify me," he said. "And I did *not* kill Lucy. You must know that."

She stared into his pleading eyes. As a patient, he had never wanted to acknowledge the truth about himself. He had flirted his way through their sessions without doing any transformative work. And now, twenty-one years later, he was still the same man who had walked into her office grudgingly. She had treated so many men like him. They went a little too far with a female employee, endangered their career, and did their "rehabilitation" time with her. But they never really changed. At best, they just got a little more careful. But Merchant hadn't been careful. "What about Baiba Lielkaja?" she asked.

He leaned forward. "I didn't kill Baiba," he whispered.

"You know what? I almost believe you. You know why? Because you don't like them dead. You just like them playing dead."

He looked at her coldly. "That is not a therapeutic thing for you to say, Constance."

"You said you didn't need a therapist anymore."

"Why are you provoking me?"

She wasn't going to answer the question, but at least she was willing to admit the truth to herself. Despite his massive flaws of character, she had felt a powerful attraction to him all those years ago. She had imagined becoming the commanding wife who would keep him in check. But he had married Lucy Merchant. And after all these years and all his bad behavior, Constance still wished he had chosen her.

Eighteen months ago, when she'd sat beside him on her office couch and showed him the layouts of two available suites in Nostalgia for his wife, she'd still felt that attraction. As his dark eyes compared and contrasted the features of the two apartments available for his wife, she'd inhaled the scent of his subtle expensive cologne, and when he turned those eyes in her direction, she'd felt an exquisite little explosion of adrenaline in her chest. "Which rooms get the best light, Constance?" he had asked, and although the words were a question, his tone was a confident statement. *I know you want me.* His knee had brushed hers "accidentally," and her excitement had turned into pulsing desire. She still wanted him, she thought now, but he had shown far more interest in Baiba than in her.

Hodges stared at his wine glass. She examined her fingernails and resisted the urge to bite them. "I just don't like to see you act like a fool," she said. "It doesn't become you. Why do you do it? Why do you feel the need to dominate every woman in your life?"

"I don't," he said.

"You do," she insisted. "And now you're trying to dominate me with this Eldercare deal. But I'm not Lucy. I'm not your daughter. I'll fight back, Thomas. I'm not going to let you destroy my career."

He narrowed his eyes, and she could see the anger in his clenched jaw and tight mouth.

"How many times did you drug her, Thomas?" Hodges pushed him even harder. "Lucy, I mean."

"Stop it, Constance."

"You shouldn't have asked me here if you didn't want me to go all the way. We're both grown-ups. I know you, and you know me. There are very few secrets here. So why don't you tell me why you really called me."

When he didn't answer after a full minute of silence, she leaned across the table and said, "Then I'll tell you why. You can control everyone else, but you can't control yourself anymore. You went too far with Baiba. You knew it was foolish, and yet you couldn't stop yourself."

"I had *nothing* to do with her death."

Hodges shook her head. "Maybe not, but you're in trouble and you're terrified. And inviting me to lunch is as close as you can come to asking for help."

Merchant finished the rest of his wine, waved at the waiter, and asked for a bourbon. He didn't speak for the four minutes it took the waiter to return with the glass. Then Hodges watched him drink it in two large gulps. "You really piss me off, Constance," he finally said.

"That's not my problem."

"Talk to the press. Tell them I've been there for my wife."

"Kill the Eldercare Elite deal," she countered. "Do that, and I'll tell them anything you want me to. You can write my script."

Merchant signaled the waiter and pointed to his glass. "Fine," he finally gave in. "Schedule a five o'clock press conference and consider it killed."

CHAPTER 65

Julia looked surprised and a little nervous.

"May I come in?" Codella asked.

"Of course." Julia opened the door tentatively.

"Thank you." Codella walked in. The young woman was still wearing pajamas. Her hair was uncombed. She looked as if she'd just gotten out of bed. "I wanted to give you an update on our progress," Codella explained.

Julia sighed. "I've read all the papers. It's so upsetting. I can't believe Baiba is dead, too. Please, have a seat." She gestured to a gold couch, but Codella remained standing. "Can I get you some water? Coffee?"

"Water would be great."

When Julia disappeared into the kitchen, Codella walked around the spacious living room. The decision-making of a talented professional interior designer was evident in the lush upholstery, carpeting, and curtain patterns that complimented each other. She noticed the fresh-cut flowers in a vase on the fireplace mantle. She saw the shopping bags on the floor near the built-in bookshelves. She read the titles of novels on the shelves and studied the souvenirs that had come from many continents. Julia Merchant had been raised in privilege, and she continued to enjoy it.

Julia returned with a glass of sparkling water and set it on a Museum of Modern Art coaster on the glass coffee table in front of the couch. Then she sat and stared at the detective.

"We're making progress," Codella told her. "I think we're actually close to knowing how your mother died."

"It was murder, wasn't it?"

"Yes, it was murder." Codella sat.

"Who do you think did it? Was it Brandon Johnson? Was it the nurse?" She paused. "Or was it my father?"

Codella sipped the sparkling water. "I can't tell you that, Julia. I'm not really at liberty to tell you everything we've got, but you have to trust me. We're going to have a resolution soon. We'll arrest the person responsible for your mother's death. I give you my word on that." She smiled. "But I need your help."

"Of course," said Julia. "Anything. What? Just tell me what you need."

"When you first came to my office, you showed me a video you recorded on a hidden alarm clock camera, the video that jump-started this investigation. You remember?"

"Of course. How could I forget that?" Julia nodded earnestly. She pushed her long hair behind her left ear. "I'm just so glad I looked at that recording."

Codella nodded. "Have you ever heard the term chain of custody, Julia?"

"No. What is it?"

"It's an expression police and prosecutors use. It refers to the evidence we collect. Every piece of evidence we use to build a case and convict someone of a crime has to meet chain of custody rules. For example, when you brought those rug fibers to my office on Monday afternoon, they did not meet chain of custody. I couldn't have stood up in court and testified that those fibers truly came from your mother's room. I couldn't prove it. I had to go back to Park Manor and collect my own samples, put them in an evidence bag, fill out forms, and then voucher them before I sent them to toxicology. Now every time those fibers move from one individual to another, they will be signed for, and the chain of custody will be unbroken. You understand? That makes for solid evidence."

Julia nodded, but her look seemed to say, *Why are you explaining all of this?*

"I've also got to establish chain of custody for the video you showed me. That's an important piece of evidence in this case. We'll use it to convict your mother's murderer."

"So you do think it's the caregiver—or the nurse?" she asked.

Codella ignored her question. "I need the camera that took that video, Julia. Otherwise, I can't prove my case."

"I see."

"You still have it, don't you?"

"Yes," she said. "Yes, of course."

"Good," said Codella, and she pulled a form from her jacket pocket. "Then we can establish the chain of custody right now. Can you go and get it?"

Codella watched the flare of Julia's nostrils on the intake of a breath. She saw the paralysis of her diaphragm as she held the air in and the blankness of her eyes in panic. "Who are you going to arrest? Is it Brandon or the nurse—or is it my father?"

Codella placed her palm on Julia's knee. "Listen to me. You have to be strong in this. Whether it's a stranger or someone close to you, that person is a murderer who *must be punished.* You can't protect them. You need to help us."

Julia nodded. "Yes, of course. I know that."

"Get it now," Codella insisted, and she watched the young woman rise slowly and uncertainly from the couch.

CHAPTER 66

Hodges deposited her coat on the waiting room chair in front of Heather Granahan's desk. Then she walked straight to the powder room at the end of the hall, locked the door, set her purse on the sink, and reached inside for the small bottle she'd purchased yesterday evening. She broke the seal and drank. How was she any worse than Merchant downing his two bourbons an hour ago? They both needed shoring up right now. They would cooperate, and they would get through this. He would call off the Eldercare dogs, and she would attest to his loyalty. Codella would find out who had killed his wife and Baiba. It couldn't be him. It couldn't possibly be him.

She dropped the empty miniature into her purse, combed her hair, and poured mouthwash from a large bottle into one of the small white cups kept on a tray for that purpose. She swished the mouth-stinging liquid around and spit it into the sink. Then she wiped her lips, applied fresh lipstick, and smiled at herself. Anxiety almost immediately loosened its grip on her mind and muscles. But then, out of nowhere, a chilling question entered her mind: What if Thomas *had* done it? What if she had just made a deal with a murderer?

She stepped out of the powder room and into her office, shut the door, and sat on her couch. What if he had used Baiba to murder his wife, and then killed Baiba to keep her from talking? But why? It always came down to that. Why would he kill his wife? She was harmless to him. And by keeping her here, he looked like the devoted spouse. It was in his best interests for so many reasons to keep Lucy alive and well cared for—unless Baiba had threatened to tell his dirty little secrets if he didn't marry her. Had she coerced him into a violent act? Had he, in a moment of desperation, conspired with Baiba to kill his wife and then murdered Baiba, too?

Don't think about it, Hodges told herself. All that mattered was Park Manor—not the place, but *her* place in it. If she lost her position, where could she possibly go? No other institution would have her after a scandal like this. She was fifty-four years old, she had no husband, and without Park Manor, she would have no role or status in this status-conscious city. People would cease to ask her to cocktail parties or invite her to sit at their fundraiser tables. The older men of Park Manor would no longer wink at her. She had even entertained the idea of marrying one of them. Why not? It was a better retirement plan than her 401(k).

If she left Park Manor, she would soon be forgotten. That was the painful reality of life on this island. You were what you had and what you did, and if you had or did nothing, you didn't belong anymore. You didn't really exist. And Constance couldn't handle that. She had to shield Thomas so that he would protect her.

She called Michael Berger. "It's time for us to address the press."

CHAPTER 67

Codella sat in her car and listened to the voicemail messages from McGowan and Detective Cooper. She called Cooper back first. "That Juice Generation cup on Lielkaja's table?" he said. "It contained oxycodone."

"So we've got a loose connection between the deaths. Very loose. But it's a start."

"The CSU guys think it's suicide, and the autopsy revealed no evidence that someone forced her to swallow the drug. So it looks like maybe she killed Lucy Merchant and then she killed herself."

"No. That's *not* what happened, Cooper. I don't care what anyone says. I think I *know* what happened."

Five minutes later, she called back McGowan. "Where are you?" he snarled. "Get the hell up here. I want to talk to you."

She was in his office doorway ten minutes later. "You must have really pissed off Merchant yesterday," he said.

"What makes you say that?"

McGowan stuffed his hands in his pants pockets. "Because his attorney called the DA's office to complain about you, and then I got a call from One Police Plaza. I don't like getting calls from 1PP, Codella."

"Who complained? Martinelli?"

"Whatever her name is. She accused you of trying to intimidate her client. Jesus Christ, Codella."

"That's bullshit."

"Bullshit or not, it's what she's saying. And they're listening. I told you that you were playing with fire."

"It means he's feeling the heat."

"And so am I," snapped McGowan. "I'm clipping your wings. You're off it. Lielkaja's a suicide—I just got the report—and Fisk will take over the Lucy Merchant investigation."

"But I've almost got it wrapped up. I just need one more day."

"You're out of days," he said. His right hand came out of his pocket, and he wagged a finger in her face. "This is what happens when you try to go it alone. You never learn, Codella. Now go write up your notes and turn them over to Fisk. That's an order."

"You can't do this, Lieutenant."

"I just did." He turned away.

CHAPTER 68

Brandon was sitting in the Dunkin' Donuts on Tenth Avenue and Thirty-Sixth Street when Maybelle Holder called his cellphone. "Where you at, Brandon?"

He told her.

"Oh man, everybody got something to say about you today."

"Yeah, well, it's all lies. I didn't do anything."

"I believe you," assured the caregiver. "But Merchant got Hodges on his side now."

"What do you mean?"

"They doing a big press conference here at five o'clock."

"A press conference?"

"Right outside the building. Her majesty call everybody together and tell us nobody allowed to come and go from the building while it going on—even on our break."

Brandon stood up and tossed his coffee cup into the trash. "I'm coming up there. I'll talk to you later. Thanks, Maybelle."

"You watch yourself, Brandon."

Brandon caught the Number 7 subway at the Hudson Yards, transferred to the Number 6 at Grand Central, and was in front of Park Manor twenty-five minutes later. A large crowd had gathered just around the corner from Madison Avenue in front of Park Manor's main entrance. Cameramen held heavy camcorders on their shoulders. At least six or seven reporters gripped microphones connected to satellite uplink vans nearby. A crowd of curious onlookers had gathered as well. Brandon positioned himself at the back of the crowd.

They all waited at least twenty more minutes in the cold. The sun had descended now, and bright lights mounted on tripods illuminated the steps to Park Manor. Finally, several people emerged from within the building. Brandon spotted Constance Hodges and Thomas Merchant among them.

Hodges stepped in front of a microphone stand and introduced herself. Her hair was perfectly coiffed. She had applied fresh lipstick. She stared into the crowd confidently and said, "As you know, a sad event occurred at Park Manor on Monday morning. Lucy Martinelli Merchant passed away. I can tell you that all of us at Park Manor are honored to have provided a caring, comfortable home to Mrs. Merchant in the last eighteen months of her life. We share her loving family's deep grief, and we join them—Thomas and Julia—in extending our condolences to everyone around the city and around the world who also mourn her death."

Hodges paused and stared at the faces in the crowd. She was a polished speaker, Brandon thought, but everything she said was a lie.

"There are still unanswered questions surrounding Mrs. Merchant's death," Hodges acknowledged, "and Park Manor is working hand-in-hand with the police and the Merchant family to answer those questions." She paused before adding, "The recent suicide of our care coordinator Baiba Lielkaja has come as an additional shock to our Park Manor community, and we mourn her loss as well." She gave a tight smile that Brandon knew from experience was completely insincere although others, he surmised, would interpret it as fortitude. "Watching a loved one face devastating illness is not for the faint of heart. As the executive director of Park Manor, I have seen many residents take their final journeys. I have watched family members struggle to come to terms with loss. I have observed many courageous acts of love and loyalty. Lucy Merchant's family has stood by her throughout her illness. Thomas Merchant is here with me today, and I'd like to turn the microphone over to him with a message for all of you."

Brandon watched the carefully choreographed movements of Hodges and Merchant as they traded places on the Park Manor steps. Merchant had to bend slightly to be closer to the mics. He spoke confidently and with no script. "I first saw Lucy Martinelli on the stage of the Majestic Theater when she was performing *Vegas Nights* in 1993, and I had the honor of going backstage to meet her after the show. What can I say except that Lucy was beautiful inside and out. She was a brilliant performer. And she was a loyal friend, wife, and mother. I will always treasure the years we had together."

He paused, took out a handkerchief, and wiped at his left eye before he continued.

"My wife, as many of you know, was uncompromisingly committed to the arts. I remember the day we were dining in our favorite restaurant, the Four Seasons, and she insisted we do something to help struggling artists. Her vision became the Lucy and Thomas Merchant Foundation, and through it we have supported independent theater productions around the country, ensuring that young artists have hundreds of small venues in which to perfect their craft. While I am personally devastated to have lost my beautiful wife, I'm happy that the foundation we started together lives on in her name."

Merchant scanned the faces in the crowd, and Brandon ducked behind a taller man to ensure that their eyes did not meet.

"When my wife began to exhibit the signs of early onset Alzheimer's disease two years ago, I learned firsthand what that illness does to victims and their families. I created another foundation—the Lucy Martinelli Merchant Alzheimer's Research Foundation. In the last year alone, that foundation has funneled twenty million dollars into research to help speed new drugs to the market. I just wish I had started that foundation in time to help Lucy. We have got to eradicate this terrible disease that strips people of their minds and robs them of years of productivity."

He paused again—for effect, Brandon thought. He was a liar. But he was a bold and convincing liar. Everyone in the crowd was nodding at his words. He would get away with his lies. People would focus on the millions of dollars he had given away. He would look like a hero. It wasn't fair. Who was going to put the hard questions to him? *If Lucy meant so much to you, why did you fuck Baiba Lielkaja, and who else did you fuck?*

Brandon wanted to push his way through the crowd, shove Merchant aside, and shout into the microphones, *Let me tell you the truth about this man. He didn't just take his wife to the Four Seasons. He also wined and dined Baiba Lielkaja there, and then he took her home, fucked her, beat her up, and turned her head around with expensive jewelry and flowers.* Brandon would tell them how Lucy Merchant really felt about her husband. He could tell them about the time Merchant came into her room and she screamed, *No, Daddy, no!* He could tell them how she had once picked up a framed photo of him and smashed it on the floor.

Merchant was speaking again. "And as you can imagine, this has not been an easy time for my family, and I ask all of you to respect our need for privacy as we mourn. We also want answers to how Lucy died, and we will do everything in our power to get those answers. Nothing is more important to me than finding out the truth. I want to end my statement by thanking everyone out there who has sent messages of love and condolence our way. They are comforting to my daughter and to me, and I know that Lucy would be so grateful for them. Thank you all." Then he turned his back to the microphones as questions roared from reporters in the crowd.

CHAPTER 69

"Just tell me, am I right?" Codella knew her words sounded more like a plea than a question. She was now disobeying McGowan's direct order.

Muñoz moved the glossy four-by-six photograph under his desk lamp and stared at it long and hard. "You're right. You're definitely right. What does it mean?"

"It means I've been lied to all along and didn't see it coming."

"It's understandable."

"It was *stupid*. I ignored the signals." She shook her head and slapped Muñoz's squad room desk in frustration.

"We're only three days into this," he reminded her. "We've sifted through a lot."

"I don't care," she said. "It ends today. I'm going to make an arrest. I'm out of time."

"But you don't have anything that will stick. What are you going to do?"

"I'm going to talk to Merchant. I think he knows." When Merchant had come to Manhattan North, she'd asked him all the wrong questions. The answers she needed, she realized now, were not concealed in the events of the past few days or weeks. They were buried in the dirt-black past. And if she didn't dig them up soon, someone else would die.

"You want me to come?"

She shook her head. "No. I want you to get a search warrant."

CHAPTER 70

Brandon sat on a bench against the stone wall separating Fifth Avenue from Central Park. Behind the wall was the Central Park Zoo, which was shut down for the winter. In front of him, cars and buses streamed south in an intermittent flow dictated by the timing of traffic lights. And across the avenue, Merchant's building sat like a stately palace. Numbers on a crisp green awning announced the exclusive address. Meticulously groomed shrubs decorated the base of the limestone façade. Intricate wrought-iron railings secured windows at ground level. And two doormen in caps, coats, and white gloves anchored the picture of fortified elegance.

Each time a resident arrived, one of the doormen held the door. Whenever a car pulled up, one of them flew curbside to assist. What would they say when he walked across the street and asked them to put Mr. Merchant on the house phone? More important, how would Merchant respond when he said, *Let me come up or I'll hold my own press conference. I'll tell my story, and you won't like it a bit.*

The last streaks of pink had faded into the inky black sky by the time he worked up the courage to cross Fifth Avenue. He stepped under the awning, and the two doormen turned. "I'm here for Mr. Merchant," he told them. "I—"

One of the doormen pointed his finger toward Sixty-Fourth Street. "Side entrance," he said.

Brandon gave him a confused look.

"The penthouses have their own elevators, young man."

Brandon nodded and walked around the corner to an equally stately entrance guarded by a third doorman. "I'm here to see Mr. Merchant."

The eyes looked at him suspiciously. "He isn't home."

"Are you sure?"

The eyes looked annoyed. "Yes, I'm sure."

"When will he arrive?"

"I couldn't say."

Brandon wasn't sure he believed the doorman. Where else would Merchant have gone after the press conference? He stepped outside and stood against the wall just beyond the doorman's view. He would wait. He would have his audience.

CHAPTER 71

Codella crossed Central Park at Eighty-First Street, turned onto Fifth Avenue, weaved around the M1 bus, and pulled the car in front of Merchant's building. A doorman came out at once and said, "You can't stay here, ma'am."

She showed him her shield. "Is Mr. Merchant home?"

"His entrance is around the corner."

Codella turned the corner and parked in front of the side entrance. And then she saw him in the shadows. He was leaning against the building, wearing the same green parka he'd worn to the station last night. She lowered her window. "What are you doing here, Brandon?"

He walked over. "Waiting for him."

"Waiting for him why?"

"To talk." She heard the resolve in his voice.

"Just talk?"

He didn't respond.

"Get in the car. Right now."

A doorman approached. "Is there a problem here?" His eyes darted from Codella to Brandon and back.

"No problem," said Codella.

"Because I can call the police if—"

"That won't be necessary." She showed her shield again. "This young man is with me. Is Mr. Merchant at home?"

The doorman's eyes went to Brandon.

"Is he, or isn't he?" Codella demanded.

The doorman nodded ever so slightly.

"You liar," Brandon hissed at him. "Everyone either lies to me or about me. I'm so sick of it."

"Get in the car," repeated Codella.

The doorman retreated to the lobby.

Brandon sauntered toward the passenger side and got in. He slumped in the seat next to Codella and said, "You should have seen that press conference."

"What press conference?"

"At Park Manor. An hour ago. Starring Merchant and Hodges. What a show. How come they can get away with their lies and no one believes me? I told you—"

Codella held up her hand to stop him. "I believe you, all right. I know you didn't kill anyone."

He turned.

"I know you're innocent, Brandon."

"You do?"

"Now I need to go have a talk with Merchant. Can I count on you to wait for me in here?"

He nodded. She got out of the car and went into the building. "I'm going up to Mr. Merchant's floor," she told the doorman.

"The elevator opens directly into his apartment. I need to call him first."

"Then do it," she said.

He picked up a house phone and dialed. Then he hung up. "There's no answer."

"When did you see him?"

"Forty-five minutes ago?"

"Was he alone?"

"Yes."

"Has anyone else gone up to his apartment?"

"Not that I know of," he said.

"Could they get to his apartment without you knowing?"

"Only if they went in through the Fifth Avenue door and used the fire stairs or service elevator," he said. "And only if Mr. Merchant left his entrance to the stairs and service elevator unlocked."

CHAPTER 72

Codella found him lying facedown on a king-size bed in a large bedroom to her right off the elevator. She felt for a pulse at his neck. His skin was warm, and her touch caused him to turn his head and moan.

She quickly scanned the large room. Ice-frosted windows faced Central Park. The bed was on the south wall, and at the north end were twin love seats facing each other in front of a restored gas fireplace. On a coffee table between those couches sat two Starbucks cups. She went over and looked at the cups. "Fuck!" she said under her breath. There had been too many strange liquids in the bottoms of cups and glasses. She turned back to Merchant. How long did he have, she wondered, before whatever he'd swallowed pulled him into death's grip?

She took out her cell phone and called 9-1-1. Then she looked around for the phone and called down to the doorman. "An ambulance is on the way for Mr. Merchant," she said. "Send up the young man sitting in my car. He has EMT training. Do it now." Then she hung up.

She left the bedroom and made her way to Merchant's living room where the vaulted ceilings gave the room a cathedral-like feel and the floor-to-ceiling windows were an altar to New York City. She walked through the dining room, kitchen, and study and climbed the spiral stairs to a second-floor balcony that led to seven spacious rooms. They were all empty.

She found Merchant's master suite on the top floor of his triplex. It was decorated with dark wood panels on the walls and a raised bed. She searched his intricately tiled bathroom and opened the door to his cedar-scented walk-in closet where dozens of suits and monogrammed shirts hung in neat rows across from racks of polished Italian leather shoes. And then she paused to think.

If she was right about who had killed Lucy Merchant and Baiba Lielkaja—and she *had* to be right—then why was Merchant lying unconscious on that bed? Had he always been the intended third target?

She went back to his kitchen. The door to the fire stairs and service elevator were unlocked. She unsnapped her shoulder holster and kept her hand on her gun as she opened the door. She found herself staring into a small landing in front of the service elevator. At one end of the landing sat a blue recycling bin and a large gray garbage can. At the other end was a closed door labeled "Fire Stairs." Codella turned the doorknob, but the door was locked from her side. No one had left Merchant's apartment via these stairs.

Brandon Johnson found her staring into the landing. "What is it?" he asked.

"You need to be with Merchant," she snapped.

"He's okay for now. Semiconscious."

"I think he just took whatever was in one of those cups on the coffee table. Don't touch anything in there, Brandon. Just stay at Merchant's side until the EMT arrives. He might get worse. He might stop breathing. Someone might have given him a narcotic. You may have to resuscitate him, you understand?"

Brandon nodded.

"Don't let him stop breathing. We need him alive. I'm trusting you. Don't let me down. I'm going to find whoever's responsible for this."

"How?"

"Never mind. Just *go*."

She watched him turn, and when he was gone, she called the service elevator. The motor that powered the pulley whined as the car ascended. When it finally arrived and the door opened, she stepped inside and the strong smell of garbage hit her. She took only shallow breaths as the elevator descended. It moved slowly, like the elevators at Park Manor, and when it finally jerked to a stop, she wanted to rush out, but she held herself back. Who was out there?

She squeezed the grip of the Glock, still in its holster. She exited slowly. The drone of the building's boiler drowned out all other sounds. Ahead of her was a long, narrow corridor with doors off to either side. She would have to open each of those doors and search the rooms one by one. Under any other circumstances, she would not be doing this. It was foolhardy to come down here alone. It was wrong to leave Brandon with Merchant. The right thing to do was get back in the elevator, go to the lobby, and call for assistance. But this was her chance to put the last nail in the coffin. She had disobeyed McGowan's order to cease her investigation, and if she didn't come out of here with her handcuffs around the killer, her career in homicide would surely be over. It might be over even if she did.

Three-foot-long fluorescent ceiling strips bathed the corridor in light, and that, at least, was a relief. She stepped to the first door marked "Bike Room" and turned the knob. It was locked. If anyone were in there, they had unlocked the door with a key, and it wasn't likely that Merchant's visitor had that key handy.

The metal door beyond the bike room was ajar. Codella pulled her Glock from its holster as she pushed the door open with her boot. The room was dark, and she stuck her hand inside and slid her palm up the wall until she hit a switch and the room became flooded with fluorescent light. Tools of every kind hung from hooks on pegboard: hammers, mallets, saws, chisels, cable cutters, and an entire row of screwdrivers. A worktable in the center of the room was covered in sawdust. Her eyes moved quickly around the room, but no one was hiding in there.

Codella returned to the corridor and continued on. When she turned the next doorknob and pushed open the door, the first thing she saw was a row of tan aluminum lockers. She stepped inside. On the left was a worn-out couch—more threadbare than the one in Cheryl O'Brien's apartment—an old Panasonic television, and a small kitchen area with a table, chairs, refrigerator, and microwave. To her right was another door.

She stared at that door. She took another glance into the corridor, and then she stepped across the staffroom and stood next to the door. Adrenaline made her heart pound as she listened for sounds on the other side. Then she raised her weapon, pulled the door open, and looked in.

Behind the door was a small pedestal sink and a toilet with the seat up. A roll of toilet paper sat on top of the toilet tank, several squares dangling down like a paper tail. The overwhelming smell of urine told her men had missed the bowl in here many times and that no one had disinfected the tiles recently.

She returned to the brightness of the corridor. Then, as she considered her next move, all the brightness was extinguished and she was standing in darkness as black as a mineshaft. She heard the flick of something. A lighter? A flashlight? She turned. And then pain exploded in her skull, and the blackness in front of her eyes became blackness inside her brain.

CHAPTER 73

Brandon heard the squawk of radios as the paramedics stepped off the elevator. He came out of the bedroom. "He's in here. Hurry! His breathing is shallow."

They followed him to Merchant. "How long has he been like this?"

"I don't know. At least twenty minutes, I think."

"What happened?"

"A detective was here. Detective Codella. She found him. She told me to tell you he might have been drugged with a narcotic. He was partly conscious until a little while ago."

Brandon watched the paramedics strip off Merchant's silk shirt. One paramedic checked his pulse and airways. The other one prepared an IV.

"Do you have Naloxone?" asked Brandon. "If somebody gave him a narcotic, Naloxone would help, wouldn't it? It couldn't hurt to try it."

One of the paramedics lifted Merchant's eyelids. He nodded. "Let's do it."

As they dug into their equipment, Brandon backed out of the room. He was no longer needed. He went to the kitchen and pressed the lighted service elevator button. When it came, he stepped in and pushed the button for the basement. When he reached the bottom, the door opened onto darkness.

"Detective?" he called tentatively, but Codella did not answer. He stepped out. He called out for her again. Had she already found whoever she was looking for? Had she gone up to the lobby?

The darkness was absolute. It felt alive and malevolent. He reached for his iPhone and flipped on the flashlight app. Its little beam was no match for the black cave in front of him. He turned and looked for the illuminated elevator button, but it wasn't where it should have been.

Instead, his little iPhone beam illuminated the gray barrel of a weapon pointed at his face.

"Step back," said the voice, "three steps and put your hands in the air. If you hesitate at all, you're dead."

CHAPTER 74

She felt as if she were swimming in quicksand. Each time she broke the surface of consciousness, she sank right back. *Sleep*, a voice said. *Just sleep.* There was really no need to get up, she thought. She could just lie here for a while. But she wasn't comfortable. Her feet were cold. Her fingers were cold, too. And her head was so heavy. All she could hear was an ear-splitting roar. What was that noise? An alarm clock? Maybe she should get up. Yes, she had to get up.

She opened her eyes. The room was dark. What time was it? She reached one arm out to turn off her screaming alarm clock, but her hand hit something hard and rough. She slid her palm down the surface. What was that?

She pushed herself into a sitting position, and then her head erupted in so much pain that she lay back down and curled into a fetal ball and rocked herself. She remained like that for several moments until it occurred to her that something was very wrong and that she was not in her bed or anywhere near it.

Her hand moved instinctively to the Glock in her shoulder holster. Her gun was not there. This awareness triggered a warning in her brain. Adrenaline gave her a surge of energy, and her lethargic mind grew more focused and alert. She reached behind her into her IWB holster. Her concealed backup gun, a Smith & Wesson, was still there, and she breathed a sigh of relief. *Think,* she told herself. *Put it back together.*

She rubbed her eyes. She had come to Thomas Merchant's apartment. He'd been lying on the bed. She had left him there—with the caregiver, Brandon. Now she was in the basement of Merchant's building. How long had she been lying there?

As soon as Codella stood, the blood rushed out of her head and she saw so many pinpoint particles of light in front of her eyes that she was certain she would faint. She bent over. A tide of nausea flooded her, but she held down the vomit and stayed as quiet as she could. She lowered herself back to the floor, sat against the cinderblock wall, and waited for the lightheadedness to pass. Her eyes were adjusting to the darkness now, and at the opposite end of the corridor, she noticed a thin strip of light under a door.

She pulled the Smith & Wesson out of its holster. Then she got to her feet again, more gingerly this time, and leaned against the wall until she was sure she wouldn't faint or throw up. Then she tiptoed slowly down the dark corridor, one delicate footstep at a time on the concrete floor, careful not to cause any sound to disrupt whatever was happening in that lighted room.

She stopped when she came close enough to hear the voices within. "Why are you doing this?" She recognized Brandon's voice.

"You wouldn't understand. You're just her stupid twenty-dollar-an-hour caregiver. You thought you knew her, but you didn't. You knew nothing about her."

"But why would you kill her? And Baiba? What did Baiba do to you?"

"You don't get anything, do you? You know what I found in her room yesterday? A pair of Tiffany clip-on earrings. I looked them up online. They cost him twenty-five thousand dollars. Almost six carats' worth of diamonds. She was cashing in. Don't feel so sorry for her. Don't be so naïve."

"You won't get away with this, you know."

"Oh, yes I will. Thanks to you. He'll take the blame for both murders, and you can be the jealous caregiver who tried to avenge Baiba's death. You can kill the cop who was coming to arrest him. You'll shoot Codella in cold blood. And then you'll shoot yourself. You made this so easy for me by showing up here. It's a much better ending than trying to sell another suicide."

"It's too late. The police are on their way. You'll never get away with it."

"Maybe I won't, but maybe I will," she said. "They'll see a bunch of dead people and you'll be holding the gun. I might just slip through. You never know." She laughed. "Now get up!"

"No!" shouted Brandon.

"Get up," she said again. "You have a cop to kill."

Codella gripped her gun with both hands. Brandon would come first through the door. She would kick him aside and shoot quickly. That was her only chance.

"I'm not leaving here," said Brandon. "Just shoot me now."

"Get up!"

"I told you, I'm not doing this. I'm not going to let you frame me. You're not going to get away with it. Just shoot me if you've got the nerve. Do it, because I don't really care anymore."

Codella wanted to scream at him, *Quit playing the martyr. Get out here and let me end this.*

"You're the crazy one," Brandon said.

Then Codella heard the *thud* of something hard. Gunmetal against flesh, she guessed. Brandon moaned. Codella didn't wait any longer. She kicked the door open. Julia Merchant swung her arm around wildly and fired Codella's Glock, but the round hit the cinderblock above Codella's head. Codella fired the Smith & Wesson once—steadily, accurately—just nicking the side of Julia's hand and sending the Glock to the floor.

Julia fell and reached for the gun, but before her fingers closed around it, Brandon pulled her back. Julia threw wild punches until he pinned her to the ground. Codella kicked the Glock out of Julia's reach and aimed the Smith & Wesson straight at her. "That's enough." Then she took out her handcuffs and fastened them around Julia's wrists. "This is over."

CHAPTER 75

The paramedics wanted to look at her. "I'm *fine*," she insisted. But she felt like hell.

"No, you're not," said the tall, thick one who'd probably played football or rugby and suffered his own share of concussions. "You need a staple in your scalp, Detective."

"A staple? Jesus Christ!"

"Maybe two. You've got an inch-long gash there." The thin black paramedic pointed. "Let us take you to the hospital."

"No," she said abruptly. "And I'm not getting any staple if it means you have to shave my head. This head never gets shaved again." She looked at Haggerty. "Tell him."

He turned to the paramedic. "She means it."

"How's Merchant?" she asked the paramedics.

"On his way to New York Presbyterian. He'll be okay. He kept calling out someone's name."

"Who?" asked Codella.

The paramedics looked at each other. "Somebody named Constance," said the tall thick one.

"Constance? He asked for Constance Hodges?"

The paramedic shrugged. "Constance. That's all."

Codella asked Haggerty, "Are they taking Julia Merchant straight to Manhattan North?"

He nodded.

"Good, because I can't wait to talk to her." Then she closed her eyes and thought of McGowan. He had shut her down. She had disobeyed his command. She might not be talking to anyone. "Oh, God, Brian. I'm so fucked. He could suspend me over this."

Haggerty put his arm around her. "He's outside. And so is the press."

"That's great. He can publically humiliate me." She buried her head in her hands. "Shit, I could use some Advil."

"You could use a hospital bed and, dare I say it, some oxycodone."

She laughed, but the laughing hurt. "What are you doing here, anyway?"

"Muñoz called me. He didn't like the idea of you coming here alone. He said you sent him to get a warrant and I should come over here. I got here ten minutes after you. They were carrying Merchant out on a stretcher. No one knew where you were. Whatever they gave him revived him, and he was going crazy."

"We might as well go out there. I have to see McGowan sooner or later." She took Haggerty's arm, and he pulled her to her feet. "If I face him while my head's split open, maybe he'll cut me a little slack. You think?" But she doubted it.

They got on the elevator along with the paramedics. The lobby was crowded with uniforms. Haggerty stopped her. "I should duck out. This isn't my scene."

She nodded. "It's gonna be a long night for me. See you tomorrow."

When he was gone, she looked past the officers in the lobby. Outside were flashing lights and cameras. She stepped through the front door and spotted McGowan. He shook his head in disgust when their eyes met. She fished in her pocket and felt for her shield. Would he make her relinquish it right in front of the cameras?

She reached him just as a Channel Two reporter stuck a microphone in her face. "Can you give us a statement, Detective? Is it true you've arrested Julia Merchant for the murder of her mother and the Park Manor staffer?"

"That's correct."

"How did you solve the case so quickly?"

And then Codella turned to McGowan. He was waiting to see what she said, and in that moment, she knew what she had to do. "The lieutenant should answer that," she said staring into his eyes. "This was his plan. His strategy. He deserves the credit." She smiled at him, stepped away from the microphone, and got into her car.

CHAPTER 76

The lights outside her office were dim. Heather had gone home two hours ago. Hodges debated whether to answer the phone. It had been ringing off the hook since the press conference. She wanted to get out of this place, go home, and pour a real glass of something. She lifted the phone reluctantly. "Park Manor."

"Ms. Hodges?"

She recognized Codella's voice. "Yes, Detective?"

"You'll be hearing it on the news soon. I thought I should tell you myself. Julia Merchant has been taken into custody. She just attempted to murder her father."

Hodges felt her heart speed up. She willed herself to speak in a calm and detached voice. "What happened?"

"We need to sort out the details, but we think she gave him a narcotic."

"Does that mean she's also the one who killed Mrs. Merchant?"

"We believe she's involved in the deaths of Lucy Merchant and Baiba Lielkaja. I can't really tell you more than that right now."

"And Thomas? Will he be all right?"

"The paramedics revived him. The ambulance took him to New York Presbyterian."

Hodges closed her eyes and sighed quietly.

"I'm curious about something, Ms. Hodges."

"What's that?" Hodges sensed more than simple curiosity in the detective's tone.

"I'm curious about why he asked for you while he was lying on the stretcher."

"He asked for me?" As soon as the words were out, Hodges realized she had said them with a little too much enthusiasm. "I don't know," she added quickly.

Codella was silent for several seconds.

She knows I'm lying, Hodges thought. "Look, he's a flawed man, Detective. But I knew he wasn't a murderer. I just never imagined that Julia could do this. I didn't see it."

"We see what we want to see," said Codella. "This is a good reminder to all of us. Let the facts tell the story. I've got to go."

Hodges heard her break the connection. She got her coat from the closet beside Heather's desk and walked through the first floor of Park Manor, smiling at the residents drinking cocktails and listening to a pianist play show tunes as if nothing else mattered. On Madison Avenue, the cold air made her shiver. She hailed a cab. Thomas had asked for her. All those years ago, she had known they would somehow end up back in each other's lives. She was stronger and smarter than Lucy Merchant. She was a much better match for Thomas. He needed her, and she would help him. And in return, he would help her. Everything would be all right, she told herself as she climbed into the taxi.

CHAPTER 77

Julia had not asked for an attorney, but Codella expected Pamela Martinelli to burst through the door at any moment, and if she did, the interview would be over and all the threads she wanted to unravel would stay tangled up forever in a defense attorney's fiction. She gestured to Julia's bandaged hand. "Does it hurt?"

"Don't pretend to be kind."

"Do you understand why you're here?"

"I'm not an idiot." Julia shot her a withering look.

"Of course not. But it must be hard for you." Codella purposefully spoke in a soft, soothing tone.

"Hard?"

"To think clearly," said Codella. "To remember things."

"What the fuck are you talking about?"

"Your memory," said Codella as if this were perfectly obvious. "I assume you're already showing the signs of your mother's condition?"

Julia glared. "How dare you say that to me! There's nothing wrong with my memory."

"No?" Codella allowed confusion to play across her face. She felt Julia's eyes watch her carefully, suspiciously. "You see, when we spoke in my office on Monday afternoon—when you came here and claimed to know me—you also claimed you installed a surveillance camera in your mother's room right after she came to Park Manor—that very same week, you said. Do you remember that?"

"What are you getting at?"

"I'm getting at the fact that there was a *different* clock in your mother's windowsill when she first moved in. A different clock was there for at least two months before you made a switch. I know because I saw a time-stamped photograph. I have it right here." Codella reached into her jacket pocket. She brought out the photo of Lucy Merchant that she had removed from the bulletin board outside Baiba Lielkaja's office. She slid it slowly across the table.

Julia glanced into the prescient eyes of her mother staring up from the glossy print. She looked away. "So?"

"So maybe you got confused about the facts because of your condition."

"I don't have a *condition*, Detective."

"Then you lied to me?"

"May I have a glass of water?" Julia asked.

Codella ignored the request. "You didn't go to Park Manor the morning of your mother's death just to say good-bye to her. You went there to retrieve the camera and slip her necklace charm out of the drawer. You knew the camera would show Brandon giving medicine to your mother—you'd done your homework. And you knew the missing charm would cast suspicion on him—and you needed to cast suspicion on someone to get this whole investigation started."

"I need a glass of water," Julia demanded again.

Codella still ignored the request. "You didn't find a spill in your mother's carpet that morning, did you? Your mother hadn't slapped the cup hard enough to cause a big spill. *You* poured the oxycodone onto the carpet. That was part of your plan, too, so you could bring the suspicious fibers to my office."

Codella stared into Julia's insolent eyes. They were heavy with mascara. "You were setting me up. You wanted me to investigate your mother's murder. But you didn't want me to

find out that *you* had done it. You wanted someone else to ultimately take the blame. You wanted to frame your father."

"You can't prove that."

"I don't have to," said Codella. "You confessed it all to Brandon in the basement of your father's building."

Julia crossed her arms. "It's his word against mine."

"Not quite," said Codella. "I was right outside that door. I
heard everything you said."

"Yeah? Well, who believes cops anymore? You all tell lies.
And that photo's irrelevant. I got the alarm clock camera shortly
after it was taken."

Codella shook her head. "I think you bought it within the
last few weeks."

Julia twisted the band of her Rolex.

"And I'll prove it," Codella added. "I'll pour over every
receipt, credit card statement, and online transaction you've ever
made. We'll contact the clock manufacturer and find out when
your unit was built and where it was sold. And we'll find out
when you bought it. You used premeditation in the murder of
your mother and Baiba Lielkaja, and I'll make sure the DA can
prove that to a jury."

Julia repeated, "I need some water."

Codella got up and left the room. Muñoz was waiting outside the door. "You been watching?" she asked him.

He nodded. "I got here five minutes ago."

"Did you get the warrant?"

"Cooper and a team are there now."

"Did they find anything?"

"She was grinding oxycodone pills in a little spice grinder."

"What about the charm?"

"It was right where you saw it—in the miniature Coliseum
on the bookshelf."

She got a glass of tap water and returned to the interrogation
room. As she watched Julia sip, she thought of Lucy Merchant
swallowing the adulterated diazepam, Baiba sucking a deadly

smoothie through her straw, and Merchant sipping a tainted Starbucks latte—all at the hands of Julia Merchant. "Did you really think you'd get away with this?" Codella asked.

"I *deserved* to get away with it," Julia answered. "You have no idea what it was like to live under my father's thumb. He thinks he has the right to control *everything*. Where I live. Where I go. Who I see. What I spend. He has billions of dollars, but all he gives me is a little monthly stipend. Last winter he threatened to write me out of his will if I didn't get tested for the Alzheimer's genes. He would have done it, too. I had to go along or get cut off. And guess what? Now I have to live with the fact that I have the same mutation my mother did."

Her eyes filled with tears. Codella could see the terror in them. "How do you think it feels to watch your mother's mind disintegrate and know that the same thing is probably going to happen to you?" Julia didn't wait for an answer. "After that, I hated looking at her. And I despised him."

Codella thought of her cancer. Would she have wanted to know decades in advance that malignant cells would stealthily proliferate inside of her one day? She leaned forward. "Is that when you started to plan your revenge?"

"I had to make it believable," Julia said with a hint of pride. "Obviously my father could never have killed her alone. Someone at Park Manor would have to have helped him. And when he started fucking Baiba Lielkaja, the whole idea fell into place."

"How did you know he was fucking her?"

"I know my father, Detective. I've seen so many of his little sex toys. He used to bring them home at night when my mother was out of town. She'd be touring or in LA or London. He'd introduce them to me and say they were working. He'd shut them up in that guest suite and a little while later he'd come into my room with a glass in his hand. *Daddy has a drink for you*, he'd say. *Daddy's drink will make you sleep better.*"

"How old were you?"

"Five, seven, ten. It went on and on. I've slept through all kinds of things, Detective. Who knows what I've slept through."

Her laugh was a hard wall of rock. But then a reservoir of tears broke through. She tried to wipe them away, but more tears erupted and flowed down her cheeks.

"It's a terrible thing to suffer at the hands of a parent." Codella spoke softly. "If we can't trust a parent, who can we trust, right?"

Julia didn't speak.

"You wanted him to pay," said Codella sympathetically. The guilty needed permission for their crimes.

The young woman nodded. "I just had to wait for my moment."

"The moment when you could get into the dispensary," said Codella. "It was you who went in there Sunday night, wasn't it? Not Baiba. You caused Dottie Lautner to fall so there'd be a big commotion."

"No. You're wrong about that. The old lady fell on her own. I watched it happen. It was like a gift from the gods, a sign that I was supposed to act."

Codella nodded appreciatively. The guilty wanted to believe they had fooled you. "You managed to get in and out of Baiba's apartment without anyone seeing you," she noted in a congratulatory tone. "She must have been pleased that you brought her one of her favorite Juice Generation smoothies."

Julia smirked. "She actually thought I was there to *commiserate* with her."

"There's just one thing I don't understand," Codella said in a "help-me-out-here" tone. "If you wanted to frame your father, if you wanted to make him pay for his cruelty to you, why did you kill him?"

Julia lifted the water glass and stared into it as if it were an expensive goblet of reserve Bordeaux. She inhaled a deep breath through her perfect nostrils. "He called me today. He wanted me to stand beside him at that charade of a press conference in front of Park Manor. When I said no, I expected him to get furious and threaten to cut me off again, but he didn't. He got very quiet instead. He just said, 'All right, Julia. We'll talk when it's over. We have a lot to talk about, don't we? Come see me.' Something had clicked in him. He knew. I could hear it in his tone. He knew. And when I watched his speech, I knew something else, too. I knew you were never going to arrest him for the crime. There wasn't enough evidence, and he would call in favors and manipulate public opinion the way he always does. I'd never get out from under him."

"So you decided to make him the next suicide?"

"I had to get free. What did I have to lose? I'd either be in his prison or I'd be in yours, and there was always the chance I'd get away with it."

Codella watched a tear roll slowly down her left cheek. *We never get free from the past*, she wanted to say. *It just doesn't happen that way.*

Julia gazed at something in front of her eyes. A spot on the drab wall? Her reflection in the one-way mirror behind which Muñoz and McGowan were watching? A scene from the distant past? She had executed her act of revenge, but the act had not set her free. She would spend the next few decades in a cell even smaller than this interrogation room, and her memories would eat away at her mind long before her genes activated any self-destruct script.

Codella got up from the table. "I'm sorry you couldn't think of another way out."

Julia shrugged. "Just arrest me. Let's get this over with."

FRIDAY
THE LAST DAY

CHAPTER 78

Codella met him at nine AM in the narrow coffee shop on Greenwich Street behind the Borough of Manhattan Community College. There was really no need for the meeting—Brandon had already given a detailed statement at Manhattan North—but Codella wanted to see him one last time. They sat across from each other in a tight booth for two, and he waited for her to speak first.

"I let myself suspect you for a little while," she confessed.

He shrugged. "It's understandable. I held the cup, and I didn't tell you I'd gone back to Baiba's that night. I'm sorry about that."

"It's not important. But I wanted to thank you."

"For what?"

"For saving my life."

He looked surprised.

"You did. Just before Julia hit me over the head, I heard the elevator coming. She must have heard it, too. Who knows what she would have done to me if you hadn't come downstairs. So I owe you my life."

He looked down shyly.

"I'm thanking you," said Codella. "You're supposed to say you're welcome."

He smiled.

"You have a great smile. You could show it more."

The waiter came. Codella ordered tea. Brandon ordered coffee.

"You saved Thomas Merchant too, you know. He probably would have died without the Naloxone. I'm not sure whether or not you're happy about that."

They both laughed.

"Ironically, I read about Naloxone while I was in Baiba's apartment that afternoon," he said. "I was trying to study for a test next week, and I couldn't concentrate at all, except for that sidebar. I found it interesting, and I read it twice." He rubbed his bristly chin. Was he trying to grow a goatee, she wondered. "I wish I could have saved her instead of him," he added.

"I know. But we don't get to choose who we save, and we can't save people from the needs that compel them to do self-destructive things."

"I did love her," he blurted out like a guilty confession. His throat sounded dry.

"I know. And it's good to admit your feelings. It's liberating." She thought of that night long ago when Haggerty had told her about the woman he'd loved and how she had humiliated him. She thought of all the shameful history she had kept to herself until Haggerty had teased it out of her.

Brandon nodded. "What's going to happen to Merchant?"

Their drinks came. "Nothing, I suppose."

"Shouldn't he be arrested for what he did to Baiba?"

"Should he? Yes. But there's no proof. All we know is that they were together on Monday night and he went to see her on Wednesday. The rest is he-said-she-said. His punishment will come in the form of Pamela Martinelli. She might have been on Merchant's side two days ago, but last night she showed up as Julia's pit bull and that woman will tear out anyone's throat. She'll make sure Julia has the best defense attorney money can buy, and the public isn't likely to forgive and forget about Merchant's transgressions when they get done spinning stories of Julia's traumatic childhood."

She watched Brandon add sugar to his coffee. "What will you do now, Brandon?"

His spoon circled the inside circumference of his cup. "I'm going to have my surgery in three weeks," he said. "Before all this happened, Baiba gave me three thousand dollars. At first I wasn't going to use it because I figured it probably came from the jewelry Merchant gave her. How else would she have had that kind of money? But then I decided if that was true, if she went to the trouble of selling the jewelry, then she was at least trying to get free from him. And she wanted me to have it. If I use it, a little bit of her will stay with me."

Codella nodded.

"And after I recover from the surgery I'll do my hospital internship, and hopefully they'll hire me on."

"You're very courageous."

"Not really," he said.

"Oh, yes. You are. In so many ways. You saved me. You saved Merchant. And you have saved yourself."

She saw his eyes become shiny with tears he wouldn't shed. She put her hand over his. "We come from all over to live in this city. We're all running away from something. Fortunately this place is big enough to absorb all our sorrows and all our bad memories. You're going to do just fine." She smiled, and she was thinking about her own younger self, the eighteen-year-old who had come to New York with no one and nothing except a dismal past she'd wanted to outrun. She leaned forward. "Can I tell you what I've learned from this case?"

He sipped his coffee and nodded eagerly.

"I've learned that you shouldn't try to forget the things that have happened. Bad or good. Don't try to forget them. Just deal with them. Otherwise, they come back in ways you never expected."

She stood and grabbed the check. She touched his shoulder. "Good luck with everything, Brandon. You know where to find me if you need anyone."

Then she drove back uptown. Part of her was tempted to detour to the East Side, stop at Park Manor, and see Constance Hodges. But why? What would she say to the woman? *I know you? I understand why you are so unhappy? I saw the same unhappiness in my mother?*

Hodges was a sad, pitiful woman trapped in a subservient job the same way her mother was trapped in a subservient marriage. Neither one of them had Brandon's courage or the resolve to break away. Their only self-expression was self-medication.

She steered the car up the West Side Highway. As she passed the light at Fifty-Seventh Street, she accelerated and the Upper West Side loomed on her right past the cliff of Trump Towers. She inhaled deeply. She was going back to *her* part of town, and she felt an unanticipated appreciation for this city that had taken her in and allowed her to start a new life. New York City could be so forgiving in that way.

Her head was still pounding, and she desperately wanted to sleep, but she turned off the highway at Ninety-Fifth Street and drove to the 171st. She found a parking spot right in front of the precinct, got out, and went inside. Behind the bulletproof glass, officers were doing what they always did. The rhythm of life in a precinct station never changed.

She climbed the stairs. Haggerty was sitting at his desk. He was on the phone, but when he saw her, he smiled with an "I'll-be-right-off-don't-go-away" wave of his hand. She stared into his blue eyes and waited for him to hang up.

"Well? Did he suspend you?" he asked when he got off.

"No."

"Did he scream?"

"No."

"How did you manage that?"

"Watch the news on Channel Two."

"Only if I can watch it with you."

She smiled.

"So are the two of you friends now?"

"More like two wolves who know their territory." She reached in her pocket. "And speaking of territory." She pulled out the small ring of keys she'd been carrying for the past two days. She set it on his desk in front of him, and he looked at it.

"What's this?"

"You know."

"Why?"

She sat on the edge of his desk and touched his face. "So you don't have to ask the doorman to let you in anymore."

ACKNOWLEDGMENTS

My family, Cynthia Swain, Cameron Swain, and Matthew Swain
My agent, Kathy Green
My editor, Matthew Martz
S. J. Rozan, for sharing her magic
Warren Hecht, for getting it all started
Constance Smith, my sister
Ret. NYPD Det. Matthew O'Donnell

Elizabeth Avery, Sue Foster, Jackie Freimor, Ann and Mark Gallops, Helen Graves, Sunil and Marcela Gulati, Sue Lund, Michelle Menzies-Abrash, Mandy O'Donnell, Ilaria Papini, Lorena Vivas, and Jane Young—for their friendship, insights, and talents

Sera and Tom Reycraft and all of my Benchmark Education colleagues—for their much-appreciated support